D1042145

Hillsboro Public Library
Hillsboro, OR
A member of Washington County
COOPERATIVE LIBRARY SERVICES

In
Hot
Water

Also available by Kate Kingsbury

Merry Ghost Inn Mysteries

Be Our Ghost
Doom With a View
Dead and Breakfast

Manor House Mysteries

An Unmentionable Murder
Wedding Rows
Fire When Ready
Berried Alive
Paint by Murder
Dig Deep for Murder
For Whom the Death Tolls
Death Is in the Air
A Bicycle Built for Murder

Pennyfoot Hotel Mysteries

A Merry Murder
A Perilous Promise
Mulled Murder
The Clue Is in the Pudding
Herald of Death
Mistletoe and Mayhem
Decked With Folly
Ringing in Murder
Shrouds of Holly
Slay Bells
No Clue at the Inn

Maid to Murder
Dying Room Only
Death With Reservations
Ring for Tomb Service
Chivalry Is Dead
Pay the Piper
Grounds for Murder
Check-Out Time
Eat, Drink, and Be Buried
Service for Two
Do Not Disturb
Room With a Clue

Raven's Nest Bookstore Mysteries

(writing as Allison Kinglsey)

Extra Sensory Deception
Trouble Vision
A Sinister Sense
Mind Over Murder

Belle Haven House Mysteries

(writing as Rebecca Kent)

Murder Has No Class
Finished Off
High Marks for Murder

In Hot Water

A MISTY BAY TEA ROOM MYSTERY

Kate Kingsbury

CROOKED
LANE

NEW YORK

This is a work of fiction. All of the names, characters, organizations, places and events portrayed in this novel are either products of the author's imagination or are used fictitiously. Any resemblance to real or actual events, locales, or persons, living or dead, is entirely coincidental.

PUBLISHER'S NOTE: The recipes contained in this book are to be followed exactly as written. The publisher is not responsible for your specific health or allergy needs that may require medical supervision. The publisher is not responsible for any adverse reaction to the recipes contained in this book.

Copyright © 2021 by Doreen Hight

All rights reserved.

Published in the United States by Crooked Lane Books, an imprint of The Quick Brown Fox & Company LLC.

Crooked Lane Books and its logo are trademarks of The Quick Brown Fox & Company LLC.

Library of Congress Catalog-in-Publication data available upon request.

ISBN (hardcover): 978-1-64385-770-1
ISBN (ebook): 978-1-64385-771-8

33614082435164

Cover illustration by Greisbach/Martucci

Printed in the United States.

www.crookedlanebooks.com

Crooked Lane Books
34 West 27th St., 10th Floor
New York, NY 10001

First Edition: October 2021

10 9 8 7 6 5 4 3 2 1

As always, to my husband, Bill. You are constantly there for me, with all the ups and downs, and I would not be able to do this without you. I love you.

Chapter One

The victim lay on the rocks, sprawled facedown, his outstretched arms having failed to slow his deadly descent from the sixth-floor balcony of the Blue Surf Hotel. Detective Lieutenant Tony Messina pursed his lips. The guy wore a bright-pink negligee that partly covered his body. This, Messina told himself, was going to explode headlines across the front page of the *Journal*.

The quiet seaside town of Misty Bay nestled on the Oregon coast, and although it had its share of tourists, especially in the summer months, the only sensation that had recently made headlines in the local newspaper was a messy invasion of rabbits.

Messina lifted his gaze to a small group of avid spectators. Turning to the officer standing next to him, he nudged his head at the onlookers. "Go talk to them. Maybe one of them saw something that might help."

The officer headed off, and Messina took a long look around the beach. A few early risers jogged along the shoreline, while a couple of less energetic folks watched two dogs scampering in and out of the ocean.

In the summer months the beach would have been a lot more crowded, even at this hour. But this was late September. The kids were back in school, and the tourists had thinned out.

Messina took a deep breath, filling his lungs with the cool, salty air. A thick mist still hovered over the rocky cliffs, blocking out the sun. By midmorning the fog would burn off, leaving the town to bask in a pleasant, warm glow for the rest of the day.

Closer to the water, the hungry gulls swooped low over the sand, hunting for their breakfast. Their haunting cries sounded desperate, and Messina's stomach growled at the thought of food. So far, all he'd had this morning was a mug of coffee.

The officer strode back to him, shaking his head. "Nothing. No one saw anything, except for the guy who saw him tumble over the balcony. He still says he didn't notice anyone else up there." He looked down at the corpse and grinned. "That dude was either a cross-dresser or he was really living it up before he croaked. What a way to go."

The detective scowled at him. Ken Brady was a good officer but a bit of a moron when it came to sensibilities. "Watch your mouth, Brady. Let's have a little more respect."

"Yes, sir. Sorry." Brady glanced up at the balcony. "You think he jumped?"

"Guess that's something we'll have to look into." Messina gazed up at the balcony. The hotel was fairly new, having opened less than two years ago. Just six floors but impressive, with its gleaming white walls and aqua-blue balconies enclosed by railings that in his opinion should have been built higher.

There had been an uproar in town when the hotel was being constructed. The majority of residents had resented a large commercial building in what was basically a sleepy, peaceful community. They tolerated the visitors in the summer for the economy, and they treasured the off-season. They were afraid that the hotel would bring an influx of noisy intruders year-round, destroying their idyllic lifestyle.

So far, their fears had not materialized. The hotel blended in rather well with the backdrop of rugged cliffs and forested hills. Although there had been a somewhat larger crowd of tourists this summer, making parking in town a headache, the town had gradually emptied out through September, and things were relatively back to normal.

Except for this. Messina was willing to bet that this man's death was no suicide or accident. He dug in his pocket for his phone and thumbed in the number for the county's Major Crime Team. After getting an assurance that the medical examiner would be there ASAP, he ordered Brady to stand guard over the body and then headed for the hotel.

He had work to do, and he had the feeling that things were going to get pretty complicated before this was over.

*   *   *

Vivian Wainwright folded her arms and cast a critical eye over the eight tables set out in the dining area of the Willow Pattern Tearoom. Snow-white tablecloths, pale-pink napkins, English bone china teacups and saucers, and small vases of white daisies—everything essential for a traditional British afternoon tea.

Still missing were the teapots, milk jugs and the tiered cake stands bearing delicate crustless sandwiches and delectable pastries, and of course, pots of strawberry jam and cream for the scones. All of which would be placed on the tables after the customers were seated.

Although the tourist season had wound down, all the tables had been booked for this afternoon. The locals had made the tearoom a popular place to spend a leisurely hour or so indulging a sweet tooth.

The sun aimed its full strength at the windows in the afternoons. Vivian had recently found white curtains patterned with delicate pink and blue wildflowers that shaded the glare without blocking the light. They reminded her of an English garden, like the childhood garden in London her mother had described to her. So much nicer than the pink-striped ones she'd bought when she'd opened the tearoom two years ago.

Everything was ready in the kitchen, so she had a few minutes to relax before her customers arrived. She was debating whether or not to open the carton of tea towels that had arrived from the UK this morning when the doorbell tinkled.

"Sorry I'm late!" The vigorous woman striding across the room thrust a heavy strand of black hair away from her face. "I stopped by the wine shop on my way here, and you know how Natalie gabs. Took me twenty minutes to get out of the store with this." She waved a bottle of wine at Vivian. "That woman's flapping tongue will get her in trouble one day. She needs to button it once in a while."

Vivian hid a smile. Natalie Chastain owned the Sophisticated Grape just down the street and was notorious for knowing everything that was going on in town long before anyone else. If you wanted to know something about somebody, you asked Natalie. What she didn't know, she'd move heaven and earth to find out—just to be first to spread the news.

"It's okay. No one's here yet." Vivian took a closer look at her friend. Jenna Ramsey had been her assistant and consultant since the day she'd opened the Willow Pattern. It was Jenna who'd suggested the name, pointing at the willow-pattern plates Vivian had lovingly placed on the walls of the tearoom.

The plates had belonged to Vivian's late mother, Angela, who'd met her future husband when he was stationed at an American air base near her home in the UK. Although she spent most of her life in America, Angela never lost her accent or her hometown traditions.

Growing up with an English mother had instilled in Vivian the British customs and culture that fostered her lifelong dream of opening a tearoom. It had taken more than sixty years, but now the dream was hers.

Its success was largely due to the tall woman standing in front of her. She loved Jenna like a daughter—almost as much as she adored her own two daughters.

"Are you okay?" Vivian frowned. "You look a bit flustered."

For an ordinary person, that wouldn't be surprising, knowing how annoying Natalie could be. But Jenna was not an ordinary person. She rarely showed emotion, though she was very good at rattling other people.

Jenna was blunt to the point of rudeness at times, but she was a hard worker, a loyal friend, and if someone was in need, always the first to offer help. Right now, however, her flushed cheeks and overbright eyes suggested she had more than Natalie's gossiping to worry about.

Obviously, she wasn't ready to share, however, as she dumped her bottle on the counter, declaring, "I'm fine. Just irritated by that airhead." She looked around at the inviting tables and across the room to where imported British foods and gifts filled the shelves, tempting customers to buy. "Where's Gracie?"

"I sent her out to the bank with the deposits. She should be back soon. I—"

Vivian broke off as the bell jingled again and the door flew open.

"You'll never guess what I heard!" The young woman bounced into the shop, her cheeks flushed with excitement. Her short pinkish-blond hair stuck up in spikes all over her head, and her bright-red lipstick matched the black sweater she wore, which hung down from one shoulder.

She was practically jumping up and down like a wayward yo-yo. For Gracie Jackson, this was nothing new. Impulsive, unpredictable, and ready for whatever adventure waited for her around the corner, she was constantly in a state of excitement.

Jenna rolled her eyes. "Don't tell me. The president's coming to visit."

Gracie stared at her. "What? No! Wait. Is he really?"

"Yeah, and he's invited us all to dinner."

Gracie uttered a derisive snort. "You wish." She jogged across the floor to the counter and dipped behind it to stash her oversized purse. Raising her head above the surface, she added, "I've got awesome news. Just in case you want to know."

"Why don't you tell us," Vivian suggested, with a glance at her watch. The first customers would be arriving at any minute, and she needed to get this drama over with as soon as possible.

Gracie stood and folded her arms. Triumphant now that she had both women's attention, she took a second to savor the moment. "They found a dead body on the beach this morning."

A nasty spasm hit Vivian's stomach. "What? Who found it? Who was it? Where on the beach?" Aware she was jabbering, she shut her mouth and looked at Jenna.

"Well," Jenna said, after a breathless pause, "Natalie will be steamed she missed this one."

"I don't know much about it." Gracie walked out from behind the counter. "They were talking about it in the candy store. They didn't know much either—like, it was a man, and he'd fallen from the top balcony of the Blue Surf."

Jenna made an odd little sound, then quickly coughed.

The sound struck a chord in Vivian's memory. "Isn't that where Dean's working now?"

"Yes, he's doing maintenance work there. That won't last long. He lost three jobs in the five years I was married to him." Jenna's voice mirrored her disgust, making no secret of her aversion for her ex-husband.

Vivian turned to Gracie. "Did they say who the victim was?"

Gracie shook her head. "I don't think anyone knows."

Hearing the doorbell one more time, Vivian gave Jenna a nudge. "Here come our customers. We'll talk about this later." She hurried forward to greet the newcomers, leaving her two assistants to head to the kitchen.

After taking orders for the full afternoon-tea experience, Vivian returned to the kitchen to find Jenna loading kettles of water onto the stove while Gracie carefully arranged sandwiches of fish paste and watercress, along with egg and tomato, on the cake stands.

"I wonder if he jumped," Gracie said, as she placed an Eccles cake onto each silver stand.

The words slowly penetrated Vivian's mind, which was focused on the small pots of clotted cream she was taking from the oversized refrigerator. "What? Who?"

"The dead guy." Gracie picked up a loaded cake stand with each hand. "I wonder if he'd had enough of life, decided to end it all, and threw himself off the balcony."

Vivian raised her eyebrows. "That's a bit melodramatic."

Pouring boiling water into the teapots lined up in front of her, Jenna uttered a growl of disgust. "Do we have to discuss this now?"

She sounded totally exasperated, and Vivian threw her a worried glance. Something was obviously upsetting her friend. She'd have to tackle her about it later. Right now, her customers were waiting, and that took precedence over everything else.

Fortunately, Gracie seemed unfazed by Jenna's irritation. Pasting a smile on her face, she sailed from the kitchen to present her loaded cake stands to the eager customers.

Vivian was kept too busy for the next three hours to speculate further on Jenna's sour mood. Between the sandwich making, refilling of teapots, clearing tables, and chatting briefly with the guests, she barely had time to even look at her assistants.

Once the last table had been cleared, however, she followed Jenna into the kitchen, anxious to find out exactly what was going on with her. Two of the tea party customers were now in the rear of the tearoom, browsing the shelves, while Gracie waited behind the counter.

Vivian headed for the sinks, seizing the moment alone with her friend. "I can tell something's bothering you, Jenna. Want to talk about it?"

"Not really." Jenna's voice was muffled as she bent over to retrieve a napkin she'd dropped on the floor.

"Okay." Vivian began cleaning one of the cake stands. "But I'm always ready to listen. Just in case you change your mind."

Jenna didn't answer, and giving up, Vivian concentrated on her task, leaving her friend alone to stack the dishes in the dishwasher.

The sound of the doorbell told her that the last customers were leaving. She would ask Gracie to finish cleaning the cake stands while she checked out the shelves to see what needed restocking.

When Gracie appeared in the doorway, however, she looked as if she'd just bitten into a sour lemon.

"What is it?" Vivian dropped the wet sponge onto the counter. "Did you break something?"

Gracie shook her head. "It's a cop. He wants to talk to Jenna."

Jenna dropped a plate into the dishwasher with a loud clatter, making Vivian wince.

"I knew it," Jenna muttered as she strode to the door.

Vivian exchanged a puzzled glance with Gracie, then hurried after her friend.

Jenna stood just inside the doorway, talking to a dark-haired officer. Vivian had met the detective only once, at a fund-raising Christmas bazaar, but he had left a lasting impression.

Lieutenant Tony Messina towered at least four inches above Jenna, who had once confessed to Vivian that she was just under five feet ten.

It wasn't the detective's height, however, that had intrigued Vivian. He had the most penetrating eyes—dark-brown orbs that seemed to bore right through her mind and into her soul. His features were craggy, with a slightly hooked nose and a firm jaw, all very pleasing to the eye.

She'd also noticed a shiny gold band on his left hand. That, and the fact that he was a good twenty-five years younger than her, prevented any romantic illusions she might have had. Nevertheless, she was stunned by her reaction to him.

Her husband, Martin, had been dead less than three years. He had gone suddenly, with a massive heart attack. The shock had immobilized her for months. Even now she had moments of disbelief.

The idea that she could be attracted to another man, much less one young enough to be her son, had completely floored her. She'd felt guilty for days afterward, until her sense of humor had kicked in and she was able to joke about it with Jenna.

Right now, however, it didn't seem as though the detective's visit was anything to joke about.

Jenna's raised voice echoed across the room. "I don't know anything about it. We've been divorced for over a year."

Messina murmured something Vivian couldn't hear.

Jenna's voice rose another notch. "Yes, I was at the hotel this morning. He was supposed to meet me to pay me the alimony he owed me. He never showed, so I left. I never saw him. I don't know what happened to him."

Thankful that the last customers had left the shop, Vivian hurried forward. "Jenna? Is everything all right?"

Messina's dark gaze sliced across her face. "Ma'am, this doesn't concern you."

Ignoring him, Vivian turned to her friend. To her dismay, she saw an unfamiliar tear glistening in Jenna's eye. "Oh, Jenna. I'm so sorry. It's Dean, isn't it?"

"Yes." Jenna raised her chin. "I always knew that jerk would come to a bad end one day."

Vivian winced and shot a quick glance at the cop. His eyes had narrowed as he stared at her friend.

"It was Dean they found on the rocks this morning," Jenna said. "He was probably drunk and fell over the balcony."

"No, ma'am," Messina said softly. "There were signs of a struggle. We believe someone pushed him over. We're looking at a murder case. I need you to come down to the station with me. There are a few questions you need to answer." He gave Vivian a meaningful look. "In private."

Jenna stared at him. "You're arresting me? Are you nuts? I just told you, I had nothing to do with this."

"I'm just taking you in for questioning, that's all. I suggest you don't turn this into a battle."

Apparently hearing the warning in the detective's voice, Jenna shrugged. "Okay, then."

"Wait!" Vivian held up her hand. "You need a lawyer. You don't have to answer any questions until you have one."

Jenna smiled. "Don't worry, Vivian. I don't need one. I didn't kill Dean."

"That's beside the point. This is a murder investigation. Trust me. You need a lawyer."

Messina cleared his throat. "Ma'am, this is police business. If you're smart, you'll butt out."

"It's okay." Jenna took hold of Vivian's arm. "I'll be fine. Don't worry. I didn't do anything wrong, and I want this over with. We'll talk when I get back."

"*If* you come back," Vivian said under her breath, with a dark glance at Messina. With a bad feeling growing in her gut, she watched her friend walk out the door, closely followed by the detective. Remembering Jenna's bad mood this afternoon, for a second or two she wondered if her assistant knew more about Dean's death than she was willing to admit.

In the next instant, she obliterated the thought from her mind. She knew Jenna. There was no way that woman would have killed her ex-husband.

"Is she being arrested?"

Gracie's anxious voice right behind her made Vivian jump. She spun around and made an effort to sound calm. "Of course not. He just wants to question her, that's all."

"Then why couldn't he just do that here?"

Gracie's eyes were wide with worry, and Vivian hurried to reassure her. "It's police protocol, that's all. They have to bring sus . . . people in to question them so they can put it in the report."

She wasn't even sure if that made sense. She just wanted to take that haunted look out of the young woman's eyes.

Gracie, however, seemed anything but reassured. "You were going to say *suspects*, weren't you?"

"Yes, I was. But Jenna's not a suspect. She's just a possible lead to what happened." Vivian shook her head. "I just wish she'd asked for a lawyer." She took hold of Gracie's arm. "Come on, let's go have a cup of tea. I've been staring at those Eccles cakes all afternoon. I'm dying to eat one."

She pulled her assistant into the kitchen and sat her down at the small dinette table in the corner by the window. After putting the kettle on to boil, she opened the container of leftover pastries and set it on the table in front of Gracie. "Here, help yourself."

The young woman stared at the cakes but made no move to take one. "You don't think she did it, do you?"

Her voice trembled over the words, and Vivian plopped down on the chair opposite her. "Of course not. Jenna would never do something like that."

"She hated him."

"Yes, I know." Vivian let out her breath. "But I know Jenna. She may be outspoken and tends to argue a bit too much at times, but she'd never be violent." She looked down at her hands, which were clenched in her lap. "Has she ever told you about her past?"

"Her past?" Gracie sounded surprised. "She said she was married five years before she got divorced. Oh, and that she grew up in a Texas border town. She doesn't talk about herself much."

Vivian hesitated, uncertain if she were doing the right thing. "I don't know if she'd mind me telling you this," she said at last, "but I think it will help you understand her better."

Gracie's eyes widened. "Tell me what?"

Vivian sighed. "Well, she didn't ask me to keep it a secret, so I guess it's okay to tell you." She paused again, then added quietly, "Jenna had a rough childhood. Her mother died when Jenna was thirteen, leaving her father to raise six kids."

"Oh, that sucks." Gracie looked ready to cry. "I know how she feels. I was sixteen when my mom died. I thought the world had come to an end."

"I know." Vivian gave her a nod of sympathy. "I'm sorry, Gracie. I didn't mean to upset you."

"It's okay." Gracie dashed a tear away with the back of her hand. "At least there was just me and my brother, and we were practically grown up. It must have been a lot tougher on Jenna."

"It was. Her father went off the rails after his wife died and drowned his sorrows in whiskey. Unfortunately, he was violent when he was drunk. Jenna was the oldest kid and protected the rest of them, so she took the brunt of the punishment."

Gracie's expression had slowly darkened as she listened. "That's so sad."

"There's more." Vivian reached for an Eccles cake. "Jenna played basketball for her high school team, and her junior year they made it to the championship finals. When Jenna got home that night, she found her youngest brother lying in the flower bed in front of the house. He'd been beaten by his father."

Gracie's sharp gasp of horror seemed to echo around the room.

Vivian swallowed. It was even more difficult to talk about it than it had been to hear it. "Jenna went to a neighbor's house to call 911. Her brother died in the hospital the next day."

"No!" A tear ran down Gracie's cheek, and she brushed it away with the back of her hand. "What happened to her father? Did they arrest the toad?"

Vivian nodded. "He ended up in jail, and the kids were split up to go to foster homes."

"That must have just about totaled her."

"I think it did. The problem is, she blames herself for not being there to protect her brother that night."

"That's crazy."

"I know. I tried to tell her that, but it's going to take more than my words to heal her. That tough-guy attitude is an act to convince herself that nothing can hurt her again. Underneath it all, there's a warm heart and a caring soul."

"I hope so." Gracie raised her head, and her pale-blue eyes were clouded with worry. "I'd hate to see her go to prison for that miserable creep. He treated her like she was garbage. What about her family? Where are they now?"

"They all still live in Texas, I believe. I think Jenna keeps in touch with them, but I don't think she visits. She's obviously trying to bury the past."

Gracie shook her head. "I can't figure out what she saw in Dean Ramsey."

Vivian took a bite of her cake and chewed for a moment before answering. "She told me she never thought she'd get married, but then she met Dean. I think she saw a need in him for someone to straighten him out. She'd never admit it, but Jenna is a caretaker. She's compelled to help people in trouble."

"Well, she should have picked someone better than him. I hope someday she'll find him."

Vivian smiled. "I seriously doubt that. I don't think Jenna will ever trust a man again."

"That's a real downer."

"You're right. It's sad." The kettle on the stove shrilled, alerting Vivian that the water was boiling. She put down the cake, then got up and hurried over to stove. After pouring a small amount of hot water into the teapot, she left the kettle boiling while she swirled the teapot around, then emptied it.

"I'm sure once the detective has questioned her, Jenna will be right back here, swearing about the time she wasted answering him." Vivian popped two tea bags into the teapot, then poured boiling water over them until the pot was almost filled.

"She told him she was at the hotel this morning."

"She said she went there to meet Dean, but he never turned up, so she left." Vivian poured a small amount of milk into two teacups, then filled them with tea.

"Why would she go see him if she hated him so much? Why couldn't he have mailed her the money?"

"You'll have to ask her about it. But don't be surprised if you get a rude answer." She carried the cups and saucers over to the table and set one in front of Gracie. "Look, I don't know what happened any more than you do. If Jenna feels like talking when she gets back, we'll find out more then."

Gracie was about to answer, but just then the shop doorbell jingled, making them both jump.

"Maybe that's her now." Gracie shot up from her chair. "I'll go see."

Vivian wasn't about to sit there and wait. She got up and followed her assistant out into the shop.

Gracie had halted halfway across the room. The woman standing just inside the doorway wore a snazzy gray suit and purple shirt. Her blond hair was pulled back into a neat bun, and thick black lashes framed a pair of piercing blue eyes.

Behind her, a younger man stood holding an oversized video camera, and Vivian's stomach dropped. Reporters. That's all they needed right now. Hurrying forward, she prayed Jenna wouldn't come back until after she'd gotten rid of the intruders.

"I'm Rita Mozell, reporter for KAKN News." The woman waved a hand at the man behind her. "This is Jim, my cameraman."

The man gave a brief nod of his head and went back to adjusting his camera.

"We'd like to speak with Jenna Ramsey," the reporter said. She started to walk toward them but halted when Vivian raised her hand.

"She's not here."

"Oh." The woman looked disappointed. "Do you know where I can find her? She's not at home."

So, they'd already been snooping around Jenna's house. Vivian folded her arms. "I have no idea where she is."

The reporter signaled to Jim, who raised his camera and pointed it at Vivian. "How long have you known Jenna Ramsey?"

"Long enough to know she wouldn't want me talking about her behind her back. Now, if you'll excuse me, I have a business to run." She turned her back on the couple. "Come, Gracie. We have work to do." Taking hold of her assistant's arm, she marched her back to the kitchen.

The doorbell tinkled again, and she exchanged a worried look with Gracie. Either that was the reporter leaving or Jenna had walked into an ambush. For several long seconds she held her breath, then let it out when nothing but silence followed.

"Thank heavens. They're gone." Vivian sank onto a chair, and Gracie plopped down opposite her. "I hope they stay away."

"I was afraid Jenna was going to walk in on them." Gracie lifted her cup from its saucer. She took a couple of gulps of tea and put the cup back down.

"She wouldn't have talked to them anyway."

Gracie's giggle sounded a little strained. "She would have told them where to shove their camera."

"I'd have liked to see that." Vivian took a few sips of her tea and put down the cup. "I hope they don't keep her at the police station too long. It's almost closing time. I don't want to lock up until she gets back here."

Gracie swallowed the last of her tea and got up, holding the cup and saucer. "I'll finish the cleanup for her."

"I'll help." Vivian pushed herself up from her chair.

"Thanks." Gracie headed over to the sink to finish stacking the dishwasher.

Vivian opened the closet door and pulled out the vacuum. Normally Jenna would take care of the dishes, vacuum the floors, remove the tablecloths and replace them with clean ones, and dust all the surfaces.

Gracie's job was to take care of the shelves, serve customers, and order the packages of English tea, candy, cookies, jars of marmalade, lemon curd, and pickled onions. Other shelves held, among other things, delicate porcelain figurines, miniature London buses filled with candy, brightly patterned tea towels, bone china mugs, and a variety of British toiletries.

Both women also waited tables and helped in the kitchen. Pushing the vacuum across the floor, Vivian reflected on how lucky she'd been to find them both. Things had been more than a little crazy when she first opened the tearoom. She'd had no experience in running a business and she was flying blind for a while, learning the ropes as she struggled to keep up with the hundred and one details that went into managing a restaurant and shop, even one as small as the Willow Pattern.

Jenna and Gracie had been her lifesavers, especially Jenna. The three of them worked well together, sharing the workload when things got busy. She couldn't have asked for better employees.

Hearing the faint sound of the doorbell above the vacuum's hum, she turned off the machine and looked at the door.

Jenna walked slowly toward her, her face white and drawn.

Vivian's spirits plummeted.

Gracie called out from the kitchen, "Is that Jenna?"

Vivian answered her with a loud, "Yes!"

Gracie appeared in the doorway, and Vivian looked back at Jenna. "What happened?"

Jenna lifted her hands, palms out, then dropped them again. "I've been ordered not to leave town. I'm the main suspect in Dean's murder." Her eyes were bleak as she looked at Vivian. "Detective Messina is convinced I killed him. I'm going to prison for something I didn't do."

Chapter Two

Gracie's anguished cry blended with Vivian's shocked gasp. "That's ridiculous." Vivian grabbed Jenna by the arm. "Come into the kitchen and sit down. I'll make some more tea."

"I need something a lot stronger than tea," Jenna muttered as she allowed herself to be propelled into the kitchen, followed by an anxious Gracie.

"I have that too." Vivian dropped her hand. "Wait here. I'll run upstairs and get it."

"No!" Jenna grabbed her arm. "I can have something later. Right now, I need to just sit here and try to get my head around what's happening."

Vivian sat her down at the table and lowered herself onto a chair. "Tell us everything that happened."

Jenna sighed and buried her face in her hands for a moment. Finally lowering them, she said quietly, "I hated Dean for what he'd done to me, but I'm truly sorry he's dead. I wouldn't have wished that on him, and I sure as heck didn't kill him."

"We know you didn't," Gracie said, taking the last chair. "Why does that stupid cop think you did?"

Jenna shrugged. "I didn't hide the fact that I hated the jerk." She made a guttural sound of disgust in the back of her throat. "Did you know he was wearing nothing but a woman's negligee when they found him?"

Gracie sucked in a breath. Vivian stared at Jenna, speechless.

Jenna nodded at their reaction. "Right. The detective believes I caught Dean with another woman, got into a fight with him, and shoved him over the balcony."

Vivian shook her head. "Why would he think that?"

"Because I was seen at the hotel this morning. Dean had stopped sending my alimony money, so I texted him yesterday, telling him I was going to report him if he didn't pay up. He texted me back real early this morning and said to meet him in the hotel lobby and we'd work something out."

"And you believed him."

Jenna shrugged. "I need the money. I figured it was worth giving it a shot. Anyway, when I got there, he wasn't in the lobby. I waited for half an hour and he didn't show up, so I left."

"And that dim-witted moron cop didn't believe you," Gracie said, her voice harsh with contempt.

"No. He thinks I found out Dean had spent the night there with this woman and flew into a rage." She shuddered. "I asked him why on earth he would think I cared, and he said that thing about *hell hath no fury.*"

"*Like a woman scorned,*" Vivian finished for her.

"Yeah." Jenna sighed. "He's convinced I went to the hotel this morning to break things up between him and this woman, whoever she is. He thinks Dean grabbed her nightgown to cover himself and backed out onto the balcony, where I shoved him to his death."

"While this woman stood by and watched?"

"Messina thinks she took off while Dean and I were fighting."

"Well, he must know who she is. Someone must have booked the room."

Jenna shook her head. "I asked him that. He said that according to the records, the suite was vacant last night."

"But what about Dean's phone? Wouldn't his text to you show up on there?"

"I asked him that too." Jenna propped her elbows on the table and covered her face with her hands again. "He said I could have sent the message to myself before I left the hotel."

Gracie uttered a loud sigh. "Too bad that man is such a moron. He's a real hunk to look at."

Jenna sent her a lethal look. "That's all you ever think about."

"Yeah?" Gracie sat up. "Well, there's no harm in looking."

"Okay. So, did you ask for a lawyer?" Vivian resisted the urge to remind her friend that she'd recommended that earlier.

"I was going to, but then he said I was free to go, though if I tried to leave town I'd be arrested."

"So he doesn't have enough evidence to hold you," Vivian said.

"Because there is no evidence." Jenna's voice had risen just a notch. "But he believes I killed my ex-husband, and I know he's going to do everything in his power to put me in jail."

"Well, then you definitely need a lawyer."

Jenna stared at her for a moment, then burst out, "I *hate* lawyers! My divorce lawyer made me feel like something that crawled out from a rock."

"I'm sorry you had such a bad experience with him," Vivian said gently. "They're not all like that."

"Well, I don't trust them. Any of them. Besides, I can't afford that kind of money for a lawyer."

Vivian sighed. "The way I look at it is this. You can either hire a lawyer or . . ."

She let her voice trail off, and the other two women stared at her.

"Or what?" Gracie said.

"Or we do a little investigating ourselves and try to find out who really pushed Dean over that balcony. After all, you know Dean better than anyone on the police force."

Gracie cheered and raised a fist. "Yeah! I'm in!"

Jenna, however, had doubt written all over her face. "I don't know. We don't know anything about police work, and it's probably dangerous to go poking around a murder case. We could all end up in even worse trouble."

"Well," Vivian said, trying to sound modest, "if you remember, my husband was a prosecuting attorney in Portland. I've followed several of his murder cases, and I've learned a thing or two. Plus, I've read enough mystery novels to know how to go about an investigation. One thing I do know is that perpetrators always make mistakes, and it's those mistakes that lead to their arrest."

"So you're saying we should hope for mistakes that will lead us to Dean's killer." Jenna still looked unconvinced.

"Something like that." Vivian sat back, feeling a thrill of excitement. "With hard work and a little bit of luck, we might be able to track him down."

"Even if we do get that lucky, and it's a long shot at best, we still have to convince Detective Messina." Jenna shook her head. "He seems determined to charge me with murder."

"You can get free legal aid," Gracie said. "I know someone who did that."

Jenna looked at her. "And how did that go?"

"Not good. He lost the case."

Jenna rolled her eyes. "See what I mean?"

"Well, we have to do something," Vivian said, making her voice ring with conviction. "We just can't sit here twiddling our thumbs while Detective Messina drums up a case against you."

Gracie leaned forward, her earnest expression making her look vulnerable. "Please, Jenna. You can't end up in jail for something you didn't do."

"She's right, you know. You could very well spend the next twenty years of your life in prison." Vivian sat back and watched her friend struggle with indecision.

Finally, Jenna sighed. "I guess we could look into it. As long as we back off at the first sign of trouble. The last thing I want is for anyone else to get hurt."

"Done." Vivian looked at Gracie. "Are you sure you want to do this?"

Gracie grinned. "Just try and stop me."

"Okay." Vivian got up and fetched a notepad and pen from one of the kitchen drawers. Bringing it back to the table, she sat down and opened the notebook. "Now, let's write down what we know." She scribbled Dean's name at the top of the page. "All we know at this point is that Dean was wearing a women's nightgown when he was killed, which means he'd probably spent the night with her."

"I think that's pretty obvious," Jenna muttered.

"I just can't imagine Dean in a woman's nightgown." Gracie shook her head. "He was so macho, with all those big muscles and that scruffy beard. You'd think he would have grabbed something a little less goofy to wear."

Vivian coughed. "I hate to ask this, Jenna, but is it at all possible Dean had a . . . you know . . . a liking for women's clothes?"

Jenna's eyebrows shot up.

"Absolutely not! Dean was no angel, but he had no hang-ups like that. I lived with the jerk for five years. I would have known. Besides, even if he did, why on earth would he spend the night all by himself in the fanciest suite in the hotel?"

"You're right, but I had to ask." Vivian paused, then added, "What I'd like to know is how that detective thinks you're capable of shoving a man that size to his death."

"I'm not that weak." Jenna hunched her shoulders. "Especially when I'm steamed. Dean sure gave me enough to be steamed about. He cheated on me at least twice that I know about. Heaven knows how many other times there were before I found out what he was and dumped him."

"Not to mention the gambling," Vivian reminded her.

"Yeah, that too." She leaned back in her chair. "One way or another, Dean probably made a lot of enemies. Jealous husbands, betrayed girlfriends, maybe someone he cheated out of money. It won't be easy finding out who killed him."

"Well, there's one woman, presumably, who can help us. The one who most likely spent the night with him."

"But when she finds out Dean's dead, wouldn't she talk to the cops?" Gracie asked.

Vivian sighed. "I think if she was going to get involved, she would have done so by now. In any case, we can't wait for her to make up her mind to come forward. We have to find her, and that means tracking down anyone who had connections with Dean."

Jenna made a face. "Not looking forward to that." She heaved a heavy sigh. "Look, I know you guys want to help me, and I'm really grateful. But right now, I'm bushed. I really want to go home, take a shower, and crawl into bed with a book."

Vivian's practical mind zeroed in on the essential. "What about dinner? You have to eat."

"I'll find something to eat."

"What about the reporters?" Gracie sat up on her chair. "They're probably waiting for you at your home."

Jenna's eyes widened in alarm. "What reporters?"

Vivian told her about the TV reporters. "They had already checked out your house," she said. "Gracie's right. They could be camped out there now. You don't have to talk to them." She looked at Gracie. "We'll go with you and see that you get past them."

"Yeah!" Gracie jumped up. "We'll show them who's in charge. Just let them try to stop us."

Jenna rose from her chair like an avenging warrior. "You don't need to come with me. I can handle this. If they want a fight, I'll give them one."

Vivian sighed. "And you'll convince them that you're a bad-tempered shrew, capable of murder."

Jenna's scowl faded. "Yeah, maybe you're right."

"All right, then." Vivian stood up and picked up her cup and saucer. "What we need is a show of support and calm authority. I'll ride with you, and Gracie can follow behind." She looked at Gracie. "You can drop me off here on your way home."

"I really don't need—" Jenna began, but Vivian stopped her with a look.

"We're coming, so quit arguing. These reporters can be aggressive."

Apparently realizing she was fighting a losing battle, Jenna relaxed her shoulders. "Okay. But I'm not making any promises."

Vivian sighed. The best she could hope for, she told herself, was for Jenna to keep her cool and not escalate an already hazardous situation.

*   *   *

Detective Messina sat at his desk, tapping a finger on the keyboard in front of him. This case was the biggest to have come his way since he'd transferred from Portland to the quiet peace of Misty Bay.

At first, after the chaos of crime in the city, the slow pace had unsettled him. It was almost like being on vacation, to the point of being boring. His purpose in making the drastic change, however, was to put the past behind him. Although the memories still haunted him and probably would always linger, the pain was slowly easing.

He'd taken one day at a time and slowly learned to relax. His body no longer jolted at the sound of a slammed door or the screech of brakes. He could wake up in the morning now with an easy mind instead of the feeling of dread that used to greet him.

It was hard for him to comprehend that it had been more than three years since he'd turned his back on city life. He could count on one hand all the assaults, car thefts, and robberies he'd dealt with during that time, along with maybe a dozen or so burglaries. The dead body he'd seen this morning was the first one he'd laid eyes on since the day his life shattered into tiny pieces.

He shook his head, mentally chasing away the ugly vision. This was now, and all he had. This murder, with a suspect who fit the bill.

Yet his reasoning was splintered with doubts.

On the surface, it seemed cut-and-dried. Furious ex-wife, big fight, tragic outcome.

Jenna Ramsey had shown him the message she'd sent her ex-husband yesterday and the one she'd received back from him this morning. He wasn't convinced. He'd seen too many incidents where phone texts had been manipulated.

The more likely story was that when Jenna Ramsey received no answer to her text yesterday demanding money, she'd gone to the hotel where he worked to have it out with her ex. Somehow she'd discovered he was planning on spending the night with a woman.

He'd probably bragged about it. How he was going to use the bridal suite, which he could access easily enough, since he worked maintenance in the hotel. Apparently the card-coding system didn't keep records.

When Jenna Ramsey found out about the other woman, she worked herself up into a rage overnight and went back to the Blue Surf early this morning to wreak her revenge and break up his little romance.

During the fight that followed, she killed her ex-husband, then sent the text to herself from his cell phone. The girlfriend, meanwhile, had bolted.

It was a tidy little scenario, and normally he would have gone with it, setting out to prove his theory. Something about the woman, however, made him second-guess his conclusions.

His twenty years of experience in the police force had taught him never to judge a book by its cover. He'd learned to look past an aura of innocence and vulnerability and find the devious malice hidden underneath.

In the case of Jenna Ramsey, it wasn't that simple. She'd made it clear that she bitterly detested her ex-husband and that his death wasn't going to ruin her life. Although she hadn't enlarged on that, Messina had the impression that Ramsey was a scumbag and that this woman was well rid of him. He knew a strong woman when he met one, and he had no doubt that Jenna knew how to stand up for herself.

At the same time, he was confused by her honesty about her feelings. If she were guilty, would she be so open about her hostility toward her ex?

Unless it was all an act. When he'd talked to the hotel manager, the guy had seemed convinced that Ramsey still had feelings for his wife. There was always the possibility that she was the owner of the negligee and had slept with her ex-husband in an attempt at reconciliation and something had gone terribly wrong. She could be pretending to hate him to throw suspicion off her.

Somehow, he didn't think that was the case. He'd questioned her for almost an hour, and her answers had been short and to the point. He'd had a strong inkling she was hiding something, yet his doubts about her involvement in Dean Ramsey's death had deepened.

He'd ended the session with a stern warning, making sure she understood she was his main suspect in the case. His only suspect until he investigated further. She'd had motive, means, and opportunity. Hopefully he'd uncover some evidence that would reveal more suspects and take the heat off Jenna Ramsey.

First, if his original theory was right, he needed to find the other woman involved. From what he'd heard about the victim, he seriously doubted that Ramsey would spend the night by himself, wearing a woman's nightgown, in the most expensive suite in the hotel.

So, where was this woman? Why hadn't she come forward? Was it possible she was the killer? Or was there someone else in the picture? The woman's husband, maybe? Found out his wife was having an affair and killed his competition?

Or was all this conjecture and he'd had the perpetrator right the first time?

Complicating things was the fact that by the time he'd made it to the suite to check it out, the room had been thoroughly cleaned. The bedsheets had been changed, and likewise the towels in the bathroom. They'd found no viable traces of DNA and the smudged fingerprints had been inconclusive. Even without that, investigating hotel rooms was hard enough, given the number of people who occupied them over a short span of time.

His only hope was the negligee, hopefully giving him the DNA of its owner before Dean apparently snatched it up in the confusion.

A vision of Jenna Ramsey wearing it popped into his mind, and he hastily shut it down. He had to admit, there was something about her that intrigued him. He was looking forward to digging further into her life, finding out more about her and what it was that she didn't want him to know.

* * *

"You're so lucky you live over the shop," Gracie said as they waited outside for Vivian to lock up. "No commute. Must be nice."

"Most of the time." Vivian turned the key in the lock and dropped the keys in her purse. "Though in nice weather I envy you your drive along the coast road in the mornings." Rentals were hard to find in Misty Bay, and Gracie lived in Newport, a fifteen-minute drive. Jenna lived in the hills overlooking the town in a house inherited from her parents.

The apartment over the tearoom was small but cozy. Just one bedroom, a bathroom, and a combined kitchen and living area. From the bedroom window, Vivian had a view of the ocean, and that was all she needed to be content. Unlike the four-bedroom house she'd sold in Portland, her home was easy to clean, quiet and peaceful for the most part, and just a few steps from where she worked. The fact that the rent was included in the lease for the tearoom was icing on the cake.

She turned to leave just as a shrill voice rang out from farther down the street.

"Yoo-hoo!"

"Oh, help," Jenna muttered. "Here comes blabbermouth."

Vivian watched Natalie totter toward them on her ridiculously high heels, her long, bleached hair flowing in the breeze. She wore skintight black pants, a bright-orange silk shirt, and a cream cropped jacket. Passing by a group of visitors in casual beach clothes, she looked totally out of place.

But then, that's how Natalie Chastain liked it. She soaked up the sidelong glances and the open stares. Wherever the owner of the Sophisticated Grape wine shop went, she was onstage, out to impress everyone who entered her realm.

As she drew closer, Vivian could tell by the woman's face that she'd heard about Jenna's encounter with the police and was positively salivating at the prospect of learning more.

"I'm going to puke," Gracie said, clutching her throat.

"Better not do it on her." Jenna crossed her arms. "She'll sue you for everything you've got."

Natalie reached them and paused, a triumphant smile spreading her orange lips. "Oh, you're back," she said to Jenna. "I thought you were in jail."

"Sorry to disappoint you," Jenna said, pasting on a false smile.

Hoping to avoid a confrontation, Vivian hurriedly intervened. "Natalie, I hear you're thinking of remodeling your store."

"Yes, I am." Natalie focused her black-rimmed eyes on Vivian. "Who told you that?"

"Hal Douglass mentioned it." Hal owned the Furry Fun pet supplies store down the road and seemed to know almost as much as Natalie about the residents of Misty Bay.

"Really. I can't imagine why." Natalie sniffed, then turned back to Jenna. "I'm sorry you're in this trouble. It must be terrifying, being arrested for murder."

Gracie stepped forward, eyes flashing fire. "She wasn't arrested. She didn't kill her ex, and nobody says she did, so you should just button up."

Natalie raised her chin. "Well, excuse me. I'm just repeating what I heard."

"As usual," Jenna said.

Deciding it was time to smooth the waters, Vivian softened her voice. "You were misinformed, Natalie. I'm sure you're relieved that Jenna had nothing to do with this, right?"

Natalie puffed out her breath. "Well, of course I am," she said, sounding deflated. "Not that I'd blame you," she added, flapping her thick eyelashes at Jenna. "If I had a husband who cheated on me like Dean cheated on you, I'd want to tear his heart out and feed it to the gulls."

"Really." Jenna's smile was pure evil. "Then it's probably a good thing you can't find a husband."

Natalie stared at her for a moment. "Well, what I'd like to know is who owns the negligee your ex was wearing. It's strange that she simply disappeared." She paused, then added, "Unless it was your nightgown."

Her face darkening, Jenna took a step toward her. "It was not my nightgown, and this is none of your damn business, so I'll thank you to keep your mouth shut. If that's at all possible."

"Jenna—" Vivian laid a warning hand on her friend's arm.

"It's all right, I'm going." Natalie tossed her head. "I understand why Jenna's upset. I just wanted to say that if there's anything I can do to help, you just have to ask." With that, she flounced off back down the street.

Jenna threw her head back and growled in frustration. "How does she always make me look like the bad guy?"

Vivian smiled. "She's a lot smarter than people think. I do believe her heart's in the right place. She just can't help being an annoying know-it-all."

"It's people like her who spread fake news around town," Jenna said, as Gracie led the way to where the cars were parked on the side street.

"Maybe." Vivian reached Jenna's ancient and battered Honda and waited for her to unlock it. "But it's precisely someone like her who can help us in our investigation. If she doesn't know the answers, she'll do her best to find them."

"But can we trust her not to spread it all over town?" Jenna opened the door on the driver's side. "Apart from the wrong people finding out what we're doing, if Detective Messina learns we're nosing around his murder case, he'll go ballistic."

"Natalie doesn't have to know we're tracking down Dean's killer. She'll just think we're interested in the case, for obvious reasons." Vivian frowned. "She does have a point, you know. The woman who spent the night with Dean must have been there when Dean was killed. He wouldn't be wearing her nightgown if she'd left already."

"Unless she forgot it and left it behind."

"That could be, though there's another possibility."

"What's that?"

Vivian stared into Jenna's anxious eyes. "She could be the killer. You know Dean had a temper. Maybe they got into a fight and she sent him over the balcony. Which could be why she hasn't come forward."

They stared at each other for another long moment, and then Vivian climbed into the car and waited for Jenna to settle herself behind the wheel.

"I'd just like to know why Detective Messina is so sure I killed Dean," Jenna said as she turned the key in the ignition. "Why isn't he looking for Dean's girlfriend?"

"He probably is looking for her, if he's any kind of detective." Vivian made sure her seat belt was securely fastened. Jenna's driving was erratic at the best of times. "But the most important thing right now is for us to find that woman. We need to talk to the staff at the Blue Surf. We could go tomorrow, which would give us more time, but I think we're more likely to find the regular crew on a weekday. So, how about Monday morning?"

"Okay. I'll meet you at the shop. Okay?"

"Sounds good. Try and make it by eight." Since they didn't open the Willow Pattern until noon, that would give them plenty of time to talk to the hotel staff.

Jenna pulled the car out into the street and cruised down to the curve that led out of town. After making a sharp right that swung Vivian against the door, she took off on the winding road leading into the hills.

Vivian tried not to look at the steep drop on her side as they roared around the bends way too fast. The views from up here were spectacular. A long line of beaches stretched way into the distance. The sun glinted on the white sand and sparkled on the blue-green water. Jagged rocks soared out of the ocean, some of them over a hundred feet, providing a home for puffins, cormorants, and the ever-present gulls.

Towering cliffs bordered the beaches, thick with pine and cedar trees, with the occasional house peeking out from the lush green woods. Behind them, the majestic mountains of the coastal range kept watch over the coastline. It was a vision that Vivian knew she'd never get tired of, no matter how often she saw it.

A quick glance in the side mirror told her that they'd left Gracie's red Mazda far behind. They were approaching Jenna's house now, where no doubt the hungry reporter with the yellow hair would be waiting.

She spotted the black SUV as they rounded the last curve and entered the narrow, tree-lined lane where Jenna's cottage sat at the end of a row of small houses.

"That's probably Rita Mozell," she said, as Jenna slammed on the brakes. Her words ended in a grunt as she jerked forward.

Jenna peered through the windshield. "Who?"

"The reporter. She's on KAKN News."

"You know her?"

"No, but I've seen her a few times on TV."

Jenna sighed, then drove up behind the parked car.

The driver's door of the car opened and the elegant reporter stepped out, patted her hair, smoothed down her skirt, and then closed the door. On the other side of the car, the cameraman hauled his equipment out and slung the strap over his shoulder.

"This doesn't look good," Jenna muttered.

"Don't worry. I know your rights. You don't have to talk to them. In fact, the less you say, the better." Vivian opened her door just as Gracie's car zoomed around the bend and sped up to them.

Gracie cut the engine and jumped out as Rita approached the cars. Ignoring Vivian, the reporter headed straight for Jenna. "Jenna Ramsey? I'm Rita Mozell, KAKN News. This is my photographer, Jim. We're sorry to hear of your ex-husband's death. Will you tell us your version of what happened?"

She thrust her microphone in front of Jenna's face. Jim was already training his camera on Jenna, and she put a hand up in front of him. "No comment."

"But wouldn't you like your side of the story to be heard?" Rita insisted. "After all, you're a suspect in your ex-husband's murder."

Vivian stepped forward and mimicked her late husband's official tone. "Mrs. Ramsey has not been formally charged. She is innocent of the crime and will prove that in due course. Until then, she has nothing to say to anyone. Thank you." Taking hold of Jenna's arm, she pushed rather rudely past the cameraman, dragging her friend behind her.

They had reached Jenna's front door, with Gracie right behind them, when Rita called out again. "Mrs. Ramsey! Did you kill your husband?"

Despite Vivian's warning shake of her head, Jenna turned to face the woman. "No, I did not," she said, her tone dripping ice. "If I was going to kill him, trust me, I would have done it a lot sooner than now."

Vivian groaned, while Gracie smothered a yelp of laughter.

Jenna fished her key out of her purse and unlocked her door.

Vivian practically shoved her inside, casting a glance over her shoulder. To her relief, the reporter was climbing back into her car. They'd earned some breathing space, but she had a nasty feeling that Rita Mozell was not about to give up on the hottest story to hit the sleepy town of Misty Bay in decades.

Chapter Three

Jenna's home was like its owner—clean, uncluttered, no frills. A gray couch and armchair sat in front of the TV, and a small bookshelf displayed an assortment of books and videos. An imposing painting of a lighthouse hung between the two windows of the living room; otherwise the walls were bare.

As Gracie closed the front door, a black cat strolled into the room, surveyed the visitors, twitched its tail, and then headed for the armchair.

Vivian watched it jump up and settle itself on the sea-blue cushion. Jenna told her some time ago that she'd picked up a stray. Vivian was surprised her friend kept it. Jenna had met Dean and married him when she was past thirty—too old to have kids, she'd told Vivian—when they were sharing a late nightcap soon after the opening of the Willow Pattern.

Vivian got the impression that Jenna had never been interested in becoming a mother. Knowing her friend's history, Vivian suspected that Jenna didn't trust herself to protect and take care of her own children.

The way things had turned out, it was a good thing she hadn't. Right now, she had only herself to worry about, and the ball of black fur now sleeping peacefully on the armchair.

"Oh, it's so cute!" Gracie rushed over to the chair. "What's its name?"

"Her name is Misty," Jenna said, as she threw her purse on the couch. "She was a stray. I found her a couple of months ago and brought her home to feed her. She's stayed ever since."

Vivian smiled. "She knows where she belongs."

"You named her after the town?" Gracie gently stroked the cat's neck. Misty raised her head and purred.

"No. It was misty the day I found her. I heard her mewing and discovered her crouching in the weeds at the side of the road."

"Oh, poor little thing." Gracie scooped the cat up in her arms.

"Not poor anymore." Jenna sighed. "She eats more than I do."

Vivian laughed. "Speaking of eating, we'd better get going." She glanced at her watch. "I promised the printers I'd have the brochure ready for the anniversary of our opening. I still haven't finished designing it yet and the celebration is only two weeks away."

Jenna shook her head. "I can't believe we've been open for two years already. Where did that time go?"

"I say that every year. The older I get, the faster time seems to fly by."

"I'm so looking forward to the anniversary." Gracie lowered Misty to the chair and brushed a hand down her sweater. "That should be fun."

40

"I hope so." Vivian leaned down to fondle the cat's ears. "Right now, I still have some planning to do, so I'd better get working on it."

"And I have a date," Gracie announced as she danced over to the door.

Jenna looked at her. "I hope it's not that punk with a ring through his nose that you brought into the shop last week."

Gracie snorted. "No, it's not. He's my brother's friend. They were down from Portland on a visit. I don't even remember his name."

"Well, good. I didn't like the look of him."

"You don't like the look of any man. Besides, I don't have to get your okay for who I date. You're not my mother."

Jenna rolled her eyes. "Thank heaven for that."

"We're going," Vivian said firmly as she gently pushed Gracie out the door. She was used to her assistants sparring with each other. Fortunately, it was entirely without malice and she suspected they both did it purely for the fun of it. She was actually relieved that her revelations to Gracie about Jenna's past hadn't changed that.

Glancing back at Jenna, she added, "I'll see you at the shop on Monday at eight."

Gracie halted, turning around to look at them both. "You're opening up early on Monday?"

"No, we're going to the Blue Surf to ask some questions," Vivian said, stepping outside.

"Why didn't you tell me?" Gracie sent Jenna an accusing glare. "You didn't want me to come with you?"

41

"We didn't think you'd want to get up that early," Vivian said, feeling guilty that she hadn't included her.

"Of course we want you to come." Jenna raised her hand and slapped at a bee that was trying to get into the house. "We need your flowing tongue to charm people into giving us the answers we want."

"As long as it doesn't flow too freely," Vivian warned, remembering Gracie's habit of blurting out thoughts before she'd considered the impact.

Gracie's face broke out in a smile. "Awesome! I can't wait. Why can't we go tomorrow? The tearoom is closed and we'll have all day."

"Because Sunday is most people's day off," Vivian said.

"Oh, right." Gracie looked disappointed. "Monday at eight, then. I'll be there."

"Good." Vivian nodded at Jenna. "See you then. Don't open your door to anyone."

"Don't worry, I won't." Jenna closed the door, and Vivian hurried after Gracie, who was already in the car.

Monday, she told herself, was going to be an interesting day. Hopefully, they would get a lead on the mysterious woman who owned the nightgown found on Dean's body. Who was she, and what did she know about Dean's death? That, to Vivian, was the burning question.

* * *

"I think we should talk with the manager of the hotel first," Vivian said as Jenna pulled into the parking lot of the Blue Surf Hotel on Monday morning. "Have you met him?"

"Yes, I have." Jenna switched off the engine and unfastened her seat belt. "I was in the hotel quite a bit before the divorce. His name is Reggie Lambert. That's if he's still the manager. He's a bit of a pompous ass, thinks he's God's gift to women. Dean loathed him, but then he didn't like anyone telling him what to do."

"Neither do you," Grace piped up from the back of the car. "At least you had that in common."

Vivian winced, knowing that Gracie had meant it as a joke and just as certain that Jenna would take offense.

Jenna's head spun around to glare at Gracie. Before she could say anything, Vivian said loudly, "Well, let's go find Reggie Lambert and see what he can tell us."

Gracie opened the car door and hopped out, leaving Jenna to shake her head before she, too, got out of the car and slammed the door shut.

Vivian eased out more slowly, nursing a twinge of the arthritis in her knee that bothered her now and again. The sea breeze fanned her face, and she took a moment to savor the view. The tide was out, and people swarmed around the huge rocks, looking for tide pools. Far out to sea the ghostly shape of a cargo ship was making its way north to Seattle.

In the distance she could just make out the outline of the Peace Rock Lighthouse, no longer alight with its warning lamps but still watching over the water.

She'd always loved the ocean, and even now she found it hard to believe she actually lived within a few short minutes of the beach. The fragrance of seaweed and sand and the cool, salty air never failed to lift her spirits.

It had been the perfect solace she'd needed after losing Martin. She'd kept herself busy during those dark days with the opening of the Willow Pattern, but it was her strolls along the water's edge, watching the tide roll shells and sand crabs onto the sand, that had helped ease her aching heart.

Giving herself a mental shake, she turned to follow her assistants. The women were already heading for the hotel's imposing entrance, and she hurried after them, anxious to get her first look inside the fancy new building.

Jenna paused at the door, waiting for Vivian to catch up with them. "Do you know what we're going to ask him?" she asked as Vivian reached her.

"Not a clue," Vivian said cheerfully. "But I'm sure we'll think of something."

Jenna rolled her eyes and Gracie snickered. The young woman was wearing a loose-fitting black-and-yellow-striped shirt over skinny jeans, reminding Vivian of a giant bee. She danced inside the door and into the lobby, then stared around with wide eyes.

Following behind her, Vivian's first impression of the entrance was warmth. From the patterned gold carpeting to the cherrywood-paneled walls and the soft glow of lights embedded in the ceiling, the room welcomed guests with an aura of comfort and relaxation.

Large pots of ferns hugged the windows, a wide vista of the ocean behind them. Comfortable wicker chairs invited visitors to sit and enjoy the view, and Gracie headed for one of them and plopped herself down.

"Look at her," Jenna muttered. "She acts like she's on vacation instead of trying to rescue her friend from a fate worse than death."

"You're not going to prison," Vivian said, with a lot more conviction than she felt. "Come on, let's go talk to this Reggie person."

The young woman behind the counter greeted them with a smile as they approached. "Welcome to the Blue Surf!" she sang out. "Are you checking in? I'm afraid your room won't be free until three PM, but I can check you in now, and you're welcome to enjoy the facilities until then."

It was a well-rehearsed announcement, one she had probably made a thousand times, Vivian thought as she returned the smile.

"Actually," she said, "we're here to see the manager. Is he available?"

The desk clerk's smile vanished. "Is something wrong? Is there something I can help you with?"

"Yes," Jenna said shortly. "You can summon Reggie Lambert. I want to talk to him about my dead husband."

The clerk stared at her for a moment, then sent a shocked glance down the counter. Apparently reassured that no one else was within earshot, she looked back at Jenna. "Excuse me?"

Vivian leaned forward and lowered her voice. "This is Jenna Ramsey. She's the ex-wife of the man found dead in front of your hotel Saturday. We need to speak with the manager immediately."

The clerk paled. "Oh. Of course." She reached under the counter, presumably for the call button. "He'll be here in a moment. Perhaps you'd like to wait for him over by the windows?"

Vivian could tell the woman was anxious to get them away from the counter and any arriving visitors. "Thank you," she said, and motioned to Jenna with a jerk of her head. "Come on, let's go sit with Gracie."

"I could sit here all day," Gracie announced as they walked up to her. She waved a magazine at them. "I could even order coffee and doughnuts." She nodded at a sign propped against a potted cactus on the table in front of her. "Talk about service." She flung a hand out toward the window. "Just look at that view!"

"When you're finished raving about the place," Jenna said, sitting down next to her, "you might want to remember why we're here. This isn't exactly playtime."

Gracie sobered at once. "Sorry. Are we going to talk to the manager?"

"Here he comes now." Jenna nodded her head in the direction of the counter, and Vivian turned to look.

A tall, trim man, wearing a stylish blue suit and a crisp white shirt, stood talking to the desk clerk, who looked as if she needed an immediate visit to the bathroom. After a moment or two he glanced at Vivian and her companions, ran a hand over his thick, light-brown hair, and then nodded at the clerk before sauntering over to them.

Nodding at Jenna, he murmured, "Good morning, Jenna. I'm deeply sorry for the trouble you're in with the police. If there's anything I can do to help, please don't hesitate to ask."

Jenna faked a smile. "Thank you, Reggie."

Vivian studied him for a moment before saying, "Mr. Lambert? I'd like a word with you, please."

The manager turned his head to look at her. "Yes, of course. How can I help you, Ms. . . . ?"

"I'm Vivian Wainwright, Ms. Ramsey's counselor, and I'm here to ask a few questions about the murder of Dean Ramsey."

A look of wariness flickered in the man's eyes. "Um . . . I really don't know much about it. I was on my way back from LA when it happened. My wife told me that my night clerk had called her earlier to tell her the police were investigating a death and that the man had apparently been pushed from a balcony." His hand wandered to his throat, revealing a tattoo on the back of it.

Squinting at it, Vivian could just make out an eagle carrying a rose in its beak. The bird was tinted dark blue—an odd color for an eagle, she thought. But then, everything about this man was over-the-top.

"You can imagine the shock when I found out the victim was my maintenance man," Reggie said. "I mean, this is a respectable hotel. And to use the bridal suite for his sordid little joyride is unforgivable."

Vivian raised her eyebrows. "Your maintenance man was staying in the bridal suite?"

Reggie sighed. "He had no business being in there, of course. The suite has been unoccupied for at least a month. He must have coded a key card himself to get in."

"And no one saw him up there?"

The manager flicked a sideways glance at Jenna. "No one except Jenna, from what I understand."

Jenna's eyes blazed. "I was never in the bridal suite with Dean—or anywhere else with him, for that matter. I haven't seen him in months."

"Oh." Reggie looked confused. "I'm sorry. I thought I heard the detective say you were seen leaving the hotel that morning about the time the murder happened, and Dean made no secret of the fact that he wanted a reconciliation, so naturally I assumed—"

"Well, you assumed wrong. Detective Messina assumed wrong. Everyone is damn well assuming wrong." Jenna stepped closer to him, poked her nose close to his face, and snarled, "I did not kill my ex-husband."

Reggie backed off a couple of steps, his cheeks warming. "Of course you didn't. I can't imagine where I got that idea."

"Neither can I."

Jenna still looked as if she wanted to throttle the poor man, and Vivian decided it was time to intervene. "Mr. Lambert, you have security cameras in the hotel, right?"

The manager stretched his neck as if his shirt collar was too tight. "Er . . . yes, we do. But they were turned off around midnight."

"Turned off?"

"Yes." Reggie finally tore his gaze away from Jenna's fierce glare and turned to Vivian. "I imagine Dean turned them off so his little escapade in the bridal suite wouldn't be discovered. They were turned on again before the police arrived. We didn't realize they had been off all night until the detective asked to check them."

Vivian frowned. "One more question, Mr. Lambert."

"Reggie." The man smiled, revealing a deep dimple in his left cheek. "Everyone calls me Reggie."

"Reggie." Vivian cleared her throat. "You say that Dean was anxious to get back with Jenna?"

"Oh, yes, definitely." Reggie kept nodding his head to emphasize his words. "He told me he was trying really hard to win her back."

Vivian nodded with him. "That's odd, because we heard that he was heavily involved with another woman."

"Oh?" Reggie's voice rose just a shade. "I wasn't aware of that at all."

"Did you happen to see him with another woman? Here in the hotel, or perhaps somewhere else?"

"I did not." Reggie shook his head. "No, I can't believe that. Dean wanted to get back with Jenna. He told me that."

"That's a bunch of crap," Jenna muttered. "He was lying to you. The only time I've had any connection with him was when I had to remind him that he owed me money. And it was never in person."

"I see." Reggie pursed his lips. "It appears he has hood-winked me on more than one occasion."

"Yeah," Jenna said, her voice heavy with resentment. "He was like that."

Just then the door of the lobby flew open to admit a small group of boisterous young adults, all talking and laughing with voices that echoed throughout the lobby.

"Well, thank you, Mr. Lambert," Vivian said, nudging her chin at Gracie to get out of the chair. "I appreciate your help."

"My pleasure. And it's Reggie."

"Right. Reggie."

Gracie jumped up and grinned at the manager. "There's such an awesome view from here."

Reggie's smile widened. "It is rather spectacular, isn't it? Quite my favorite spot on the coast."

"Me too." She waved her hand good-bye at him. "See you."

"Yes." He looked confused again. "You also."

"He's a bit of an old poop, isn't he?" Gracie said, as she followed Vivian down the steps to the parking lot.

Vivian winced as Jenna, walking behind her, grunted. "Yeah. He's got to be at least forty-five years old."

Gracie halted. "I meant he acted like an old poop. I didn't mean he was actually old. I mean . . ."

Jenna shook her head at her, but she was smiling. "Forget it, shrimp. I know what you meant. The guy's a jerk."

"Actually, I thought he was kind of cute. Wait, where are you going?"

Vivian paused as she heard Gracie's voice behind her. "To the tradesmen's entrance. We need to talk to more hotel staff."

As she had pretty much expected, the few employees who were willing to talk with them could tell them nothing useful. One member of the housekeeping staff, a fresh-faced young woman, seemed fearful of working in a hotel where a murder had occurred.

"I keep looking over my shoulder," she told Vivian, "in case he's still lurking around, and I'm scared to go into the rooms now, in case he's hiding in there."

Vivian did her best to reassure the woman. "I'm quite sure that whoever killed your maintenance man is far away by now.

If I'd killed someone, I certainly wouldn't hang around the crime scene waiting to be arrested."

The woman managed a smile at that, but Vivian could tell she wasn't convinced. "Well, I'm sorry I can't help you," she said. "I'd really like to see him caught, but I didn't know Dean that well and I haven't a clue who might have done it."

"Did you ever see him with a girlfriend?"

The woman shook her head. "He was always working when I saw him."

Vivian thanked her and went in search of her two assistants, who had spread out to question whoever would talk to them.

"Nothing," Jenna said, when Vivian caught up with her. "Nobody's talking. They either don't know or they're afraid to speak up."

Gracie said much the same thing as they walked out into the parking lot. "I'm sorry, Jen," she said, as they reached the car. "I wish they could have helped."

"Yeah, well, at least we tried." Jenna raised her chin to look at the sky. "I'm screwed."

"No, you're not," Vivian said, as she pulled open the door of Jenna's car. "We'll get there. Just not today."

Minutes later they were on the road and heading into town. Gracie chattered on about the hotel and how she would love to stay there while Jenna said nothing, her gaze firmly on the road ahead.

"I loved it when you, like, told Reggie you were Jenna's lawyer," Gracie said, as they entered Main Street. "He might not have talked to us otherwise."

"I didn't lie." Vivian twisted her head to look behind her at Gracie. "I told him I was a counselor. That could mean a lot of things other than a lawyer. It could refer to a therapist, a teacher, a mentor, or simply an adviser. It's a title that sounds official, that's all. It's up to Reggie how he interprets it."

"Clever," Jenna said, finally speaking up. "I like it."

"Wow, me too." Gracie grinned. "This is fun."

"You won't think so if it gets dangerous," Jenna warned. In the next instant she slammed on the brakes as an elderly couple stepped off the curb ahead of her. "Why can't these people use the freaking crosswalks?" she muttered, as Vivian rubbed the elbow that had smacked painfully against the dashboard.

She'd sounded agitated, and Vivian patted her arm. "It's okay. You stopped in plenty of time."

"They were lucky I didn't run over them. They're not going to live much longer if they don't pay attention to the traffic."

Vivian studied her as the car surged forward. "Are you okay?"

"No."

For a moment, Vivian thought that was the only answer she was going to get, but then Jenna added, in a torrent of words, "Reggie Lambert believes I killed Dean. The cops believe I killed him. It was all over the news on TV last night. The whole town probably has me convicted and locked away already. I didn't do anything. Why are people so quick to blame me for something I didn't do? Am I that bad a person that they find it so easy to believe I'm a cold-blooded murderer?"

Her voice had gradually risen, and the car had gathered speed. Worried now for their safety and that of the pedestrians strolling the sidewalks, Vivian said firmly, "Jenna, slow down. Relax. We'll talk about this when we get back to the tearoom."

To her relief, Jenna immediately braked to a normal speed, and they arrived back at the Willow Pattern without any more incidents. Gracie had been unusually quiet, and Vivian guessed the young woman was thinking about the conversation they'd had a couple of days ago about Jenna's past.

The moment Vivian stepped inside the tearoom, she began to relax. The aura of serenity that always greeted her when she walked through the door never failed to settle her nerves.

It wasn't exactly the way she'd felt when she'd first set eyes on the property.

At that time, it was operating as a small eatery called the Beach Bums Café. The owners had decorated it with a Hawaiian theme and had gone overboard with the decor. Gaudy posters of dancers in grass skirts and tiki bar huts covered the walls, plastic palm trees crowded the corners, while nets slung from the ceiling held glass fishing floats, fake pineapples, and coconuts.

All very Hollywood, and not at all to Vivian's taste. She'd closed her eyes to envision the atmosphere she hoped to create—something with a little class and distinction. All things British, in a welcoming haven of appetizing delicacies and the soothing elixir of fine tea.

Her dream had eventually become a reality, and now she could reap the rewards. And she felt rewarded every time she entered the tranquility of the Willow Pattern Tearoom.

"Have either of you had breakfast yet?" she asked, as she led the way past the immaculate tables to the kitchen. "I can fix an omelet for you both."

"I'm not hungry," Jenna said, dropping her purse onto a chair. "I feel like I should be doing something, but I'm not sure what."

"I ate before I came." Gracie pulled a chair out from the table and dropped down on it.

"Okay, then. I'll make some tea and we can talk. Decide what to do next."

"I think we should talk to Madison," Jenna said. "She's the night clerk at the Blue Surf. She was probably there at the hotel when Dean was killed."

"Yes, she was." Vivian filled a kettle with water and placed it on the stove. "Remember, Reggie said the night clerk called his wife Saturday morning to tell her the police found the body."

"I still can't believe Dean is dead." Jenna shuddered. "I detested that man, but I would never have wished that on him."

"I know." Vivian walked over to the table and sat down. "Jenna, not everyone thinks you killed him. The people who matter to you don't believe that. And when Detective Messina starts hauling in more suspects, people will soon focus on them."

"*If* he finds more suspects."

"Well, if he doesn't, we will." Vivian peered at her watch. "We can go talk to Madison now, if you like. We still have time before we open. Do you know where she lives?"

"No, but I have her cell number. I had to get ahold of her once when Dean was too sick to go to work."

"Why don't you give her a call," Vivian said, "and ask if we can meet somewhere." As if answering her, the kettle shrilled, steam bursting from its spout. She got up, adding, "Maybe she'd like to come here and have some tea with us."

Gracie laughed. "You act like a cup of tea solves everything."

"It got the British through two world wars, so yes, I think a lot can be achieved over a good cup of tea." She walked over to the counter and took the lid off a teapot.

"I'll call her," Jenna said, "but don't be surprised if she doesn't want to talk to us. She's not the chatty type."

"She'll talk to me," Vivian said. "Just get her to meet us." After swishing the teapot with hot water, she emptied it, popped in three tea bags, and filled it from the boiling kettle.

Meanwhile, Jenna had thumbed a number into her cell phone. After a moment or two she muttered, "She's not answering. She probably doesn't want to—" She broke off, then raised her voice. "Madison? It's Jenna. Ramsey," she added, as an afterthought.

She listened for a moment, then said, "Thank you. I appreciate that." She flicked a glance at Vivian. "We were wondering if you'd like to stop by the Willow Pattern for a scone or something. We'd like to talk to you about what happened."

She listened again, then looked at Vivian. "She's shopping at the grocery store. She says she doesn't know anything anyway."

Vivian walked over to her. "Give me the phone." She took it from Jenna's outstretched hand and put it to her ear. "Madison? I'm Vivian Wainwright, Jenna's counselor. I believe you were there when the detective was in the hotel?"

Madison's voice sounded shrill when she answered. "Yes, I was. I was the one who told him Jenna was in the hotel Saturday. He was asking questions about Dean, and I'd seen Jenna leave the lobby that morning and it just slipped out. I didn't mean to get her into trouble."

"I know you didn't," Vivian said, making her voice soothing. "She understands that. Did you see her come into the hotel?"

"No, I didn't. I just saw her as she was going out the door." Madison paused, then said in a rush, "Maybe Paula saw her. She was in the hotel early Saturday morning."

"Paula?"

"Reggie's wife. She's our assistant manager."

Vivian sent Jenna a questioning look, which she answered with a nod. "I see." She paused, then added, "Madison, did you happen to see Dean lately with a woman companion?"

There was a long silence at the end of the line, and then Madison said faintly, "No, I haven't seen him with anyone." Her voice sank to a near whisper. "I'm so sorry."

"Thank you, Madison."

"Please tell Jenna I'm sorry. For everything."

"I will." Vivian handed the phone back to her friend. "She feels very badly about telling Messina that she saw you leaving the hotel. She said to tell you she's sorry."

Jenna shrugged. "She was only saying what she saw. By the way, Paula is Reggie's wife."

"Yes, Madison told me. Have you met her?"

"Only once." Jenna wrinkled her nose. "She isn't what you'd call sociable."

"Madison said that Paula was in the hotel early Saturday morning."

"She's the assistant manager. She does all the hiring of employees and takes care of any problems with them. She takes over at the hotel when Reggie's off on one of his business trips. Did Madison see Dean with anyone?"

"No, she didn't."

Jenna tucked her phone back in her purse. "So, what now?"

"Now we'll have a cup of tea, and then we'll discuss our options." Vivian got up to pour the tea, trying to decide if she wanted to open a pack of Scottish shortbread to go along with it.

Behind her, Gracie asked, "You think Dean turned off the security cameras?"

"Probably," Jenna said. "After all, he worked on them often enough. He'd know how to do it without getting caught. Actually, I'm surprised he was that careful. He sure wasn't too smart when he cheated on me."

"I'm so sorry, Jenna." Gracie sounded as if she were close to tears. "That must have been such a bummer."

Jenna shrugged. "I'll survive."

Hearing the note of defeat in her friend's voice, Vivian hurried over to the table with the brimming cups of tea. "Here. Drink this, and you'll both feel better."

She went back for her cup and saucer and carried it back to the table. "Now then," she said, "we have to decide what to do next. The sooner we get to the bottom of this, the sooner we can all put it behind us. Positive thinking is positive action, as my mother was fond of saying."

"I'm trying to think positive," Jenna said, as she lifted her cup, "but I have a bad feeling this isn't going to end well."

For once, Vivian was at a loss as to how to answer her. How could she make promises when she wasn't sure if she could keep them? What if Jenna was convicted of murder? She wouldn't be the first innocent person to go to jail.

She gave herself a mental shake. She couldn't afford to let the doubts creep in. The truth was out there, and they would keep digging until they found it. Come what may.

57

Chapter Four

Deciding that it was time to get down to basics, Vivian made an effort to sound confident. "What about Mr. Lambert's wife? I think we should talk to her. She might have seen Dean with someone in the hotel."

Jenna took a sip of her tea before answering. "It's worth a shot, I guess." She put down her cup. "I tell you one thing, this was no one-night stand for Dean. He went to a lot of trouble and took a big chance on being caught. He could have been charged with trespassing and heaven knows what else. He wouldn't have taken a risk like that unless the woman was special to him."

Vivian nodded. "I had the same thoughts. I think he was having an affair and this has been going on for a while. So, I would say our best course of action is to do everything we can to find this woman. She either killed Dean or she knows who did and is afraid to tell anyone. Otherwise she would have come forward."

"Unless she's married and doesn't want her husband to know she was having an affair." Jenna picked up her cup. "Whatever—she's the answer to this mess."

"Maybe she's dead too," Gracie said, her voice hushed.

Vivian stared at her. "I hadn't thought of that."

"Well, if she is," Jenna said briskly, "somebody will report her missing, or her body will turn up sooner or later, and this time Detective Know-It-All Messina won't be able to blame me."

"There's that, I suppose." Vivian stared thoughtfully at her cup. "We need to keep a sharp eye on the news. Meanwhile, we'll talk to Paula Lambert. We can look up her address online."

"We could just call her," Jenna said.

"Do you have her number?"

"I have the hotel number. Or maybe Madison will tell us what it is."

"If she knows." Vivian shook her head. "It will be better if we talk to Paula face-to-face anyway. It's too easy to just hang up a phone. Besides, people tend to give more away when you can see them."

"Okay. I do know where she lives. Dean showed me Reggie's house one time." Jenna wrinkled her brow. "At least, I think I remember where it is."

"I'll check it out to be sure." Vivian looked at Gracie. "It's too late to go now. How about this evening?"

Gracie shifted on her chair. "Er . . . well . . . okay. What time?"

Vivian peered at her face. "You already had plans for tonight?"

"Don't tell me," Jenna said. "You've got a date."

"Nope." Gracie reached for her cup and drained her tea.

"It's okay if you do." Vivian glanced at Jenna. "We can talk to Paula Lambert. You don't have to be there. We can fill you in tomorrow. Right, Jenna?"

To Vivian's relief, Jenna nodded. "Sure. It's okay, Gracie. No big deal."

"Well, yeah, it is a big deal," Gracie said, putting down her cup with a clatter that made Vivian wince. "Like, clearing your name is more important than anything else. It's just that . . . well . . . I'm supposed to be . . . somewhere tonight, and it's not a date."

Feeling sorry for the poor woman, Vivian leaned toward her. "Gracie, all we're going to do is talk to Paula. We don't even know if she'll be at home. Go to your appointment. We'll tell you everything tomorrow."

Gracie still looked doubtful. "Well, if you're sure."

"We're sure," Jenna told her.

"Okay. Thanks." Gracie sprang up from her chair. "I'd better go and unpack that shipment that came in this week. I need to restock the shelves before we open." Before anyone could answer her, she shot across the kitchen and disappeared into the storeroom.

Vivian turned back to Jenna, who was staring after Gracie, her forehead creased in a frown.

"That was odd," Vivian said. "She's not usually that secretive."

"Yeah. Something's going on there that she doesn't want us to know about."

"I just hope she's not sick, or in some kind of trouble." Vivian glanced back at the storeroom door.

"Well, I guess if she'd wanted us to know about it, she would have told us." Jenna rose to her feet, her empty cup rattling in the saucer in her hand. "Knowing Gracie, she can't keep anything secret for long. Sooner or later she'll spill it." She picked up Gracie's cup and saucer and carried them, along with her own, to the counter.

"Well," Vivian said, "we'll pay Paula a visit tonight. Hopefully we'll have something to tell Gracie in the morning."

Jenna's sigh was audible. "I'm not looking forward to talking to Paula. She's even more snooty than her husband. It's a sure bet that she believes I killed Dean."

Vivian got up from the table, bringing her cup and saucer with her. "I could go alone; then you wouldn't have to deal with her."

Jenna's smile transformed her gaunt face. "You're sweet, but I'm not letting you do this alone. This is my problem, and I have to deal with it. I just hope you know how grateful I am for helping me like this. No matter how it turns out."

Vivian cleared her throat. "It's going to turn out just fine. I'm a strong believer in justice." And she would see to it that justice prevailed, she promised herself. She would not give up as long as she had a single breath left in her body.

*   *   *

There had been a time when Tony Messina hated Mondays. That was in the days when he was married and the weekends were a treasured respite from the mayhem. Now and then the peace would be interrupted with an emergency, but for the most part he could enjoy some leisure time with his wife and daughter. Time when he could forget, for a while, the pressure and stress of his job, until the alarm brought him back to reality on Monday mornings.

Now, however, the weekends were long, lonely, and full of memories he fought to block out. He actually looked forward to Mondays, when he could focus on the job and leave the past where it belonged.

Staring at the report in front of him, he studied the sparse details. There had to be a clue in there somewhere that would confirm that Jenna Ramsey had killed her ex-husband. Or preferably, that she hadn't. So far he was drawing a blank.

Mornings were usually quiet in town, and the three police officers were at their desks. Papers rustled and now and then someone would cough, but other than that there was little noise to disturb the peace.

Until his phone rang. He picked it up, surprised to hear the chief's voice on the line. "Messina? I need a word."

"Yes, sir." Messina got up from his desk, frowning as he walked over to the office. Visits to the chief were unusual. He usually communicated by text messages or emails. Even that was rare.

Dennis Chapman had taken over from Paul Reinhard, the previous chief, just six months ago. Messina missed Paul. They had enjoyed an easy relationship, exchanging jokes and occasionally enjoying a beer or two together at the brewery. Paul had retired, leaving Chief Chapman to fill his shoes, which he had done with efficiency and dedication but without the easy camaraderie that Messina had enjoyed with his former boss.

After a brief tap on the door, Messina walked into the office to find the chief frowning at his computer as if he were chastising a wayward rookie. "How are you doing on this murder investigation?" he demanded as Messina paused in front of his desk.

"We're digging. We don't have much to go on yet."

The chief grunted. "According to this report, you don't have anything. A corpse, and that's about it. What about the hotel room? Nothing there?"

"No, sir. By the time we got up there, the room had been wiped cleaned. Security cameras had been turned off."

"What about the victim's wallet? Anything helpful?"

"We checked out his bank account. He had a substantial balance in there. Maintenance jobs must pay well. Otherwise, nothing significant turned up. We'll be checking out a couple of his contacts today."

"Hmmm." The chief sat back in his chair. "Okay then, Messina. Carry on. Let me know if anything turns up."

"Yes, sir." Messina resisted the temptation to salute him and turned on his heel. It was unusual for Chapman to take so much interest in a case. Normally he would wait until he was presented with the final report before commenting on it.

Then again, Messina reminded himself, as he walked back to his desk, this was the first murder case under the new chief's watch since he'd arrived in Misty Bay. It wasn't surprising he was curious about the process.

He'd barely sat down when Brady wandered over, waving a sheet of paper. "Just got the DNA report from the lab," he said, handing it to Messina. "Not much there, though."

Messina scanned the lines of the report and swore under his breath. The only DNA found on the negligee belonged to Dean Ramsey.

"You still don't think he was cross-dressing?" Brady had that sickening grin on his face that made Messina's skin creep.

"No," he said shortly. "I don't. Get the car. We're going to check out that hotel suite again."

Brady's grin vanished. "Yes, sir." He ambled over to the door like he had all day to get there.

Messina filed the report in the Ramsey folder, then dropped it in a drawer and locked it. True, he didn't have much to go on so far, but experience had taught him that patience and persistence usually paid off. If Jenna Ramsey killed her husband, he'd find the proof he needed. If she hadn't, then somebody else had, and he wasn't going to rest until he chased that person down and took them into custody.

Twenty minutes later he stood once more in the bridal suite of the Blue Surf Hotel. The room had been sealed off while the investigation was ongoing, and everything looked the same as it had two mornings ago.

He and Brady had searched the entire suite from top to bottom and, except for the wallet, watch, and cell phone, found nothing they could use. All surfaces had been thoroughly cleaned, the bedding had been changed, and not even a scrap of paper lay in the wastebasket.

He could hear Brady in the bathroom, opening and closing the shower door, though what he expected to find in there was a mystery.

Seconds later, Brady emerged from the bathroom, brandishing a gold tube in his gloved hand. "Guess what I found!"

Messina looked closer. "A lipstick? How did we miss that?"

"It was underneath the cabinets. It must have dropped to the floor and rolled underneath out of sight. I was bending down to look at a stain on the floor when I saw it."

Messina grunted. He'd searched the bathroom himself on Saturday. Never thought to look under the rims of the cabinets. He was slipping. It wasn't a comfortable thought. "Good work, Brady. Get it to the lab. That thing has to be loaded with DNA."

"Yes, sir!" Beaming, Brady pulled a paper bag from his pocket and sealed the lipstick inside it.

"It doesn't mean it will solve the case," Messina warned as Brady headed for the door. "If the cleaners missed it on Saturday, it means they're not very thorough. That thing could have been lying there for months."

Brady's smile faded. "Yes, sir."

On the other hand, Messina mused, as he followed his officer out the door, it could also have been dropped by whoever had spent the night with Dean Ramsey. He sighed, envisioning the work that lay ahead of him, tracking down the DNA or fingerprints found on the lipstick. If he was lucky, it could lead him to the killer. If not, a helluva lot of work would go wasted.

Then again, that was the nature of the job. It was still infinitely preferable to the hell he'd gone through in Portland. With that thought in mind, he lightened up as he stepped outside into the fresh sea air of Misty Bay.

* * *

The rest of the morning passed swiftly for Vivian. She prepared the fixings for the sandwiches while Jenna laid the tables, filled the small china pots with imported Devonshire cream and strawberry jam, and poured milk into the delicate porcelain jugs before stashing everything in the fridge.

Soon after Vivian turned the OPEN sign face out, the customers started trickling in. Some were there for an early afternoon tea, while a couple of regulars stopped by to pick up their favorite British biscuits, sweets, or pickles. Occasionally, someone wandered in to potter around the shelves, looking among the calendars, tea towels, and pottery for the latest imports from the UK.

Vivian was in the kitchen, loading the cake stands, when Jenna hurried in, carrying empty plates and a pink teapot. "They're all looking at me like I'm going to stick a knife in their backs," she said as she placed everything on the counter.

"Oh, no. I can't believe that." Vivian looked at her in dismay. "You must be imagining it. I'm sure they don't think you're capable of hurting someone."

"Yeah? Well, one of our regular customers shrank away from me when I put the sandwiches on the table. She acted like I was contagious with some deadly disease."

Vivian clicked her tongue in disgust. "Seriously? I should go out there and set her straight."

"Don't." Jenna laid a hand on her arm. "I don't want to cause trouble. I can't blame her, really. After all, I am the only suspect. Who else is she going to blame?"

"She can reserve her judgment until the truth comes out."

"Yeah, well, not everyone is you. I'm sorry, Vivian. I'm just afraid all this will hurt your business."

Vivian turned and gave her a swift hug. "Hush. You've got no reason to be sorry for anything. I'm not in the least bit worried about the business. We'll get to the bottom of this, I promise, and then all those ignorant people out there will feel guilty for doubting you and they'll be falling over themselves to make amends."

Jenna's face broke out in a smile. "You always know how to make a woman feel better."

"Good. Now go out there and hold your head up high. You've got right on your side." She watched her friend hurry out the door, wishing she felt a little more confident. Hunting down a killer was no easy task. She had no illusions about that.

If she were honest with herself, she was doing it more to give Jenna hope than because she had any real expectations of success. When facing a disaster, it helped to feel you were doing something to help yourself rather than sitting and waiting for the ax to fall.

She had to believe that Detective Messina was still investigating the case; otherwise he would have charged Jenna. She hoped he'd find evidence that would at least exonerate her friend, if not lead him to the real killer.

Still, a part of her had to admit, she rather enjoyed the challenge. Although Martin hadn't been able to discuss his ongoing cases with her, he would go into great detail after they were concluded. She'd found it fascinating to learn how the puzzles had been unraveled. In another life, she rather fancied herself as a sleuth.

It was this interest in murder cases that fed her appetite for mystery novels. Now she was slap-bang in the middle of one herself. What could be more exciting than that?

"Your boyfriend just came in," Gracie announced from behind her, making her jump.

Vivian twisted her head, her hands still full of pastries. "What boyfriend?"

"Hal Douglass." Gracie grinned. "He didn't have a reservation, so I sat him in the corner by the shelves." Her grin widened. "You can, like, have a private conversation there."

Vivian sighed. Gracie seemed to find huge delight in teasing her about Hal. "I wish you wouldn't keep calling him that. I've told you over and over, he's just a friend. That's all."

"Yeah, a boyfriend."

Vivian wrinkled her brow. "Hal is older than me. He's hardly a boy."

"Okay, a manfriend, then."

"That sounds even more improper."

Gracie laughed. "You need to get with it."

"Are you suggesting I'm old-fashioned?"

Tucking her arm into Vivian's elbow, Gracie pulled her toward the door. "I'm just trying to help you enjoy life. You must get that Hal's interested."

"I don't know any such thing." Vivian could feel her cheeks beginning to burn. It was true that she and Hal enjoyed each other's company, but she'd never considered him anything more than a friend. She seriously hoped that Gracie was mistaken about his feelings. If he was looking for something more significant, that would just make things awkward between them. It could even mean the end of their friendship.

She was rather surprised by how much she would hate that, and she was still dwelling on it when she made her way to his table.

The moment Hal spotted her, his face lit up with a dazzling smile. "Hi, there! Hope you don't mind me dropping in like this."

"Not at all." She looked around at the rest of the customers. A group of ladies took up two of the tables and were chatting back and forth among each other, spattering the conversation now and then with shrill laughter.

At another table, an elderly couple sat quietly talking, apparently oblivious of their rowdy neighbors. She watched them for a moment as the woman reached for her companion's empty cup and filled it from her teapot.

She used to do that so often for Martin. She waited for the shaft of pain that usually accompanied such a memory and was somewhat confused when it didn't materialize.

Switching her gaze back to Hal, she summoned a smile. With his shaggy gray hair and soft brown eyes gazing at her through the lenses of his tortoiseshell glasses, he often reminded her of a huge teddy bear—dependable, cuddly, and infinitely comforting.

In the early days of opening the Willow Pattern, it was Hal who eased the agony of life without Martin. He'd been the first to make her laugh again, the first to convince her that she was doing the right thing by realizing her dream. He was a rock in the middle of her raging torrent of stress, and she'd leaned on him maybe more than she should have, which just might have given him the wrong idea.

He smiled back at her. "Do you have time to talk?"

Feeling guilty now, she gave him a reluctant shake of her head. "I'm sorry, Hal. Maybe later?"

"Sure. I just stopped by to see how you were all doing."

"You saw the news about Dean?"

"I did." He glanced over to where Jenna was hovering around the chattering women. "Is Jenna okay?"

"She will be." Vivian leaned closer, lowering her voice. "She didn't do it, you know."

Hal nodded. "I didn't think so."

"There was someone else with him that night. The three of us are looking for her. We have to find her."

Hal's expression changed. He looked over at the crowded tables, then back at Vivian. "Come by the shop when you have time. We need to talk."

Vivian's pulse quickened. "You know something that could help?"

"Maybe. We can't talk here."

"Okay. I'll stop by later."

"Good."

"You want some tea?"

"No, thanks. I have to get back to the shop." He climbed to his feet. "I left Wilson in charge, and that's never a good idea."

Vivian smiled. Wilson was young, enthusiastic, and somewhat clueless. His skills in technology were nothing short of brilliant. He could manipulate a computer or his smartphone in ways that made Vivian's head spin. Yet he couldn't tell the difference between a dog's harness and a leash.

Vivian remembered the time Hal asked him to fetch a case of dental chews to restock the shelf. Wilson came back with toothpaste, wondering how a dog was going to chew it. The fact that Hal overlooked Wilson's shortcomings in hopes that the kid would eventually get the hang of it was a testament to the older man's patience and consideration. This was Wilson's first job, and Hal wasn't going to start off the young man's working life with failure.

Spotting Jenna heading for the kitchen, Vivian nodded at Hal. "I'll see you later then," she said, then turned and hurried after her friend.

It was on the tip of her tongue to tell Jenna that Hal could have some information that might help their search for Dean's mysterious lover. She decided against it. Better not to get the woman's hopes up if it turned out to be a dead end.

She waited until the tearoom had emptied of customers and it was time to close up shop before announcing that she had an errand to run. "I'll grab something to eat after that," she told Jenna, "and I'll meet you out front at eight. Does that sound okay to you?"

"Sounds fine." Jenna picked up her purse. "I have to go home and feed Misty anyway. I'll find something to eat there and be back at eight."

"Are you sure you don't want me to come with you?" Gracie asked, as she hunted for her own purse. "I could cancel my meeting."

Noticing Jenna's eyebrows rising, Vivian said hurriedly, "No, Gracie, you don't have to cancel anything. We'll talk in the morning."

"Okay." Gracie recovered her purse from behind the counter, then dashed over to the door. "I hope you get the lowdown on Dean's lover," she called out before she disappeared outside.

Jenna wrinkled her nose. "Lowdown? She's been watching too many B movies."

Vivian laughed. "I don't think she sits still long enough to watch a movie." She sobered as she added, "She said she was going to a meeting. I just hope she's okay and there's nothing bad going on with her."

"If you're that worried about her, ask her," Jenna said. "She trusts you. She'll probably tell you."

"No." Vivian walked with her to the door. "I'll wait until she feels like confiding in us."

"And until then, you'll worry yourself sick."

Vivian smiled. "I'll see you at eight."

Jenna gave her a brief nod, then stepped outside. Looking up at the clouding sky, she murmured, "There's a storm coming in. I can feel it."

"Well, I hope it waits until we're done visiting." Vivian watched Jenna head for her car, then closed the door.

Peering at her watch, she figured she had just enough time to have a quick chat with Hal before heating up something in the microwave. Like her, he lived upstairs from his shop. He closed an hour later than she did, however, so he should still be behind the counter.

After combing through her hair, she peered closer at the mirror. It had been at least a month or two since she'd had a hairdo, and it was getting a little long behind her ears. She wore it in a bob cut and so far had resisted the urge to have it dyed, despite the sprinkling of silver in the light-brown mop.

After reassuring herself that she couldn't see an increase in the gray hairs, she dabbed lipstick on her lips, adjusted the neckline of her flowered cotton blouse, and headed out the door.

The Furry Fun pet supplies shop was just down the street, and it took Vivian less than a minute to reach the door. Stepping inside, she was relieved to see the store empty of customers. She didn't have time to wait for people to be served.

Hal greeted her as she walked over to the counter. "How did your day go?"

"Great! We had a mostly full house this afternoon." She looked around at the shelves of pet food, toys, and treats. Hanging from hooks at the end of one aisle were dog sweaters in all the colors of the rainbow, with tartan and checkered ones in between. The next aisle sported an assortment of dog boots in neon shades that made Vivian blink, and even patterned ball caps for dogs.

Vivian tried to picture a dog wearing a cap and failed. She looked back at Hal, who was studying her through his glasses with a quizzical expression. "How about you?"

"Just enough to keep me afloat." He came out from where he'd been sitting behind the counter. "Which is the way I like it."

Vivian nodded. "Not too much stress, then."

"Not a lot, no. I've had enough stress in my life. It's time to take it easy."

Remembering some of the conversations she'd had with him, she knew what he meant. "Do you ever think of retiring?"

"I retired once," he reminded her. "It didn't take."

"You were only in your fifties then, right?"

"Fifty-seven. And feeling every second of it."

"I'm not surprised." Vivian shuddered. Hal had told her about his days as a firefighter in Portland. Some of his stories had given her nightmares. Especially when he'd told her how he'd been hit by a burning tree while fighting a wildfire.

She remembered the fire. It happened about eight years ago. They called it the Cache Creek Fire. It destroyed around seventy-five thousand acres in Hells Canyon, near the Snake River on Oregon's border with Washington. She remembered Martin showing her photos of the burn, little dreaming that she would one day meet one of the brave men who had finally tamed it.

Hal had been clearing some brush when the fire suddenly flared up behind him and his fellow firefighters. Before they could escape, a tree, flaming up to its highest branches, came down on them.

Hal escaped with a broken arm and severe burns on his back. Two of his companions weren't so lucky. Hal had become emotional while telling her the story, and she knew that the death of those two friends haunted him to this day. He'd been forced to retire from the Portland Fire Bureau and had bought the shop in Misty Bay a year later. Eighteen months after that he lost his wife, Terry, to cancer—yet another emotional story from him.

After learning about Hal's past, Vivian had realized why he'd been so instrumental in helping her heal from Martin's death. He had been through the same thing himself and could understand the anguish engulfing her.

They'd shared a shattering experience and had formed a bond. And that was all it was, she constantly reminded herself.

Just a friendship. Close, maybe, but they were simply friends all the same. She had no real desire to become romantically involved with a man again. The fear and pain of losing again was too agonizing to bear.

"Come upstairs," Hal said, as he walked over to the door. "I'll open some wine. I just bought a couple of bottles of excellent Oregon Pinot from Natalie."

Badly wanting to say yes, Vivian reluctantly shook her head. "I can't. I still have to eat, and I'm supposed to meet Jenna at eight at the shop. We're going to try and talk to Paula Lambert about the murder. She's the assistant manager at the hotel."

Hal nodded. "I know. I know them both. Reggie belongs to my golf club."

Vivian stared at him. "Somehow I can't imagine that man playing any kind of sport."

Hal chuckled. "He plays at it. I think it's just an excuse to get away from the hotel for a while." He checked his watch. "How about I close up and fix you a sandwich with that wine? You still have time for that, and we need to talk anyway."

Vivian looked around. "Wilson isn't here?"

"No. I sent him home an hour ago. It won't hurt to close a bit early. It's unlikely anyone's going to come by now. It's munching time."

Giving in, Vivian smiled. "Lead the way, mister. I could use a nice glass of Pinot."

"There you go!" He was beaming as he crossed the floor and opened the door that led upstairs.

Climbing the steps ahead of him, Vivian was beginning to have second thoughts. This was the first time Hal had invited her to his apartment. Although she trusted him completely, she was a little concerned he'd get the wrong idea.

In the next instant, she chided herself for her immature anxiety. Hal was no more interested in her that way than she was in him. She was acting like a teenager on a first date, for heaven's sake.

Reaching the top of the stairs, she waited for him to reach her. They were in a narrow hallway that opened up on her right into a large storeroom, where shelves were crammed with various sizes of boxes.

"This way." Hal turned left, and she followed him down to a door and waited for him to open it.

Throwing the door open, Hal announced, "Welcome to my humble abode."

It was too late to have second thoughts now. Hoping she wasn't doing something she'd regret, she walked slowly into his living room.

Chapter Five

O nce inside the room, Vivian's attention was immediately drawn to the huge TV hanging from a wall. It dominated the room and made her feel as if she'd walked into a movie theater.

A comfortable dark-brown couch sat in front of the TV, with a beige armchair to keep it company. Two bookcases against another wall held stacks of books and videos. Vivian headed over there and studied the titles, pleased to see a couple of her favorite authors.

"I see you like mysteries too," she said as she squinted at the small print. She'd left her reading glasses at home and could barely make out the names. "I've read some of these." She pulled out a book with a gaudy cover showing a silhouette of a man against a nighttime city skyline with a dagger dripping blood over his head. "Not this one, though." She held it up for him to see. "This one looks kind of gory. I prefer the cozies."

"It is gory." Hal headed across the room to the small kitchen area. "That'll put you right off your dinner. I suggest you stick to the cozies." He opened the fridge and peered inside. "Ham and cheese okay?"

"Sounds great. Thanks." Vivian put the book back. "Can I help?"

"You can open the wine." He reached inside the fridge and pulled out a bottle. After standing it on the counter, he rummaged in the drawer below and pulled out a foil cutter. "Here you go."

She walked over to him and took the cutter, then looked at the bottle. "Ooh, nice wine. Did Natalie recommend that?"

Hal pretended to look offended. "I may not be a connoisseur, but I know what I like."

Vivian picked up the bottle. "I always did like a man with good taste."

"Yeah? Well, I'm glad I pass the test."

He sounded a little gruff, and she gave him a quick glance. His expression told her nothing, however, and she quickly looked away.

"The opener is over there." Hal gestured at the end of the counter.

Vivian carried the bottle over to where an electric corkscrew sat on its charging base. It had a clear plastic cover at the end of the tube. She liked that. She could see exactly where to place the point of the corkscrew.

The cork popped out of the bottle with ease, and then, at the push of a button, dropped into her waiting hand. "This is cool. I've seen pictures of these but never thought to buy one. I still open my wine the old-fashioned way."

"There's nothing wrong with being old-fashioned." Hal had taken ham and cheese slices out of the fridge and laid them on the counter. As she watched, he pulled a head of lettuce, wrapped in plastic, out of the fridge, and then reached in again for a couple of ripe tomatoes. "The wineglasses are up there."

He nodded at a cabinet on his right, and Vivian opened the door. Six wineglasses sat on the shelf, and she took two of them down. It suddenly occurred to her that she hadn't asked him what it was he wanted to tell her. Something significant, obviously, since he was wary about being overheard.

Feeling guilty, now, for allowing herself to be distracted from what was important, she carefully poured the wine. "So, what was it you wanted to tell me?" she asked, as she handed him a glass.

Ignoring her question, Hal raised the yellow wine. "To a beautiful friendship,"

She avoided his gaze as she answered, "I'll drink to that." She took a sip, savoring the crisp, clean apple and pear flavors. "This is scrumptious."

"Scrumptious?"

He sounded amused, and she looked up to see his eyes twinkling at her. "It was one of my mother's favorite words."

He nodded. "Good one." He turned back to the counter, put down his glass, and finished laying ham and cheese on the thick bread slices.

There was an awkward silence for a moment or two while Vivian wondered what he was thinking, and then he asked abruptly, "How well did you know Dean Ramsey?"

"Not all that well. I'd known Jenna less than a year when she divorced him. He came into the tearoom once in a while, but he didn't have much to say for himself. I got the feeling he was a bit unsociable."

Hal grunted. "Never liked the guy myself. I figure he was running with some bad company. I do know one thing. Whatever he was mixed up in got him killed." He turned his head to look at her, and his expression was deadly serious. "I'd really hate to see that happen to you."

"So would I. I still need to upgrade my apartment." Judging by Hal's expression, her attempt at humor had fallen flat. She added quickly, "It wasn't Jenna with Dean that night, so whoever it was probably knows what happened. We have to find that person. Jenna thinks that Detective Messina believes she killed Dean and that she'll end up in prison. We can't let that happen."

"I agree, but I have faith in the Misty Bay Police Department. It's early days. They'll get to the truth eventually."

"Maybe, but meanwhile, Jenna is being condemned by some of the people in this town, and it's tearing her apart. By going around and asking questions, at least she feels that we're doing something to help."

Hal straightened, holding a plate in each hand. "That's what worries me. Asking the wrong people questions can get you into trouble."

"I promise you we'll be careful."

"Well, I can't tell you what you can and can't do. Just promise me something else, okay?"

"Like what?"

"That you'll keep me posted on where you're going and what you're doing. It doesn't hurt to have someone at home base knowing what's going on."

Warmed by his concern, she smiled. "Will do."

He nodded at that, and headed over to the couch.

Still smiling, she picked up the two glasses of wine and walked over to where he was setting down the plates on a carved oak coffee table. "This is a beautiful table," she said, as she waited for him to place a coaster next to each plate. "Is it antique?"

"Probably. It was in my wife's family for decades. I do know that."

Vivian placed the wine on the coasters and gently stroked the edge of the table. "It's gorgeous. I saw one like this in Portland. It was selling for over a thousand dollars."

Hal's eyebrows shot up. "No kidding. I should put this up for auction."

"That depends." Vivian sat down on the couch and reached for her wine.

"Depends on what?"

"On what the sentimental value is to you. Sometimes that's worth far more than dollar bills."

"You're right." Hal sat down next to her. "But I can't see myself getting sentimental about a table."

"But if it was in your wife's family . . ."

His expression sobered. "Oh, I see." Leaning forward, he picked up his glass and took a sip of wine. "My wife," he said quietly, "died almost five years ago. I will always love her, of course, and I will never forget her. But that's my past, and

Terry wouldn't want me to dwell in it. I still have some good years ahead of me, and I intend to make the most of them. So, no, the table has no sentimental value to me."

She couldn't help but feel a spark of delight at his words. She might not be there yet, but she was very happy that Hal had found that peace.

Deciding that it was time to change the subject, she put down her wine and picked up her sandwich. "You still haven't told me what you wanted to tell me."

"No. I've been weighing in my mind whether or not you need to know."

Hearing the tension in his voice, her fingers tightened on her plate. "That sounds ominous. Now you have to tell me."

He sighed. "Yeah, I guess I do. You might have a problem tracking down whoever it was who slept with Dean that night."

Wondering what was coming, Vivian said warily, "Well, we never expected it to be easy. Obviously, she doesn't want to be found."

"No, I mean . . . there's more than one."

She stared at him. "What?"

He kept his gaze steadily on the wine he was holding. "I don't think the management is aware of it, but there's a secret escort service being run in the Blue Surf Hotel. Someone on the staff there is providing access to vacant rooms so that customers can enjoy the services without compromising their identity. I'm guessing that Dean was a customer. Which means his partner that night could have been any one of a number of women."

"Good Lord!" Vivian's sandwich almost left the plate as her hand jerked.

"Sorry. I didn't mean to shock you." Hal shifted his position and took a deep sip of his wine. "I thought you should know."

Vivian finally found her breath. "Yes, well, I'm glad you told me. This does complicate things."

"I thought it might."

She carefully put down her plate and picked up her wine. "Well, we shall just have to try and get a description of the . . . er . . . woman with Dean. Does Detective Messina know about this?"

Hal shrugged. "I don't think so, or I think we would have heard about it. Imagine this town if the news got out. It would shock the hell out of them."

"Have you met him?"

"Messina? No, but I've heard a lot about him. His sidekick, Ken, is a friend of mine."

"He seems a bit . . . formidable."

Hal smiled. "He's been through some rough times. Some criminal he arrested escaped from jail and set fire to Messina's home. He wasn't there at the time, but his wife and daughter died before the firemen could get them out. Ken told me the guy's still having a hard time getting over it."

"Oh, no." Vivian's heart ached for the poor man. "That must have been so awful. I can't imagine how someone recovers after something like that."

"I guess that's why he moved down here to Misty Bay." Hal put down his glass. "It's not common knowledge, so don't go spreading it around. Ken mentioned it to me when we were talking about firefighting one day. He asked me not to tell anyone." He looked at her over the top of his glasses. "But I can trust you, right?"

"Of course you can." She studied him for a moment. "You seem to have a lot of secrets. How did you know about the escort service?"

His cheeks turned pink as he sent her a swift glance, then looked away. "I haven't used their services, if that's what you're wondering. I might get lonely at times, but there are still some things I won't do."

Vivian hurriedly cleared her throat. "Of course not. I wasn't . . . I didn't think . . . I wouldn't dream of . . . oh, pish."

"Now you sound like Mary Poppins."

She stole a look at him and was relieved to see him smiling.

"I'm sorry," he said. "I know this is embarrassing, which is one of the reasons I was reluctant to tell you."

"I'm not in the least embarrassed." Vivian took a hasty sip of her wine and put down the glass. "Remember, Martin was a prosecuting attorney. Believe me, some of the stories I heard from him would make your toes curl."

"Then you should be well aware of the danger in trying to track down these people."

"I am. I also know how to avoid trouble." She smiled at him. "Don't worry, Hal. We'll be careful. That's why the three of us are doing this. There's safety in numbers."

"I hope you're right."

Her smile widened. "Didn't you know? I'm always right."

He raised his glass. "I'll drink to that." After taking a sip, he put the glass down. "By the way, I learned about the service from a friend. He thought I might want to participate. I soon set him straight."

"Oh." She thought about that. "I don't suppose you'd care to give me his name?"

Hal looked at her. "You want to talk to him? I don't think you'll get any answers from him."

"I can be very persuasive." She reached for her sandwich. "And devious when I have to be."

He looked worried. "I don't know . . ."

"It's to help Jenna." She leaned toward him. "Please, Hal. We can't let her go to jail for something she didn't do."

He sighed. "You're going to use that a lot, aren't you?"

"Is it working?"

He had to smile at that. "All right. His name is Ray Constanza. He owns the hardware store on Ocean View Road. He's usually in the office, but you might have to make an appointment to meet him."

"Thanks, I'll do that. Now let's eat. I'm starving."

She spent the rest of the hour discussing with him the economics of Misty Bay and sharing ideas on how they could expand their respective customer bases. Hal was deep into an analysis of his expenses versus his income when Vivian glanced at her watch.

"Oh, shoot. I have to go." She put down her empty glass and pushed herself up from the couch. "I'm sorry to end this enlightening and invigorating conversation, but I have to meet Jenna in five minutes."

Hal climbed to his feet and walked with her to the door. "I enjoyed it very much. We'll have to do it again sometime."

"Absolutely."

He opened the door and stood back to let her pass through. "Go ahead. I'll show you out the back way so you don't have to go through the shop."

"I'm sure I can find the door." Vivian stepped out on the hallway. "It's probably in the same place as mine."

"Probably, but I always personally escort a lady from the premises."

After what they'd been discussing, that sounded a little risqué. She quickly dismissed the thought and laughed. "Now you sound like a Victorian novel."

"A little old-fashioned courtesy never hurt anyone, right?"

"Right." She was smiling all the way down the stairs and out the door.

She arrived back at the tearoom to find Jenna waiting on the doorstep.

"I was beginning to get worried," Jenna said, as Vivian hurried up to her. "I rang the bell a few times and was just going to call you."

"I've been talking to Hal," Vivian said, trying to catch her breath. "Boy, do I have some news for you!"

Jenna's eyes lit up with hope. "He knows who was with Dean on Friday night?"

Hating to have to disappoint her, Vivian shook her head. "I'm sorry, Jenna, no. In fact, he's just made things more complicated." She glanced at Jenna's car parked in front of the store. "Are you going to drive to Paula's house, or would you like me to for a change?"

"I'll drive." Jenna marched over to the car and pulled open the driver's door.

Vivian hurried around the rear of the car and slid into the passenger seat. Fastening her seat belt, she said quietly, "It doesn't mean we won't find that woman."

"Then what does it mean?" Jenna made no attempt to start the car but sat staring at the street ahead.

Quickly, Vivian recounted what Hal had told her about the escort service.

Jenna's expression grew more incredulous as she listened to the story. She waited for Vivian to finish before saying, "I don't believe it."

"What, you don't believe there are call girls using the hotel?"

"I don't believe Dean was sleeping with a prostitute. It just doesn't sound like him. I don't think he'd ever do that."

"Well, Hal did say it was a guess. Anyway, technically, an escort is not a prostitute. The service is not illegal. The escorts are hired for companionship, and that's all. It's made clear that anything further is not included. What they do beyond that is up to them."

"Which usually means ending up in bed with the customer."

Vivian smiled. "You're probably right, but that's how these services get past the prostitution laws."

Jenna shook her head. "I just can't see Dean paying some-one to go to bed with him."

Vivian felt a pang of sympathy for her friend. "You said yourself he cheated on you twice and you don't know how many more times there were."

"I know, but I saw the two women he was involved with when we were married. They sure didn't look like hookers to me."

"They usually don't. They're glamorous and sophisticated."

"Still, that's just not Dean. Besides, where would he get the money for something like that? Isn't that kind of thing terribly expensive?"

"I guess it depends on the service."

Jenna didn't answer right away, and Vivian fastened her seat belt, wishing she could say something to take that awful look off her friend's face.

"All right, then," Jenna said at last, "so if it's true, then how in heaven's name do we find out which one was with him?"

"I don't know. I'm still finding my way with this. If we could get a description of her, we might be able to narrow it down. Maybe Paula Lambert can help us with that."

"And if she can't?"

"Then we'll have to find out more about the escort service."

Jenna shook her head. "They're not going to talk. Besides, how are we going to find these women?"

"Hal gave me the name of the friend who told him about the service, so I think we should talk to him."

Jenna raised her eyebrows. "And this guy is going to admit to a perfect stranger that he hires escorts?" Her expression changed. "Wait a minute. If the service is using the hotel, wouldn't they book the rooms?"

"Hal said someone on the staff was providing access to vacant rooms to protect the clients' identity."

"And probably getting paid to do it."

Vivian thought about it. "That's a good point. We need to talk to Paula. She might have seen Dean with a woman. And I think we should talk to Ray Constanza."

"Ray who?"

"Constanza. He's the owner of Ray's Hardware on Ocean View. He's the friend Hal told me about. If there are call girls frequenting the hotel, they probably knew Dean. They might even know the woman Dean was with that night. Maybe we can get Mr. Constanza to give us the name of one of them."

Jenna reached for the ignition and switched it on. "This is crazy. I can't believe we're doing this."

"You'd rather wait and see if Detective Messina finds the real killer?"

Jenna looked at her. "Heck no. If there's a chance of proving to him and this town that I didn't kill my ex, then I'm all for it. Let's go." With that, she slipped the car into gear and took off down the street.

About a mile down the coast road, she turned toward the hills and began the climb that eventually landed them in front of a large house overlooking the ocean.

Stepping out of the car, Vivian had to pause for a moment to admire the Lamberts' home.

The red cedar shingles covering the walls gave the whole building a warm glow, as if it were bathing in the rays of a setting sun. The entranceway was impressive, with a bright-yellow door surrounded by glass windows, a massive clay pot of cactus plants in each corner of the porch, and a yellow Adirondack chair on either side to welcome guests.

A balcony ran around the corner of the house, where more chairs sat waiting for appreciative visitors to enjoy the ocean view peeking through the pine trees.

This was a house she could enjoy living in, Vivian told herself as she followed Jenna to the porch.

Reaching the door, Jenna jabbed a thumb on the bell and was rewarded by the faint sound of a chime from inside the house. Seconds later the door opened abruptly to reveal a slender woman with sleek auburn hair falling to her shoulders and gold medallions dangling from her ears. She wore a black-and-white shirt with skinny white pants that ended inches above her ankles and gold sandals that revealed pink-painted toenails.

Remembering the suave hotel manager, this elegant, glamorous creature was exactly the wife Vivian had envisioned. She stepped forward and offered the woman a tentative smile. "Mrs. Lambert?"

Paula's expression was less than welcoming. Her disdainful glance swept over Vivian like a nutritionist eyeing a plate of fries. Then she caught sight of Jenna, and her face darkened. "What do you want?"

Before Jenna could answer, Vivian spoke up. "We're sorry to disturb you, Mrs. Lambert, but we were wondering if we might ask you a couple of questions regarding the unfortunate death of Mrs. Ramsey's late ex-husband."

The hostile green eyes focused on Vivian again. "Who are you?"

"I'm Mrs. Ramsey's counselor. I promise we won't hold you up too long."

"You won't be holding me up at all. I know nothing whatsoever about that man's death, and I can't help you."

She began to close the door, and Vivian tried again. "Can you just tell us if you saw Dean with another woman in the hotel? It would help—"

She broke off as the door slammed in her face. "Well!" She turned to Jenna, who had an *I told you so* look on her face. "What a rude woman."

Jenna shrugged. "She's an unhappy woman. Look who she married."

Vivian gestured at the house. "Well, she does have some compensations. This is gorgeous."

"I guess so." Jenna turned to walk back to the car. "Personally, I'd rather have my house. It's cozy and doesn't take a lot of work to keep up."

"That's exactly why I like my apartment. And I have a better view than she does." Vivian jerked her thumb at the coastline. "You have to squint to see the ocean through those trees." Having effectively abolished her envy, she followed her friend to the car.

Sitting behind the wheel, Jenna sighed. "Well, that got us nowhere. I think we're wasting our time. I still have a bad feeling we're not going to find out who killed Dean and I'm going to end up in jail."

"We are and you're not." Vivian fastened her seat belt. "We have Hal's friend to talk to, and hopefully he'll tell us more about the escort service. If we can get a connection from him, we can maybe find Dean's missing inamorata."

"His who?"

Vivian smiled. "Fancy word for lover. It sounds more dramatic."

"Well, dramatic or not, it's not going to be easy to track her down."

"Nothing worthwhile is ever easy." Vivian winced as Jenna stepped on the gas, sending the car forward with a jolt. "And if we solve this case and clear your name, it will be infinitely worthwhile."

"Thanks, Vivian."

Jenna sounded gruff, and Vivian shot her a quick glance. "Don't thank me yet. We have a long way to go yet. I have to tell you, though, if it wasn't for the fact that your freedom depends on it, I'd really be enjoying this."

Jenna's frown disappeared. "Spoken like a true amateur sleuth."

Vivian let out a sigh. "I just hope I can live up to that."

"Just the fact that you're trying is enough for me." Jenna looked at the dashboard. "It's still early. Want to stop by the brewery for a drink?"

"That sounds great, but I'd better not. I have accounts to catch up on before I go to bed, and I need a clear head."

"Okay. We'll do it another time." Jenna took the sharp curve at a speed that stopped Vivian's breath. "So, when do we talk to this hardware guy?"

"Tomorrow. How about in the morning? Around eight?"

"Okay. What about Gracie? She'll want to come too."

"Right. I'll give her a call tonight."

"I hope we get better luck with this guy than we did with Pompous Paula."

Vivian uttered a shout of laughter. "Good name for her. Did you see the way she looked at me?"

"She looks at everyone that way. Like they're dirt beneath her feet. I don't know what gives her the idea she's better than anyone else."

"Does she spend much time in the hotel?"

"I only saw her there a couple of times. Like I said, she goes in sometimes to check on things when Reggie's away. I think she likes bossing people around."

"Yes, she'd be good at that." Vivian clutched the armrest as Jenna bounced the car onto the coast road. Next time, she promised herself, she'd do the driving. So far, the most dangerous part of this investigation was riding in Jenna's car. She could only hope it stayed that way.

* * *

Jenna arrived at precisely eight the next morning, making Vivian wonder if her friend had sat in her car, waiting to time it perfectly. She was about to tease her about it when Gracie appeared around the corner, wearing skinny jeans and a rose-patterned oversized shirt.

"This is so awesome!" she said, after greeting them both. "We're going on a murder hunt. Can I drive?"

Vivian glanced at Jenna, who shrugged. "Fine with me."

"All right! Let's go then." Gracie led them around the corner to where she'd parked her car. "I just filled up with gas, so we're okay. You said the hardware store is on Ocean View?"

"Yes, on the corner. You can't miss it." Vivian waited for Jenna to crawl into the back seat before joining Gracie in the front. "I just hope Mr. Constanza is in the office when we get there."

"Maybe we should have made an appointment," Jenna said, sounding muffled as she struggled with her seat belt.

"I was going to, but I couldn't think of a reason to give him that would sound feasible. I was afraid he'd refuse and hang up on me." Vivian sighed. "This detective stuff isn't as easy as it seems."

"Yeah," Gracie said, as she steered the car out of the parking space. "But it's so much fun."

"It would be," Jenna said, "if we were making any headway."

"It's early days yet." Vivian glanced at her friend over her shoulder. "We'll get there."

"I hope you're right. Have you thought about how you're going to ask this guy about hiring an escort?"

"I have. I came up with it this morning, but it's going to be delicate, so I need you both to play along."

"Shouldn't you, like, let us know what you're going to say before we get there?" Gracie asked.

"I'm going to tell him we want to hire an escort for a friend as a surprise birthday gift."

For a long moment there was a stunned silence in the car, and then Gracie exploded with laughter, echoed by Jenna's shocked voice exclaiming, "You're kidding!"

Vivian sat up, feeling slightly offended. "It's a brilliant idea, and it will work. We just have to appear sincere."

"Even I'm not that good an actor," Jenna muttered.

"Oh, come on, Jenna." Gracie's voice was still tinged with laughter. "It's hilarious. I can't wait to see this guy's face when Vivian tells him."

"Well, you'd better keep a straight face when I do, or the whole thing will backfire on us." Vivian gave her a stern look, which was wasted, since Gracie was concentrating on the road ahead. "Remember, we're doing this to save Jenna from going to jail."

Gracie sobered at once. "Got it. I'll do my best."

Jenna groaned. "We're all going to be arrested."

"Nonsense." Vivian tried to sound reassuring. "Even if we can get Mr. Constanza to tell us how to get in touch with these people, no one is going to go tattling to the police about it. They are just as anxious as we are to keep it under the rug."

"Or under the sheets," Gracie said, smothering another giggle.

"Isn't that the hardware store?" Jenna tapped on her window. "Right there, on the corner."

Gracie braked, slowing the car enough to turn into the narrow parking space.

She turned off the engine, and Vivian took a deep breath. She had never been good at lying. There had been times when she'd tried to lie to Martin, like the time she'd bought him a new laptop for his birthday. When the package arrived days before she planned to surprise him with it, she told him it was a box of filters for the furnace.

He knew at once that she wasn't telling the truth and teased her, suggesting that she had bought herself a new nightgown. She'd told him what she should have told him in the first place, that it was a surprise gift for him and he'd get it on his birthday.

"Are you coming?"

Hearing Jenna's voice, Vivian looked up with a start to see both women standing outside the car, waiting for her. Scrambling out of the car, she mumbled, "Sorry. I was thinking about something."

Jenna peered at her. "Are you okay?"

Vivian answered her with a smile. "I'm fine. Let's go do this." Praying she wasn't making a mistake, she marched toward the door, her friends trailing close behind her.

Chapter Six

Inside the shop, a customer stood at the counter, talking to the salesclerk. Two more customers browsed the aisles, wandering down the shelves stacked with hand tools, locks, hinges, paint, electrical supplies, nails, and screws.

As she walked over to the counter, Vivian eyed a heavy-duty lawn mower, feeling thankful that she no longer had a lawn to mow. The clerk had finished talking to his customer, who had wandered off down the aisles.

Vivian smiled at the young man. "Good morning! My friends and I were wondering if Mr. Constanza's available?"

The clerk looked confused. "Available?"

"Yes. We'd like a quick word with him if he can spare the time."

"Er . . ." The clerk looked around as if searching for help, then looked back at Vivian.

"Could you show us to his office?"

Again, the young man seemed at a loss for words.

Gracie sidled up to Vivian and leaned across the counter. "Hi," she said in a breathy voice Vivian had never heard her use before. "You know where Mr. Constanza's office is, don't you?"

The clerk stared at her, then nodded. "Yes, but—"

"We just need to, like, talk to him for a minute." She leaned closer. "That's okay with you, isn't it?"

"Mr. Constanza doesn't usually have visitors in his office. He doesn't like to be disturbed."

"Oh, we're not visitors." Gracie flapped her eyelids at him. "We're customers. Very important customers."

The clerk still looked uneasy. "I can call him and ask him to come out." His expression suggested that his request would be met with a strong denial.

"We prefer to talk with him in his office," Vivian said, wondering what all the secrecy was about.

"I'll call and ask if he will see you."

He reached for the phone, and Gracie shot out a hand to cover his. "We want to surprise him. Everyone likes surprises. You like surprises, right?"

"Well, yeah, if they're good one, but . . ."

"Well, Mr. Constanza will be real happy to see us." Gracie gazed at the flustered clerk as if she were about to propose, and Vivian cringed. "I know he'll be grateful to you for, like, taking us to his office."

The young man seemed mesmerized for a moment, then gave her a reluctant nod. "Okay. There's the door." He jerked a thumb behind him.

"Thank you!" Gracie sent him a dazzling smile and pushed herself away from the counter. "Okay, let's go!" She bounced around the counter and opened the door.

Vivian caught a glimpse of a bearded man seated behind a desk and hurried around the counter to join her. Jenna followed close behind, and the three of them crowded into the office.

The man at the desk stared at each of them. "Who the hell are you, and what do you want?"

Jenna quickly closed the door, and Vivian approached the desk. "We apologize for disturbing you, Mr. Constanza, but we have an urgent request, and we were hoping you could help us."

"That's what my sales staff are for," Constanza said, obviously annoyed. "I don't appreciate being accosted in my office. I have strict rules not to be disturbed. Now, please leave, before I call my security and have you forcibly removed."

"It's about the escort service," Vivian said. "I believe you are a customer."

The tough attitude vanished in an instant. Constanza sent a hunted look at the door, as if he expected armed officers to burst through any minute. "Are you cops?"

Vivian smiled. "No, just potential customers."

Now the man looked bewildered. "Um . . . you do know they're all women, right?"

Vivian shifted her weight. This was even more awkward than she'd anticipated. "Yes, of course. Actually, we want to hire an escort for a friend."

Gracie stepped forward, using her breathy voice again. "It's a surprise."

Jenna must have decided she needed to contribute, as she added rather hoarsely, "For his birthday."

Constanza leaned back on his chair and studied all three of them again. "I see." He tapped his fingers on his desk for a moment, then asked, "How did you learn about the service?"

Vivian smiled. "From a friend of yours. Hal Douglass."

Constanza's expression relaxed. "You know Hal?"

"He's a very good friend. He told me to ask you about it."

"Is this . . . er . . . surprise for Hal?"

"Oh, good Lord, no!" Aware she'd sounded a little too appalled at the suggestion, she cleared her throat. "No, it's not for Hal. It's for another good friend." She tried another smile. "We just need a number we can call, that's all."

After studying her a little too closely for comfort, Constanza finally sighed. "I can't give you the number. I do have a contact who might help you."

"Oh, that would be—"

He raised his hand, cutting off her words. "On one condition."

"What's that?"

"That you don't tell her I gave you her name."

Vivian patted her chest. "You have my word."

He glanced at her friends, and she added quickly, "All our words."

He seemed satisfied with that, as he reached for a notepad and pen. After scribbling down something, he tore off the page, folded it a couple of times, and handed it to Vivian. "This visit never happened."

Vivian met his gaze. "What visit?"

With a nod of approval, he waved a hand at the door.

"Thank you." Vivian turned to go, beckoning to her friends to follow her.

She was almost at the door when Constanza spoke again. "Give my best to Hal."

"I will." She walked out into the store area, feeling uncomfortably certain that he was convinced Hal was to be the lucky recipient of the surprise birthday gift.

As she rounded the counter, she received an anxious glance from the young man at the register. "Mr. Constanza enjoyed our visit," she told him. "Thank you."

He beamed in relief. "You're welcome! Have a good day."

Outside the store, Gracie burst out laughing.

Jenna shook her head. "That was awkward."

"It was." Vivian opened the passenger door of the car. "He thinks we're hiring an escort for Hal. I hope he doesn't give him a hard time about it."

"He's a customer himself," Jenna said, opening the rear door. "I don't see how he can mess with Hal about it."

"Maybe I shouldn't have told him Hal gave me his name." Vivian slid into the car, wishing she'd kept that to herself.

Jenna crawled into the back seat. "I doubt if you'd have learned anything from him if you hadn't told him that."

"I guess so. He's very protective of himself. He probably has a wife and is afraid she'll find out about the service."

"He obviously didn't know who I am and that I'm a suspect in Dean's murder."

"No, I'm sure he didn't. I'm glad those reporters didn't get to interview you. I'm kind of surprised they haven't been trailing around after you."

"There's still time," Jenna said. "I'm expecting them to pop up behind me any minute."

"I think this whole thing is a trip," Gracie said, as she wriggled into the driver's seat. "I had a tough time keeping from laughing in there."

"You would," Jenna muttered.

Gracie glanced at Vivian before switching on the ignition. "So, what name did he give us?"

Vivian unfolded the paper she still had clutched in her hand. "It just says 'Florrie Hayes' and her phone number."

"Are you going to call her?"

"I am. But not now. I need to think about what I'm going to say to her. I guess the simple thing would be to just ask her if she knew Dean."

"You're going to ask her on the phone?" Jenna sounded surprised. "I thought you said you learn more by meeting face-to-face."

"I do, but I was talking about suspects." Vivian twisted her head to look at her. "This woman isn't a suspect. She's just someone who might or might not be able to help us."

"Do you think she's one of the escorts?" Gracie backed the car out of the parking space and pulled out onto the road.

"Probably." Vivian glanced at the scribbled note again. "Or maybe she's an organizer."

"Either way, you'd rather not visit her," Jenna said.

Vivian sighed. "Does that make me sound like a fuddy-duddy?"

"No," Jenna said. "You're out of your comfort zone with this and feeling insecure."

Vivian looked at her in surprise. "You're right. Is it that obvious?"

"No, but I'm feeling the same way. It's unusual for both of us."

"It is indeed." Vivian sat back on her seat and gazed at the glimpses of sparkling ocean between the pine trees.

"Vivian," Jenna said, her voice heavy with concern, "I'll understand if you'd rather not pursue this. I really don't want to get either of you involved in this mess. It's my problem. I'll get through it."

Vivian twisted around again to look at her friend. "Nonsense. There isn't anything I wouldn't do if it means clearing your name."

"Me too. Totally," Gracie declared. "We're in this together. All for one and one for all."

"I feel like I should be brandishing a sword or something." Jenna's words sounded cheerful, but Vivian could tell her friend was moved by the show of support. "Let's go have a cup of tea," she said, tucking the note in her purse. "We'll talk about this and decide how we're going to proceed."

"Oh, cool," Gracie said, turning the wheel to drive onto Main Street. "I can't wait to find out what happens next."

In spite of her reservations, Vivian couldn't help but agree with her. When she'd started this, she hadn't expected anything like the revelations they had uncovered. She wondered what Reggie Lambert and his snooty wife would say if they knew that an escort service was conducting business right under their noses.

She wished she could be there when they found out. That wasn't likely to happen, but it was sure to be on the news eventually. If her investigation had led her there, it was a sure bet that Detective Messina would get there too.

That would put a spark in Misty Bay. The town would be gossiping about it for months. Even Natalie would be shocked by this one. Vivian smiled as she envisioned Natalie rushing down to the tearoom to deliver the startling news.

Her smile faded again when she remembered why they were doing this in the first place. The most important part of this whole adventure was to prove Jenna's innocence. That's all that mattered. Come what may, whatever it took, that's what they were going to do.

With that, she sat back, prepared to take the next step. Wherever that would lead them.

Minutes later, Gracie parked the car in front of the tearoom.

When Vivian climbed out, she was surprised to see Natalie pacing back and forth at the door.

"Where have you been?" Natalie demanded, as soon as she set eyes on Vivian. "I've been waiting and ringing the bell for ages."

"We had to take care of some business." Vivian took out her keys from her purse and unlocked the door. "You know we don't open until noon."

"I know. But you're usually home, and I've got something really important I need to tell you."

"You could have called me."

"I did. I got your voice mail. I didn't want to leave a message, so I came down to talk to you."

Vivian pulled her phone from her purse and looked at it. "I forgot to turn it on this morning."

Natalie gave her an accusing look. "Must have been important business." She glanced at the other two women. "For all of you. Did it have something to do with the murder?"

Vivian sent a worried look down the street, afraid that reporters might be lurking nearby. "No, it didn't. What do you want, Natalie?"

"I heard something I think Jenna should know." Natalie looked around and lowered her voice. Peering up at Jenna, she announced, "I found out your ex had a girlfriend."

Jenna's eyebrows twitched, but her expression remained calm as she looked at Natalie. "That's none of my business."

"But it means she must be the owner of the negligee."

Jenna nodded. "I guess so."

Natalie looked crushed. "I thought you'd be happy to hear the news. It means someone else could be involved in Dean's murder."

"Well, thanks, Natalie, but we'd already figured that out."

"Well, excuse me for trying to help you." Flipping back her hair, Natalie turned to leave.

Vivian shot out a hand to lay on the woman's arm. "Why don't we step inside for a minute and talk about this."

For a moment it seemed that Natalie would refuse, but then she shrugged and stepped inside the tearoom.

Vivian waited until everyone was inside and closed the door.

Natalie looked around with the air of someone inspecting the premises for mice. "You've got new curtains," she announced. "They're pretty."

"Thank you." Vivian smiled at her. "So, tell us, where did you hear about this girlfriend?"

The center of attention once more, Natalie appeared to relax. "I heard it at the beauty salon. I was waiting to go under the drier, and the woman next to me was talking about the murder. She said that the victim was having an affair with some woman and that she was surprised, since they didn't seem to have anything in common."

"Did she say who the woman was?"

Natalie shook her head. "No, she didn't. I was going to ask her, but by the time I got out from under the drier, she'd gone."

"Who was the woman who said that?" Jenna demanded, earning a warning look from Vivian.

Natalie pouted. "I don't know. I don't know everybody in Misty Bay."

Vivian cleared her throat. "Natalie, perhaps you could ask the stylist for the name of that client? We'd like to talk to her."

Natalie seemed pleased by the request. "Of course! I could pop in there for a can of hair spray or something."

"Excellent." Vivian looked at her watch. "I'm about to make a pot of tea. Would you like to join us?"

Natalie shuddered. "Tea? No thanks. I only drink coffee in the mornings."

Jenna looked relieved. Gracie had already vanished into the kitchen, probably to investigate what treats Vivian had created for her customers.

Vivian nodded. "Another time, then. Thank you, Natalie. You've been a great help."

"You're welcome." Looking pleased with herself, Natalie opened the door and stepped outside. "I'll let you know if I learn anything." With that, she gave an airy wave of her hand and tottered off down the street.

Jenna shook her head as Vivian closed the door. "She didn't tell us anything we didn't already know."

"I don't know about that." Vivian led the way to the kitchen, talking over her shoulder. "We did find out that Dean had a girlfriend who didn't appear to be compatible with him."

"So that rules out the escort thing. I told you he wouldn't go for a hooker." Jenna slumped down on a chair at the table.

Gracie had already put a kettle of water on to boil and was examining the shelves of pastries for something good to eat.

"Unless he was personally involved with one of the escorts."

Jenna sighed. "That's possible, I guess."

"We have to find this woman." Vivian walked over to Gracie and paused at the shelves, then pulled out a tray. "Is this what you're looking for?"

Gracie stared at the pastries as if she'd just discovered gold. "Cherry scones! My favorite."

"Take one." Vivian offered her the tray.

Gracie needed no second invitation. She grabbed one of the sugary scones off the tray and stuffed it in her mouth. "Oh, God," she moaned as she chewed. "I think I'm going to have an orgasm."

Jenna snorted in feigned disgust, while Vivian laughed. She held the tray out to her, asking, "Would you like one?"

Jenna stared at them for a moment, then snaked out a hand to take one. "It's a miracle I don't put on a ton of weight working here."

"You work way too hard for that." Hearing the kettle's whistle begin to shriek, Vivian pushed the tray back onto the shelf and grabbed a teapot from the cabinet.

"Do you think Natalie will be able to, like, track that woman down?" Gracie asked, as she reached with one hand to the cabinet for cups and saucers. Her other hand still held the remains of her scone, which traveled to her mouth every few seconds.

"I don't know." Vivian warmed the pot, then filled it with boiling water. "But I do think I will call Florrie Hayes. If Dean was involved with an escort, she might know her."

She waited until the teacups were full and they were all seated at the table before picking up her phone. After copying the number on the note to the dial pad, she held the phone to her ear.

The voice that answered her sounded pleasant and cultured, not in the least what she'd been expecting. Though she wasn't sure quite what she'd been expecting. Two pairs of eyes stared at her from across the table as she replied, "Ms. Hayes? I apologize for this intrusion. My name is Vivian Wainwright, and I'm a friend of Jenna Ramsey."

There was a slight pause at the end of the line before the voice answered, "How can I help you?"

Vivian tried frantically to organize her words. "Well, I'm sure you've heard what happened to Dean Ramsey. I'm his ex-wife's counselor, and I was hoping you might help us learn more about the case."

Again, the pause, then the voice—more wary now. "I'm sorry, Ms. Wainwright, but I can't discuss anything over the phone."

"Then can we perhaps meet somewhere? I own the Willow Pattern Tearoom on Main Street. Or we can meet you somewhere else?"

The pause was much longer this time.

Vivian tried again. "It's vitally important, Ms. Hayes. Jenna Ramsey is being wrongly accused of murder. We need to find out the truth of what really happened, or the wrong person could go to jail."

Finally, Florrie spoke. "The brewery. Nine thirty tonight." She hung up before Vivian could answer.

"What'd she say?" Gracie leaned forward, her face alight with eagerness.

"She said to meet her at the brewery tonight." Vivian shook her head. "She's obviously uncomfortable talking to me on the phone."

"Maybe it's because she knows something she shouldn't," Jenna said, her voice rising in hope.

"Maybe. Anyway, she'll be at the brewery at nine thirty."

"I'll pick you up at nine." Jenna frowned. "How will we recognize her?"

"I think she'll recognize you." Vivian reached for her teacup.

"Well, I guess you'll find out when you get there tonight," Gracie said, brushing scone crumbs from her fingers. "I wish I could be there with you."

Jenna stared at her. "You're not coming?"

"No. Sorry. I have a meeting."

"You just had a meeting last night."

"I know." Gracie looked uncomfortable. "Sorry, but this is, like, important."

"Too important to tell us what it's about?"

Vivian hastily intervened. "It's all right, Gracie. You don't have to tell us anything."

Apparently realizing she'd stepped over the line, Jenna sighed. "Sorry, Gracie. This mess has turned me into a shrew. I just hope that if you're in trouble or something, you'd let us know. We worry about you."

Gracie's face puckered. "Aw, that's sweet, Jenna. Don't worry. I'm not in any trouble. I wish I could tell you about it, but right now I can't." She turned to Vivian. "You'll both know soon, I promise."

Still feeling somewhat concerned, Vivian nodded. "Okay. As long as you know that we're here if you need us."

"I know." Gracie's smile spread over her face. "I'm so lucky." She looked back at Jenna. "I just hope this Florrie person can tell you something that'll help."

Jenna raised her teacup. "Amen to that."

Vivian echoed the sentiment in her mind as she picked up her cup again. If they could find out who'd been with Dean his last night on earth, they could give that information to Inspector Messina and let him take it from there.

He wouldn't be too thrilled that she had been messing with his investigation, but if it led to the arrest of a murderer, he would forgive her. Hopefully. "Before we get ready to open," she said, "we need to go over the plans for the celebration. I've come up with a couple of ideas. I've ordered a case of English lavender potpourri sachets. I thought we could give one to all our women customers."

Janna nodded her approval. "I like it."

"What about the men?" Gracie demanded. "Don't they get something?"

"That's why I need your help." Vivian put down her cup. "I need some suggestions for what to give the men. Nothing too expensive. Just a token of thanks for being a customer."

"Give them something they can eat," Jenna said. "Most men love snacks."

"I'd like to give them something a bit more permanent." Vivian wrinkled her brow. "I just can't think of anything."

"What about those refrigerator magnets with the English images on them?" Gracie waved a hand in the direction of the storeroom. "We just got a new shipment in yesterday. There are twenty-four in a pack, and they only cost us seven dollars. They have pictures of London buses on them, some of the palace, and the Beefeaters, the Thames, London Bridge, and—"

Vivian leaned forward and grabbed Gracie's arm. "Perfect! Thank you, Gracie. What would I do without you guys?"

Gracie grinned. "Cool."

Vivian leaned back with a sigh of contentment. "This is going to be even better than last year's anniversary."

"And we'll make it even better each year." Jenna stood up. "That's if I'm still around."

"You'll be around," Vivian promised her. "I'll make sure of that."

"So will I," Gracie said, nodding her head.

They were both rewarded with a warm smile from Jenna. "Now I'd better get going," she said, as she got up from her chair. "Some of us have to make a living here."

The rest of the day passed swiftly. The usual rush of people eager to enjoy afternoon tea kept all three women busy making sandwiches, filling teapots, loading cake stands, and clearing tables.

By six PM the last satisfied customer had left, and Vivian was able to turn the OPEN sign and close the door.

"I'm going home to feed Misty," Jenna said, as she retrieved her purse from the kitchen. "I'll be back here at nine."

"And I'm off to my meeting." Gracie danced out the door, waving a hand while slinging her king-size purse over her shoulder.

Following behind her, Jenna gazed after her with a thoughtful expression, but said nothing before she sped off to her car.

Closing the door, Vivian leaned against it for a moment. Jenna had cleaned up the tearoom as usual, and it looked so peaceful with its vacant chairs and tables, bare except for the pots of daisies smiling at her.

This was a moment she savored at the end of every day— the sense of accomplishment, and the reminder that she was living a dream.

A light tap on the glass panel of the door turned her head. To her surprise, Hal stood outside, staring down the street with an odd expression on his face. Guilt pricked her as she remembered her conversation with Ray Constanza this morning. Quickly she unlocked the door and opened it. "Is something wrong?"

He raised his eyebrows at her as he stepped inside. "Why would you rush to the conclusion that something is wrong the second you lay eyes on me?"

"Well, you were looking a bit peevish. I just thought you might not be feeling well."

"Or maybe it's because you told Ray Constanza you were hooking me up with a lady of the night."

Vivian swallowed. This was what she'd been afraid would happen. Now she had some explaining to do, and all she could hope was that she hadn't just wrecked a beautiful friendship.

Chapter Seven

Avoiding Hal's gaze, Vivian murmured, "Come into the kitchen. I'll make you some tea."

To her relief, he sounded amicable when he answered. "No tea. How about a glass of wine? You owe me."

She sighed. So far she'd resisted inviting him upstairs, but there was a first time for everything. "It's in my apartment, if you'd like to come up there."

"Sounds like a winner."

She led him up the stairs, conscious of him behind her every step of the way.

Standing in her living room seconds later, Hal looked around with a nod of appreciation. "Very nice. I like that chair. It looks comfortable."

"It is." She glanced at the roomy club chair sitting in front of her TV. She'd bought it when she first moved into the apartment, because its wavy aqua lines on the cream background reminded her of the ocean. "Take a seat in it. I'll bring you your wine."

"You're going to join me, I hope?"

She hesitated. "I shouldn't. I'm going to the brewery tonight."

She couldn't quite interpret the look he gave her. "Hot date, huh?"

She had to smile at that. "I'm going with Jenna. We're meeting someone there who might be able to help us with the murder case."

His expression changed. "I guess you haven't found your mystery women yet."

"No, but we're hoping to remedy that tonight."

"You sure you know what you're doing?"

She laughed. "Of course not. That's the fun of it." Seeing his frown, she added, "I hope you're not about to give me another lecture."

"Would it do any good?"

"Probably not."

"Then bring on the wine. And one for yourself. I hate drinking alone."

"Okay." Smiling, she walked over to the kitchen and opened the fridge. "Chardonnay okay?"

"Perfect. I've never yet met a Chardonnay I didn't like."

"Me either." She poured two glasses and carried them over to the coffee table.

Hal stood across the room, studying her bookshelves. "You have an impressive collection of mystery novels," he said, as he walked toward her. "You're obviously an addict. No wonder you're so eager to be hot on the trail of a killer."

"That's part of it," Vivian admitted, as she set the glasses down on the table. "But it's mostly to help Jenna."

"I know." He picked up a glass of wine and handed it to her, then picked up the other one. "To a prompt and safe solution to the mystery."

"Amen." She took a sip of her wine, then sat down on the coffee-colored love seat.

Hal lowered himself to the club chair and leaned back. "I could go to sleep in this thing."

"I often have." She took another sip of wine. "Hal, I'm sorry about the misunderstanding with Ray Constanza. I had to come up with some excuse for wanting the number of the escort service, and because I mentioned your name, he jumped to the conclusion that I was going to give you a birthday surprise."

"It would have been one heck of a surprise. I'll give you that."

"I know. I'm sorry."

To her relief, he chuckled. "Forget it. Ray's been trying to get me to use that service for months. Maybe this will shut him up."

"I hope so." She glanced at the clock on the wall. She'd found it in one of the antique shops in town and had fallen in love with it. The numbers were painted on wood with an ocean background, surrounded by ceramic sea gulls and seashells. She could almost smell the sea air whenever she looked at it. "Have you eaten yet?"

Hal looked at her over the rim of his glass. "Not yet."

"I can fix something for you, if you'd like."

His smile lit up his face. "I'd like. Can I help?"

"No, thanks. It won't take me more than a few minutes. Turn on the TV and relax." She found the remote and handed it to him.

"This is what I call service." He leaned back with a sigh of contentment. "I could get used to this."

"Well, don't get too comfortable. Remember I have to be out of here by nine."

"I won't forget."

He didn't sound too happy about that, reminding her of his concern about her meeting with Florrie Hayes. It actually gave her a spurt of pleasure to know he cared enough to worry about her. She hadn't felt so protected since Martin died.

She could hear a news anchor's voice but wasn't really listening to it as she whipped up eggs for an omelet and rummaged in the fridge for ham, cheese, green onions, and a tomato.

As she turned up the heat under the frying pan, however, she heard the anchor say, "There have been no new developments in the murder case involving local resident Dean Ramsey, whose body was found on the beach this past Saturday. The police won't comment on the investigation, and so far, the only suspect in the case has not been arrested."

With a cry of dismay, Vivian rushed out to scowl at the TV. "For heaven's sake, do they have to keep going on about it? The more they do that, the worse it will get for Jenna. She's already getting weird looks from the customers."

"Calm down. At least he didn't mention Jenna's name."

"But everyone knows who he's talking about."

Hal turned off the TV and got to his feet. "All this will blow over once the case is solved."

"And how long is that going to take?" She glared at him as if it were his fault. "Meanwhile, Jenna is being treated like a leper."

He tilted his head to one side. "Is it really that bad?"

She let out her breath in an explosion of frustration. "No, probably not. I'm just anxious, I guess. I want to help, and I'm not sure I can."

"You're doing your best to find out more about the case, and taking considerable risk in doing it. I'm sure Jenna appreciates that."

Vivian felt her tension begin to melt away. "You're right, and I'm sorry for yelling at you."

"You weren't yelling at me. You were letting off steam. Does us all good sometimes." He nodded at the kitchen. "Why don't you let me help you with that?"

Smiling, she relented. "Okay, you can slice the onions and tomato."

"Sounds good. I'm an excellent slicer."

That made her laugh, and she managed to forget her worries for the next hour or so as she and Hal reminisced about their former lives.

All too soon her watch warned her of the time. Hal helped her with the dishes, then left, with another warning to be careful. Soon after that, the bell in her apartment rang, signaling Jenna's arrival at the shop door.

To Vivian's dismay, she opened the door to see rain pouring down, sending a rivulet of water down the street. Jenna stood under the eaves, which didn't really help, since the wind was blowing the rain at her like a shower head.

"Oh, come in a minute." Vivian opened the door wider, letting a blast of damp cold air into the tearoom. "I'll go get an umbrella."

Jenna pulled the collar of her jacket closer to her neck. "This is Oregon. No one uses an umbrella. Besides, my car is right outside."

Deciding that getting a little damp was better than making the effort to climb up and down the stairs, Vivian darted out into the storm.

Minutes later they walked into the warm and welcoming atmosphere of the brewery. Vivian was surprised to see so many customers at the bar on a Tuesday night. Pausing inside the door, she scanned the room. Although there were plenty of women, none of them seemed to fit the image Vivian had formed in her mind.

After buying two glasses of wine, she took another look around. "There's an empty table over there." She nodded to a far corner of the room.

"Do you see anyone who might be Florrie?" Jenna asked as they made their way to the table.

"No." Vivian sat down and hung her purse on the back of her chair. "Then again, I really don't have any idea what she looks like."

"I looked up her name on my laptop," Jenna said, taking the other seat. "There are a few pics of different women with that name, but I couldn't find anyone who lives in Oregon."

Just then Vivian noticed a slim woman with flaming-red hair detach herself from a group at a table across the room and stroll toward them. "I think she's found us."

Jenna turned her head as the woman reached them.

"Ms. Ramsey?"

Jenna nodded up at her. "That's me."

"I'm Florrie Hayes." She looked at Vivian. "You must be the woman who called me today."

"Vivian Wainwright." She nodded at the empty chair. "Please, sit down. Can we buy you a drink?"

"Thank you, but I have one at my table." Florrie sat down and flipped back her hair from her face. "This won't take long."

Vivian leaned forward, her pulse beginning to race. "You knew Dean?"

"I did. We all did."

Jenna frowned. "We?"

"The girls." A look of caution crept over Florrie's face. "You do know about the service, right?"

Vivian shifted on her chair. "Yes, we do." She sent a quick glance at Jenna, whose face was set in stone. "Was Dean a customer?"

Florrie shook her head. She looked around to make sure no one was eavesdropping before adding quietly, "Dean set up the calls."

Jenna made a sound like her bare foot had stepped on a thumbtack.

Aware that her mouth was hanging open, Vivian hastily closed it. Her mind grappled for words, while Jenna just sat staring at the call girl with a stunned look on her face,

Finally, Vivian found her voice. "Are you saying that Dean worked for the escort service?"

"I'm saying he owned it. Him and a partner."

Still struggling to make sense of the news, Vivian exchanged a look with a dazed Jenna before asking, "Can you give me the partner's name?

Florrie cast an impatient look over at her table. "I don't know who his partner was. Dean never mentioned a name."

"Does the management know about all this?" Vivian tried to imagine Reggie Lambert being okay with prostitutes doing business right under his nose.

"I don't think so." Florrie looked worried now. "I hope they never find out. That could land most of us in jail."

"I don't believe it," Jenna muttered, apparently coming back to life. "Why would Dean be working in maintenance at the hotel if he was running his own business and making all this money?"

Florrie shrugged. "I don't know. Maybe he kept the job as a cover. All I know is that he set things up for us in the hotel."

Jenna grabbed her wine and took a gulp. "I can't imagine Dean doing something like this. He wasn't a businessman. He hated office work."

Florrie smiled. "I guess he liked money. The service charges are high, and he took a hefty cut. Plus, I heard some customers paid him extra to keep their names under wraps. Some of his customers are well known in town."

Jenna's eyes widened. "Like who?"

Florrie shrugged. "Like our chief of police, for one. At least two of our county commissioners, Adam Weinberg and Philip Stedman. Oh, and Warren Lester."

It was Vivian's turn to utter a muffled squeak of shock. "The bank manager?"

Florrie nodded. "Also Mark Stanbury, the owner of Stanbury's Paper Mill. Maybe one of them can help you find out who killed Dean."

"Oh my God," Jenna muttered.

Vivian cleared her throat. "I understand Dean was romantically involved with a woman." She paused, aware how ridiculous that sounded under the circumstances. "Do you happen to know her name?"

Florrie shook her head. "I heard he was hooking up with someone but never saw him with anyone." She looked at Jenna. "I don't know how much any of this helps, but I was once accused of doing something I didn't do. I know how it feels. Someone helped me out of it, and now I'm paying it forward. So, I hope you find out who killed Dean."

For a moment Vivian thought Jenna might hug the woman, but then her friend drew back. "Thanks, Florrie," Jenna said, sounding a little choked. "You've been a big help."

"You certainly have," Vivian said, adding her thanks.

"Dean was a good guy, and someone needs to pay for what happened to him." Florrie stood up. "You have to keep my name out of this. If it gets out that I was the one giving you all this information, things could go very badly for me."

"I promise you," Vivian said, "no one will ever know."

"Thank you." She looked back at Jenna. "Good luck." She strode off before Jenna could answer her.

"She's taking a huge risk telling us all that," Jenna said, watching the woman as she returned to her table. "She dished the dirt on some powerful people."

"She did." Vivian frowned. "My guess is that she's been hurt by some of these people and she's getting her revenge by exposing them."

Jenna's eyebrows shot up. "You don't believe that bit about paying it forward?"

"Not for a minute. But then, I'm naturally suspicious of everyone's motives. Comes from being married to a prosecutor."

"The police chief," Jenna said, shaking her head. "Can you believe it?"

"And our bank manager." Vivian envisioned the scrawny, nervous young man in charge of the bank. "I wouldn't have thought he had the guts."

"What I can't believe is that Dean was actually running a business." Jenna took another gulp of her wine.

"I imagine his partner probably did most of the managing. From what Florrie said, it sounds as if Dean was in charge of setting up the appointments."

"Yeah," Jenna said dryly, "he'd be good at that."

"Well, I'm going to write these names down before we forget them." Vivian rummaged in her purse for pen and paper.

"I don't think we're going to forget them. Two councilmen, a bank manager, a business owner, and a police chief." Jenna raised her glass again and drained it. "I'm going to get a beer. Want one?"

"No, thanks. You go ahead." Vivian found the pen and pulled out an envelope that contained a survey she had long forgotten to mail. Scribbling down the names Florrie had given them, she tried to picture them. The only one she would recognize on the street was Warren Lester, the bank manager.

As for the rest of them, the names were familiar, but the faces were a blur. She didn't remember ever seeing a photo of Mark Stanbury, though she'd certainly heard of him. The paper mill hired a good percentage of Misty Bay's population as well as employees from a couple of the nearby towns.

Any of these men would be highly embarrassed, and possibly hurt, by the exposure of their connection to an escort service. It sure wouldn't look good for the police chief or the councilmen.

She watched Jenna carry her beer over and waited for her to sit down before saying, "I wonder if Dean was blackmailing one of these men."

Jenna's eyes widened. "That could be a motive for murder."

"Exactly." Vivian slipped the pen and envelope back into her purse. "Let's meet early again tomorrow and discuss our next move. I think we've just found our next suspects to question."

* * *

The following morning Gracie arrived at the tearoom brimming with excitement. Vivian had filled her in the night before on her conversation with Florrie Hayes, and Gracie was obviously raring to go on the next phase of their investigation.

They had to wait half an hour for Jenna to arrive, by which time Gracie had devoured two scones and was sipping her second cup of tea. "You're late," she told Jenna, as her friend flopped down at the kitchen table.

"I'll make a fresh pot of tea." Vivian stood up and walked over to the stove to put the kettle on again.

"Sorry," Jenna mumbled. "I'm just not used to getting up this early. It's three mornings in a row now. I'm losing my beauty sleep."

"You wouldn't know it to look at you."

Jenna stared in surprise at Gracie. "That's the nicest thing you've ever said to me."

"Yeah, well, I'm in a good mood this morning. All this excitement, like, pumps me up."

Jenna smiled. "That's a normal condition for you."

"I'm glad you two are being so kind to each other," Vivian said as she pulled a cup and saucer from the cabinet. "Because we need to have an intense discussion this morning."

Jenna got up from her chair as the kettle shrieked. "Did Vivian tell you about last night?"

Gracie nodded. "Yep. I'd just got home from my meeting when she called."

"I told her everything that Florrie said." Vivian poured boiling water over the tea bags in the teapot.

Jenna took a bottle of milk out of the fridge and tipped some into the empty cup. "Anyone else want another cup of tea?"

"Not me," Gracie said, picking up her cup. "I'm on my second one now. I'll be peeing all day if I drink more."

Vivian stirred the tea and replaced the lid on the teapot. "You'll have to swirl it around a bit before you pour. It needs to brew a bit more."

"I know." Jenna glanced at Gracie. "So, what do you think about the news?"

Gracie put down her cup. "It totally blows my mind. I just can't imagine our police chief making out in a hotel room with a call girl. I wonder if his wife knows about that."

Jenna uttered a sound of disgust. "You can bet she doesn't. Which is why he was willing to pay Dean to keep it quiet."

"You think Dean was blackmailing the police chief?" Gracie's eyes had widened. "Wow. That was gutsy."

"We don't actually know that Chief Chapman spent the night with an escort, or if he was being blackmailed." Vivian walked back to the table and sat down. "Florrie only said that he was a customer."

Jenna picked up the teapot and began swirling it in little circles. "She said some customers paid Dean to keep quiet. I'm betting that the chief was one of them."

"Well, I can't imagine us getting close enough to him to find out. Something tells me it would be a little awkward asking the police chief if he was being blackmailed for being involved in illegal activity. However, we can question a couple of the other names Florrie gave us."

"We don't know any of them except Warren Lester." Jenna poured her tea and brought the cup and saucer over to the table.

"We didn't know Ray Constanza or Florrie Hayes either, but we got a lot of information from them."

"True. But these men aren't going to talk to us. There's no way they're going to admit they had anything to do with the escort service, or if they paid Dean to keep it quiet. And if one of them did kill him, I don't think he's going to spill his guts." Jenna reached for one of the scones.

"I've been thinking about that." Vivian sipped her tea before delivering her bombshell idea. "We have to have a way of opening a conversation with them. Except for Warren Lester, none of these men know who we are."

"They'd know me. I'm all over the news." Jenna took a bite of her scone and munched as if she were trying to obliterate the problem with her teeth.

"So far no one has posted a photo of you."

"As far as we know."

"Well, anyway, what I'm thinking is that we check out what we can about the councilmen on the internet. Try to find out where they go or places they're likely to be. Then one of us approaches them and, you know, starts a conversation and mentions that you work for the escort service."

Both women at the table stared at Vivian as if she'd gone completely out of her mind.

Jenna was the first to find her voice. "You mean act like a hooker?"

"I mean act like an escort. Like I said, they're hired to be companions, nothing more. Maybe one of the men will say something to incriminate himself or someone else, and we can take it to Detective Messina."

"Are you nuts?"

Vivian bristled. "Do you have a better idea?"

"Any idea is better than that one." Jenna shook her head as if trying to rid herself of the vision. "What makes you think any of them would talk to an escort in public?"

"You just said they wouldn't talk to us if we just walked up to them. They're much more likely to speak freely if they think we work for the escort service."

Jenna uttered a word that mercifully Vivian couldn't hear. "This is crazy."

"I think it could work," Gracie said. "After all, we know that's the kind of women they like. You know, confident and aggressive."

"Exactly." Vivian was rapidly warming up to the idea. "One of us gets dressed up, puts on lots of makeup, and acts, you know, like Gracie said, confident and aggressive."

Jenna's face was devoid of expression as she studied Vivian. "And who did you have in mind to play this enviable role?"

Vivian's lips felt stiff when she smiled. "I was hoping you would."

Jenna's expression would have been comical if the stakes hadn't been so high. "Me?" An explosive sound of disbelief erupted from her mouth. "Now I know you're crazy."

"Well, it can't be me," Vivian said, trying to sound calm. "I'm too old."

"I'll do it!" Gracie shot up her hand. "It'll be a hoot!"

"That's exactly why you can't do it." Vivian smiled to take the sting out of her words. "We need someone mature. With . . . er . . . experience."

"Oh." Gracie looked crestfallen. "Yeah, you're right. They'd never believe I was an escort."

"But they would me?"

Jenna sounded offended, and Vivian rushed to placate her. "It would all be an act, Jenna. We just think you could do a better job of acting than either of us."

Jenna put the last piece of her scone into her mouth, chewed, swallowed, and then said quietly, "I'm not going to act like a call girl."

"Not even to clear your name and stay out of prison?"

"Please, Jenna," Gracie added. "I know you can do it."

"You don't have to go overboard with it," Vivian assured her. "After all, like you said, these women are sophisticated. Look at Florrie Hayes. She looked glamorous, yes, but respectable. You would never know what she did for a living just by talking to her."

The silence in the kitchen seemed to go on forever before Jenna spoke again. "What if they recognize me?"

"How would they know you aren't working for the escort service? After all, Dean was your ex. It's feasible that you could be working for him."

Again, Jenna uttered a curse under her breath. "This will never work. This isn't a mystery novel. This is real life."

"It's worth a try."

Gracie added her two cents. "Come on, Jenna. What have you got to lose?"

"My reputation, for one."

"These men aren't going to spread it around town." Seeing the doubt still heavy on Jenna's face, Vivian added, "All you have to do is mention the service. Say something like how terrible it is what happened to Dean. They might give something away, or mention who Dean's partner was, or the name of the woman who slept with him that night. Or something helpful, at least."

Jenna stared down at her hands for several seconds, then shook her head. "I'm sorry. I know you mean well, but I can't."

Vivian wasn't sure if she was disappointed or relieved. "It's okay. It's probably just as well, considering the risks involved.

You're right, it was a dumb idea." The sudden dinging of the doorbell raised her head, and she glanced at her watch. "Who can that be? We don't open for another two hours."

Jenna rose to her feet. "I'll go. I need to do something constructive right now."

She disappeared through the doorway, leaving Gracie to watch her go. "She's really bummed," she said, looking upset herself.

"She's got a lot to worry about." Vivian sighed. "And right now, I'm not sure how we're going to help her."

The sound of Jenna's raised voice out in the shop startled her. She exchanged a worried look with Gracie. "I hope it's not that nosy reporter. I'd better go see what's going on out there."

Gracie followed her as she hurried out into the tearoom. She came to an abrupt halt when she saw who was on the receiving end of Jenna's sharp voice.

Detective Messina looked calm and controlled, though the officer behind him fidgeted with obvious discomfort under the torrent of Jenna's outburst.

"I don't know how many times I've told you, I did not kill my ex-husband. Do you have any proof? If you do, show it to me. If not, leave me the hell alone."

Vivian rushed forward and laid a hand on Jenna's quivering arm. "What is the problem here, Officer?"

"It's Detective, ma'am," Messina corrected her. He handed a sheet of paper to her. "I have a warrant to collect a sample of Ms. Ramsey's DNA." He looked back at Jenna. "Give me that and I'll leave you the hell alone."

Out of the corner of her eye, Vivian saw Gracie's hand shoot up to her mouth. Ignoring her, she asked Messina, "Do you have new evidence in the case?"

"We have uncovered some DNA that could be connected to the case. We need a sample from Ms. Ramsey so that we can possibly exonerate her." All the time he was speaking, his gaze remained steadily on Jenna's face.

Whether it was the tone of his voice or the look in his eyes as he waited for her response, it had the effect of calming Jenna down. She stared back at him as if she were seeing him for the first time.

"Fine," she said, her voice so quiet Vivian barely caught the words.

The officer behind Messina stepped forward, a small plastic bag in his hand. Opening it, he produced a swab and waved it at Jenna.

"I'll take that," Messina said, and took the swab from the surprised officer's fingers.

Jenna looked apprehensive as the detective moved toward her. "Open wide," he murmured, pointing the end of the swab at her mouth.

She slowly obeyed, her gaze fixed on his face.

Messina gently swiped the inside of her cheek, then withdrew the swab. "Thank you," he said quietly.

"Yeah, you're welcome." Jenna's voice was low and husky, with just a trace of sarcasm.

Sensing that the dynamic between them had undergone a subtle change, Vivian watched them with growing interest.

Messina seemed to be in a trance, his gaze still concentrated on Jenna's mouth as if he'd forgotten why he was there. The antagonism in Jenna's face had melted, leaving only a bemused expression that disclosed her confusion.

Vivian could literally feel the tension in the air. She remembered Hal telling her that the detective was still mourning his late wife. It occurred to her that Jenna might help the poor man get past that and move on.

Impatient with her romantic mind, she shook off the idea as the police officer stepped forward and took the swab from Messina's hand. He dropped it into the plastic bag and sealed it, then stepped back again.

Messina seemed to come back to earth with a start. "You'll be hearing from my office shortly," he said, then nodded at Vivian before striding to the door, barking, "Let's go, Brady."

"Yes, sir." The officer shot out into the street behind the detective and closed the door with a loud snap.

Vivian looked at Jenna, who was staring at the door. "Well, that was interesting."

"He has the hots for her," Gracie said, her grin vanishing under Vivian's scathing glance.

"What?" Jenna turned on her. "What are you? Twelve? The man is a self-righteous idiot who doesn't recognize the truth when it's shoved in his face." With that, she took off for the kitchen and disappeared inside.

"Wow," Gracie said, shaking her head. "That was intense."

"And the less said on the subject, the better," Vivian warned her.

"Did you see the way he looked at her?"

"Yes, I did."

"And the way she looked back at him?"

"Gracie"—Vivian wagged a finger at her—"if you know what's good for you, you'll keep your mouth shut, okay? Jenna is in an intolerable position right now. She doesn't need us speculating on whatever that was between her and Detective Messina."

"He said he was trying to prove she didn't kill Dean."

"He may have just been saying that to get her to cooperate. These detectives can be devious when it comes to solving a case."

Gracie's excitement faded. "Yeah, you're right. He was probably just stringing her along to get what he wanted."

"Exactly." Vivian was pretty sure it was more than that, but she wasn't about to waste time obsessing over it now. Nor was she going to allow Gracie to turn the incident into something more meaningful. Knowing Jenna, she wouldn't want that kind of complication in her life.

"Come on," she said, "my tea is getting cold."

Gracie followed her into the kitchen, where Jenna sat at the table, her chin propped up in her hands. She sat up straight when Vivian sat down opposite her. "I guess that's it, then," she said, her eyes lighting with her smile. "My DNA will prove I'm innocent."

Hating to wipe that look of relief from her friend's face, Vivian sighed. "Not necessarily. I'm sorry, Jenna. Your DNA obviously won't prove you killed Dean, but it might not prove you didn't."

"You mean I'm still a suspect? But Messina said it would exonerate me."

"It depends on where they found the DNA they're matching it with and how certain they are that it's related to the murder. Remember, he said it *could* be connected. He didn't say it was definite."

Jenna's smile faded, and a fierce frown took its place as she thumped the table with her fist.

"He played me," she said. "Okay, then. I'll do it."

Vivian looked at her. "Do what?"

"I'll act like an escort and talk to these guys. I'll prove I didn't kill my ex if it's the last thing I do. I'll show that patronizing stuffed shirt just how wrong he can be."

"Well, I think he's hot," Gracie said, then shut her mouth when Vivian looked at her.

"Are you sure you want to do this?" Vivian studied her face. "There's one thing we haven't discussed yet."

"What's that?"

"It could be dangerous. If one of these guys did kill Dean and we start asking questions, things could get dicey. We could just tell Messina what we know and let him take it from here."

"And that could scare everyone off. If they knew the police were investigating the service, no one would talk about it to anyone."

"There's that, I guess. Though Messina won't be happy if he finds out we know something that could help him and we didn't tell him about it."

Jenna looked defiant. "We haven't found out anything yet that connects someone to the murder. Besides, we're trying to help solve the case, not hinder it. If we can hand him the killer, he'll be so grateful he'll go down on his knees and thank us."

"That's something I'd like to see." Vivian tried to picture Messina on his knees and failed miserably.

"I want to do this," Jenna said quietly. "I want to get this mess over with and get back to a normal life again. I'm tired of having people look at me like I'm a criminal, and I'm tired of dodging reporters. I can't answer my phone anymore because of them calling me. Let's do this. Now."

Chapter Eight

Vivian could understand the desperation that drove Jenna to her decision and had to resist the urge to give her a hug. "I'm sorry." she said, wishing she could take away her friend's distress. "This is so hard for you."

Gracie pulled her phone from her pocket. "What are the guys' names?"

Vivian picked up her purse, but before she could look for the envelope with the scribbled names of Florrie's customers, Jenna announced them to Gracie.

"Adam Weinberg, Philip Stedman, and Mark Stanbury. Warren Lester knows us, and Vivian's right, the police chief is totally off the list."

"Wow," Vivian said, "I'm impressed. The only one I remembered was the guy who owns the paper mill."

"Trust me, the names are imprinted indelibly on my mind." Jenna looked at Gracie. "Go ahead. Look them up."

Gracie was already thumbing on her phone.

Vivian sipped her tea and pulled a face. "It's cold, but I don't want to make another pot of tea." She turned to Jenna. "You want another one?"

Jenna shook her head. "I usually drink coffee this early in the mornings."

"Oh, well, I have coffee."

"Not now, thanks." Jenna's gaze was on Gracie, who was swiping her phone with two fingers.

Finally, Gracie lifted her head. "I found the two commissioners. They look like dorks."

She showed her phone to Vivian, who stared at the pics. One of the men was gray haired and overweight, and the other was younger, thinner, and wore glasses. "They look like perfectly respectable businessmen to me."

"Let me look."

Gracie handed Jenna the phone, and she studied it with a frown. "They both look kind of familiar."

"You've probably seen them on TV or on the internet," Vivian said. "They look familiar to me, too, but I know I've never met them."

Jenna shuddered. "They don't look the type to use an escort service. Are they married?"

Gracie took the phone back and started swiping it again. "Here's a pic of them together," she said, moments later. "It was taken in the bar of the Blue Surf Hotel."

Vivian took the phone from her and stared at it. "Somehow we have to meet up with one of them."

"Well, we could send them an invite to the tearoom," Gracie suggested. "Like offer them fifty percent off the bill."

"And what if they turn up with their wives?" Jenna sounded exasperated.

"I don't think we could have a constructive conversation

here," Vivian said. "We need to corner them in a bar or somewhere like that."

"Like the Blue Surf Hotel?" Gracie had taken back her phone and was waving it at Vivian. "It says here that they are frequent visitors in the bar."

"Then we could go down there tonight in the hopes that at least one of them is there." Vivian didn't really expect an enthusiastic response to her impulsive suggestion.

Jenna, however, sat up on her chair. "Let's do it."

"It could be a total waste of time," Vivian warned her.

"It's worth a chance. We might even be able to leave a message for the guys if they're not there so we can meet them later."

"That's possible," Vivian murmured, after giving it some thought.

Jenna turned to Gracie. "I guess you've got a meeting."

"Actually, I don't tonight." Gracie grinned. "Besides, I wouldn't miss this for anything. I'll be there."

"Good." Vivian peered at her watch. "Do you want to meet down there, or shall we go together?"

Jenna and Gracie spoke in unison. "Together!"

"That's settled, then. Let's meet here at seven. If those guys stop by the bar for a drink after work, they probably won't stay too long."

"Let's go right after we close," Gracie said. "I'll drive."

"No." Vivian looked at Jenna. "You will have to go home first and change into something flashy."

"I don't own anything flashy." Jenna frowned. "What does flashy mean, anyway?"

"You know, glitzy."

"I know what the word means. I meant, what do you consider flashy?"

Gracie jumped in. "Something bright and eye-catching. I have a silk shirt you can borrow. I'll go home and get it after we close. Wear it with some tight pants and unbutton it low."

Vivian nodded. "That'll work. And go heavy on the makeup."

"Bright-red lipstick," Gracie suggested. "And lots of mascara."

"Pin your hair up," Vivian added. "It looks more sophisticated."

Jenna groaned. "I can't believe I'm doing this."

Vivian felt a pang of guilt for putting her friend through such turmoil. "You can still change your mind. We can think of something else."

"No. I think you're right. This is the best chance we've got right now of solving this thing. Or at least, learning more about it."

"Even if we do learn more," Vivian said, "there's no guarantee it will help us find out who killed Dean."

"Maybe, but right now, the list of suspects is pretty long. If we talk to these guys, we might be able to rule out some people and narrow the list."

"Or add some to it. We don't know how many people were paying Dean to keep his mouth shut."

"True, but either way, we could learn more about the escort service, and like you said, we might even find out the name of Dean's partner or his girlfriend."

"Okay, then. As long as you're sure you want to do this, we're on for tonight. We can get something to eat in the bar." Vivian got up from her chair. "Now I have things to do. We open in less than two hours."

"I might as well stay and help," Jenna said, pushing herself away from the table.

"Me too." Gracie jumped up. "What can I do?"

Grateful for the offer, Vivian smiled at her. "You can help me make the Bakewell tarts." She turned to Jenna. "There are some boxes in the storeroom to unpack, if you could help with those?"

"Sure. It'll take my mind off tonight."

Still feeling guilty, Vivian watched her leave. It had seemed such a good idea when she'd first come up with it, but now that they were actually going to put it into action, she could see all the pitfalls. She could only hope that things didn't go terribly wrong and put her friend in danger.

Maybe she'd read too many mystery novels. Things didn't always work out the way they did in fiction. Maybe she should have just told Messina about the escort service and let him handle it.

There was always the chance that Jenna's DNA would prove her innocence, though even if that was so, Vivian was convinced that neither she nor Jenna or Gracie would be satisfied until they had discovered who had killed Dean. They were in it to the end now, come what may.

In spite of the crowded tables and hungry customers, the day seemed longer than usual to Vivian. She found it hard to focus on the sandwich fillings; her mind was too busy inventing opening comments for Jenna to use when she approached the men.

It would be easier for her if she could meet with one of them alone. To have to confront two of them would be more intimidating. Not that she'd ever seen Jenna intimidated, unless it was in front of Detective Messina.

Hastily taking her mind off that, Vivian finished slicing the cucumber for the cheese-and-cucumber sandwiches. She was pulling the roast beef from the fridge to slice up when Gracie rushed into the kitchen, her cheeks warm with the exercise.

"One of our customers just spilled a full cup of tea on the tablecloth." Gracie rushed over to the counter and started pulling wads of paper towels from the holder. "It's made a huge mess all across the table."

Vivian slid the roast beef back into the fridge. "Has it affected the food?"

"I don't think so." Gracie tore back to the door.

"Just mop it up," Vivian called after her, "then get Jenna to help you take everything off the table. I'll bring a clean tablecloth."

With a nod, Gracie charged into the tearoom.

Vivian grabbed a clean tablecloth from the closet and hurried after her. The elderly woman who had spilled the tea was red-faced, apologies spilling from her mouth as she helped move the dishes to the counter.

By the time Vivian had soothed everyone at the table and replaced the tablecloth and all the dishes and food, peace had been restored in the room. The rest of the patrons had gone back to enjoying their afternoon tea, and Gracie was looking a lot more relaxed.

Only Jenna still seemed on edge, and Vivian guessed her friend was getting uptight about the evening's adventure.

She was feeling tense herself, still wondering if her idea that had seemed so logical when she'd first thought of it would end up being a total failure, or worse, lead them into trouble.

Then again, what trouble could they be in for by talking to someone? Jenna was simply going to have a conversation with two people who might be able to help them find a killer.

And if one of them turned out to be the killer?

She wasn't going to overthink things, Vivian told herself sternly. This wasn't Chicago, or even Portland. This was Misty Bay—a quiet, sleepy town where anything more disastrous than a winter storm rarely happened.

Until three days ago, when Dean's body had been found on the beach and Jenna was accused of his murder.

* * *

Jenna arrived back at the tearoom shortly before seven that evening. She looked different with dark-green eye shadow and her hair pinned up, and Vivian tried to forget her doubts as she greeted her friend.

"You look great," she said, hoping to erase the tension in Jenna's face. "You won't have any trouble getting those men to talk."

"You could use more blush and thicken those eyelashes," Gracie said, handing her the silk shirt. "I brought my makeup back with me. I'll do it for you."

"If I put any more crap on my lashes, I won't be able see through them." Jenna took the shirt from Gracie and shook it out. The black-and-white diamond pattern was eye-catching yet sophisticated—not at all Gracie's style.

Catching Vivian's surprised look, Gracie shrugged. "It belonged to my mom," she said. "I've never worn it."

"It's beautiful," Jenna said, fingering the crystal buttons. "I've never worn anything like this either."

"It will go great with those black pants." Gracie jerked her head toward the back door. "Let's go to the bathroom, and I'll fix your makeup."

Jenna followed her out the door, leaving Vivian to pace the floor until they returned a few minutes later.

She hardly recognized her friend when she walked into the kitchen. Jenna had been transformed. With the extra makeup, the slim pants, the high heels and jazzy shirt, she looked every bit as beautiful and glamorous as any movie star.

"Well," Gracie demanded, waving a hand at Jenna. "How does she look?"

"Fabulous." Vivian studied her friend. "You'll be turning heads in there tonight."

"This isn't me." Jenna looked down at the shirt. "I'm a jeans-and-sweater girl."

"That's the whole point," Vivian told her. "You're playing a part, remember?"

"I'm not likely to forget." She looked at her watch. "Let's go and get this over with. I'm driving. I need to focus on something else for a while." Jenna led them out the door and over to her car parked at the curb.

"Do you know what you're going to say to these guys?" Gracie asked as she climbed into the back seat.

Jenna tucked a stray hair back in place and reached for the ignition. "I'm gonna say I'm a friend of Florrie Hayes, I'm planning a party for her birthday, and I want to invite them."

Gracie groaned. "That's gruesome. You need something like, 'Hi, handsome. You look lonely tonight. Want some company?' "

Jenna raised her eyebrows. "That's a bit direct."

"You're an escort," Gracie said. "They are direct."

"Gracie's right." Vivian seized the seat belt and clasped it around her. "You need to put it out there. That's what they expect, and it's what they respond to, so you might as well give it to them."

Jenna sighed. "Okay, then. I guess it's no worse than you telling Ray Constanza you wanted to hire a call girl for a birthday present."

Gracie hooted with laughter. "That was so cool. Especially when he thought it was for Hal."

Vivian winced. "Yeah, well, Hal wasn't so amused."

"Oh, rats." Jenna sounded upset as she pulled out of the parking space. "He told Hal what you said?"

"He did. Hal took it really well, though." Vivian smiled. "He's a good man."

"He is," Gracie agreed. "You should go out with him."

Vivian dismissed the suggestion with a laugh. "I'm much too busy with the tearoom to get involved with a man." She leaned forward and pointed at the window of the Sophisticated Grape as they approached. "Look, Natalie has changed her window display."

Jenna slowed to take a look, murmuring, "She needs to stock some cheaper wine. The last bottle I bought from her just about broke me."

Thankful for the change of subject, Vivian sat back and tried to relax.

By the time they arrived at the Blue Surf parking lot, however, her anxiety was at fever pitch. The more she thought about her crazy idea, the more outrageous it seemed. What was she doing, putting Jenna in a position that could not only discredit her in town but actually put her in danger?

If she'd thought she could play the part herself, she would have jumped at it. Putting herself in a questionable position was a lot easier than putting a friend in one. As Jenna cut the engine, Vivian turned to her. "Maybe we should just go home. This isn't one of my best ideas."

Gracie muffled an exclamation of dismay, while Jenna shook her head. "No way. We've come this far. We're going for it."

"What can happen to her in a crowded bar with both of us there with her?" Gracie demanded.

Vivian looked at her. "We won't be with her when she's talking to those men."

"She's not, like, going anywhere with them." Gracie shot an alarmed look at Jenna. "You're not, are you?"

Jenna smiled. "Don't worry. I'll be fine. It won't be the first time I've dealt with a sleaze." She opened the car door and thrust out a leg. "Let's go."

Gracie jumped out, while Vivian followed more slowly.

The sun hovered just above the horizon, its rays sending golden streaks across the darkening sky. In the distance, the towering pinnacles of rock looked like black sentinels guarding a calm ocean. A handful of people wandered along the shoreline, stalked by the ever-hungry sea gulls swooping overhead.

It was a scene that so often had calmed Vivian's soul. She began to feel better as she marched toward the door of the hotel. Jenna would be fine. The men would be dazzled by her and tell her everything they needed to know.

Having convinced herself of that, she sailed into the bar and scanned the room, hoping to spot one or both of the councilmen.

"Do you see them?" Gracie asked, as they sat down at a table close to a window overlooking the ocean.

Her anticipation deflating, Vivian shook her head. "Not yet. Maybe they'll come in later."

Jenna stared at the bar, her forehead creased in a frown. "Isn't that Warren Lester over there?"

Vivian followed her gaze to where a man sat slumped over the counter. "It's hard to tell from his back, but it could be."

"I'm not surprised he uses an escort service," Gracie murmured. "He's not exactly dating material."

"I thought he was married," Jenna said.

"He is, but that doesn't seem to make a difference, from what we've learned so far." Vivian picked up the menu and flicked a glance over it. "Which isn't much. We don't even know the name of the service. We should have asked Florrie."

"She probably wouldn't have told you," Gracie said.

"She told us the names of her clients," Jenna reminded her. She squinted at the bar. "I'm sure that's Warren. You can't mistake that ratty brown hair. He needs to find a decent barber."

"Well," Vivian said, "he's on our suspect list. I'm going to go over there. After all, he knew Dean. I'll invite him to the table so we can all talk to him." She got up from her chair, adding, "I'll order dinner if you tell me what you want."

"I'll have the burger and a glass of Chardonnay." Jenna looked at Gracie. "What are you having?"

Gracie quickly checked out the menu. "The Cobb salad. And a beer."

With a brief nod, Vivian took off for the bar.

She could feel two pairs of riveted eyes burning into her back as she sauntered over to the man drooped over the counter.

Scrambling onto the barstool next to him, she jogged his elbow. "Warren! How nice to see you! It's been a while."

She wasn't sure if it was the shove she'd given him or the shock of seeing her there that made him spill his beer.

He stared at her for a moment, then stammered, "Mrs. Wainwright. I didn't recognize you at first. It must be at least a year since you were in the bank."

"Has it been that long?" Vivian laughed. "How time flies. Gracie does all my banking now, so I don't go in there anymore. How are you, then? How's the bank business?"

He opened his mouth to answer, but she held up her hand. "Wait! Gracie and Jenna are over there. Why don't you come over and join us? We're just going to have a quick bite to eat."

A flush was slowly spreading over Warren's cheeks. "Oh, I couldn't. I mean, I should be getting home."

Vivian sent a pointed look at his full glass. "You've barely started your beer. Bring it over to the table and finish it there."

She realized she sounded like a boss giving orders, but to her relief, it worked. Obviously reluctant, Warren slid off his stool and picked up his beer.

Leading him over to the table, Vivian half expected him to make a run for it. Especially as they drew closer, since both Jenna and Gracie were gawking at them like hungry dogs waiting to be fed.

As she reached the table, Vivian turned to the man behind her and waved a hand at the empty chair. "Take a seat."

Warren looked at his watch. "I really can't stay long. I should be going."

"Sit down, Warren," Jenna said, fluttering her eyelashes at him. "We won't bite."

He stared at her as if he hadn't seen her before as he lowered himself onto the chair. "You look different," he said, sliding his gaze across her face as if afraid to linger there.

"I'm trying out a new style." Jenna sent him a dazzling smile, then lowered her voice to a husky drawl. "It's real nice to see you, Warren."

He gulped. "Nice to see you too, Jenna."

She leaned toward him, her gaze devouring him. "I guess you heard what happened to Dean."

Warren shot a nervous look at Vivian. "Yes, I did. Terrible. Hard to believe."

"It is indeed." Vivian sighed. "He will be missed."

"Not by me," Jenna muttered, drawing back.

Vivian loudly cleared her throat. "You knew him, didn't you, Warren? It must have been a shock to you."

Warren flicked another glance at her. "Yes, it was."

"How well did you know him?"

Warren stared across the room as if judging his chance to escape. "Not all that well. He wasn't exactly pleasant company."

Vivian nodded. "I know what you mean. Dean could be abrasive at times." She looked up as the server approached, carrying a tray. "Ah, here's our food. Can we order something for you?"

Warren shook his head and started to rise. "Thanks, but I have to leave."

"Oh, but you haven't finished your beer yet." Jenna gave him another smoldering look. "Besides, we're enjoying your company, aren't we, ladies?"

Vivian answered with a hearty, "Yes, we are!" while Gracie managed a stiff nod.

Warren gaped at Jenna for a moment, then slowly sat down again and grabbed his glass.

The server reached the table and set down the plates and drinks. Vivian had ordered the club salad with her Chardonnay. She was pleased to see that it looked as appetizing as the picture on the menu.

Gracie rolled her eyes at the size of Jenna's burger before picking up her fork to dig into her salad.

The server, a pretty young woman with curly red hair, smiled at Warren. "Hi! Your friend came in looking for you on Friday. I told him you'd just left. Did he catch up with you?"

Warren coughed, almost spilling his mouthful of beer. He put the glass down and dabbed at his mouth with the back of his hand. "Yes, he did. Thanks."

"That's great." The server looked at Vivian. "Is there anything else I can get for you?"

"I think we're good," Vivian told her.

The server nodded, then sped away, leaving an uncomfortable silence at the table, before Vivian finally broke it.

"So, you were here on Friday?"

Warren gulped down the last of his beer. The glass thudded on the table when he set it down. "Yes, I was."

"That was right before Dean was killed. I don't suppose you saw him with anyone that evening?"

"I didn't see the man at all. Like I said, he wasn't any friend of mine. Now I have to go." He shot up, mumbled something else Vivian didn't catch, and took off like he was desperate to get to a bathroom.

"Well," Vivian murmured. "That was interesting."

"It was," Gracie said, her voice bordering on a giggle. "Especially when Jenna came on to him. I just about burst trying not to laugh."

"Was I that bad?" Jenna sighed. "I thought I'd try the escort act on him, but let's face it. It's just not me and never will be."

"You did great," Vivian assured her. "You got his attention, that's for sure. He was mesmerized—until we started asking questions."

Jenna took a hefty bite out of her burger, chewed, and swallowed. "You're not suggesting that dweeb killed Dean, I hope? Dean would have flattened him with one swipe of his hand."

Vivian picked up half of her sandwich. "One thing I learned from following Martin's cases: you can never judge a book by its cover. If someone wants to kill a person badly enough, he'll find a way."

"I think Warren Lester is creepy enough to find a way," Gracie said, balancing a wad of lettuce on her fork. "You should hear him tell people why he can't give them a loan. It's like he's expecting them to rob him."

Jenna gave her a questioning look. "You asked him for a loan?"

"What? Me? No!" Gracie laughed. "I hear him sometimes when I'm at the counter. He's got one of those voices that you can hear from across a room."

"Well, I think he's on our suspect list," Vivian said. "He's a client of the escort service, and he could be one of the men who were paying Dean to keep his mouth shut. Plus, he was here on Friday night."

"But he left," Jenna reminded her. "Remember the friend who was looking for him?"

"And Dean wasn't killed until the next morning," Gracie added.

"I know, but he was definitely nervous about something." Vivian glanced out the window at the ocean, which had almost disappeared in the darkness. "It could just be that he was worried we'd find out about his membership in the escort service. Or it could be something else. Something more sinister."

"Now you sound like one of your mystery novels." Jenna picked up her wine. "It doesn't look as if the councilmen are going to put in an appearance tonight, so I say let's forget the case for now and enjoy the evening."

"I'm sorry we got you all dolled up for nothing." Vivian looked around the room. "Is there anyone here you might be interested in? It's a shame to waste all that glamour on Warren Lester."

Jenna grunted. "I'm done with men, remember? Once bitten, twice shy."

Vivian gave her a stern look. "Don't talk like that. You're still a young, attractive woman. You deserve a good man."

"Yeah? Well, if such a thing does exist, I'm not likely to find it in Misty Bay. Even if I wanted to, which I don't." Jenna took a bite of her burger, ignoring the piece of onion that fell into her lap.

"Well, I think it's a bummer." Gracie attacked her salad with a vicious fork. "I was looking forward to you seducing those men."

Jenna choked on her mouthful of food. "Let's get one thing straight. No one is doing any seducing. Especially me. I don't mind talking to these guys, but I absolutely draw the line at anything more than that."

"And we're not expecting you to do more than that." Vivian sent Gracie a warning frown. "Anyway, you're right. As long as we're here, we might as well enjoy the outing." She picked up her wineglass. "To the three musketeers."

"More like the three rookies," Jenna said, raising her glass. "Here's to us."

Gracie held up her beer. "To us."

And may we come out of this unscathed, Vivian prayed as she sipped her wine.

Chapter Nine

The rest of the evening passed swiftly as the conversation turned eventually into an animated discussion about the pros and cons of living at the beach as opposed to in the city. They were so engrossed in the argument that Vivian barely noticed the server bringing the bill to the table. She flipped her credit card onto the plate and waved away offers from the other two to pay their share.

"It's my treat," she assured them. "A little bonus for working so hard for me."

Their grateful thanks warmed her heart as she checked her watch. Shocked to see how much time had gone by, she pushed back her chair. "Much as I hate to end this enjoyable get-together, I have to leave. I need to throw some lemon curd tarts together for tomorrow."

Jenna shook her head. "I don't know how you do it," she said as she gathered up her coat and purse. "You must work half the night."

Vivian laughed. "Not really. I love to bake, and it keeps me busy. After Martin died, the evenings were the worst time to get through. I needed something to keep me occupied, to keep my mind off everything I'd lost. That's when I unearthed my mother's box of recipes and started baking." She sighed. "A lot of my neighbors put on weight that first year. Including me."

"You've lost quite a bit of it since I've been working for you," Gracie said, rising from her chair.

"I'm using up more energy now that I have the tearoom." Vivian unhooked her purse from the back of her chair. "It's a lot of work, and I love every second of it."

Gracie grinned. "So do I. It's the most fun I've ever had working."

"Me too." Jenna looked serious for a moment. "You saved my life, giving me this job. I hate to think where I'd be right now if it wasn't for you and the Willow Pattern."

"You'd be working just as hard somewhere else," Vivian told her. "I just gave you the opportunity. You're the one who made it work for you." She cleared her throat. "Now, let's get out of here before we all get tempted to have a group hug or something."

That made both Gracie and Jenna laugh as they followed her out to the lobby.

As they crossed the carpeted floor, the front door swung open and an elegant man in a gray suit strolled toward them.

Reggie Lambert raised his eyebrows as he drew closer. "Good evening, ladies," he murmured, his gaze skimming over Jenna and then resting on Vivian's face. "I hope we don't have another problem?"

Vivian smiled at him. "Not at all. We were just enjoying a drink in your excellent lounge."

"Ah." His features relaxed. "We are rather proud of the lounge. It was designed by a prominent local artist."

"Desmond Pinto," Jenna said.

"Yes, that's right." Again, Reggie's gaze swept across Jenna's face. "Er . . . well, please excuse me. I have a rather urgent appointment. Have a good evening." He nodded at Vivian, smiled at Gracie, and then hurried off in the direction of the bar.

"Probably needed the bathroom," Jenna muttered, as they stepped out into the night.

Once outside in the brisk air, Vivian closed up her coat with one hand as they crossed the parking lot to the car. She couldn't see a single star in the darkened sky. The clouds must have rolled in while they were eating. The faint orange glow from the streetlamp, however, helped light the way between the parked cars.

They had almost reached Jenna's car when Vivian halted with a sharp exclamation of dismay. "Oh no! I left my credit card sitting on the table with the bill. I have to go back and get it."

"We'll come back with you," Jenna said, turning around.

"No! You two go on. I'll be faster on my own. It won't take me a minute. I'll meet you at the car." Before they could argue, she sped off toward the hotel door as fast as her aching knee would allow.

To her relief, the table was still vacant when she rushed into the bar. Her spirits plummeted again when she saw that the plate holding the bill and her credit card had disappeared. Hurrying over to the counter, she prayed that someone hadn't stolen it. Visions of her frantically calling the bank the next morning raced through her mind as she signaled to the young woman who had served them.

The redhead gave her a brief nod and continued serving a cocktail to a thickset man with wavy gray hair, who was chatting so loudly that Vivian was sure the entire bar could hear what he said.

She barely gave him a glance as she waited with growing impatience for the server to approach her. Finally, the woman hurried over to her. "You forgot your credit card," she said. "I'll get it for you. I'm afraid I have to ask for some identification before I can give it to you."

Relief made Vivian smile. "That's fine. I'm just glad it wasn't stolen." She pulled her wallet out of her purse and drew out her driver's license. Remembering that she hadn't added a tip, she slipped a ten-dollar bill out from her wallet while she waited for the server to bring back her card.

The redhead returned, holding the card. "Your ID?"

Vivian handed over her license. "I'm Vivian Wainwright. I own the Willow Pattern Tearoom on Main Street."

The young woman's eyes lit up. "Oh, really? My mom goes there all the time. She says you make the best pastries she's ever tasted."

"That's very sweet of her." Vivian felt a warm glow of satisfaction. "Please tell her I appreciate her business. What's her name? I know most of my regulars."

"It's Lilly. Lilly Colby."

Vivian nodded. "Oh, I know her! I will mention you next time I see her. What's your name?"

"Katie. I—"

She broke off as a harsh male voice from farther down the bar demanded, "Hey, gorgeous, can I get a drink down here?"

Katie rolled her eyes and handed over the license and card, then accepted the ten-dollar bill Vivian offered her with a smile of thanks.

Shaking her head, Vivian headed out of the hotel. It was a good thing she didn't work behind a bar, she told herself. She'd be yelling at jerks all night long and would probably drive away customers and end up getting fired. Thank heavens for the peaceful dignity of the tearoom.

Stepping out into the night, she shivered in the chill from the damp fog that had begun to creep in from the ocean. It was already curling around the streetlamp and dimming the light. She could barely see past the rows of cars filling the parking lot.

Just as she reached the first row, she thought she heard the sound of footsteps behind her. She glanced over her shoulder, peering into the murky shadows. She could see no signs of movement anywhere.

Just in case, she quickened her step, and again she heard the footsteps crunching on the concrete.

She quickly turned her head and for a moment thought she saw movement to her left. Another sharp glance revealed nothing, but something told her she wasn't alone in that dark, misty parking lot.

Jenna's car was in the last row of vehicles, and with her nerves screaming at her to hurry, Vivian sped as fast as she could to where she had left her friends. In her panic she forgot where Jenna had parked and frantically rushed down the row, glancing into windows as she passed each car.

Jenna must have seen her coming, as the lights of a car ahead of her suddenly switched on, bathing the area with welcome light.

Weak with relief, Vivian rushed up to the car and pulled the passenger door open. She practically fell into the seat and pulled her legs in, then slammed the door shut and locked it. "Let's go," she said, with the little breath she had left.

Jenna switched on the ignition. "What happened? Are you okay?"

"Just get out of here," Vivian urged, struggling to fasten her seat belt. "I think someone's following me."

"Where? Who is it?" Gracie sounded excited, and Vivian turned to look at her.

"I don't know. I couldn't see who it was."

Gracie stretched her neck to peer out the window. "I can't see anyone."

"Neither could I, but I know he was there. I could hear him walking behind me."

Jenna carefully backed out of the parking space, then pulled forward to drive slowly between the rows of cars. "Are you sure? It's creepy out there with all this mist. It's easy to imagine things. The fog can distort sounds. Whoever it was probably wasn't anywhere near you."

"I know what I heard, and I know what I felt." Vivian sat back, beginning to wonder if Jenna was right. Getting mixed up in a murder case could make someone oversensitive to the most innocuous situations.

"Okay, we'll take a look." Instead of driving out to the street, Jenna turned the car and began to coast up and down the long rows of vehicles.

When they reached the final row without seeing anyone, Vivian started to relax. "I'm sorry," she said. "I guess I let my nerves get the better of me. Let's go home."

"Did you get your card?" Gracie asked, as Jenna pulled out into the street.

"I did." Vivian patted her purse. "And I found out that our server in there is Mrs. Colby's daughter, Katie."

"Mrs. Colby?" Jenna sounded surprised. "The blond woman who comes in every Wednesday with a bunch of her cronies?"

"That's her." Vivian smiled. "She said I make the best pastries she ever tasted."

"I know her," Gracie said. "She loves your Eccles cakes. I don't know how she stays so thin when she's stuffing herself with those."

"She doesn't look old enough to have a daughter working at a bar," Jenna said. "They have to be over twenty-one for that job."

"I promised her I'd mention that we met her when her mom comes in again."

"Maybe she'll bring Katie with her," Gracie said. "She seems like a fun person."

"She has to have a lot of self-control to work at a bar." Vivian fished in her purse for a tissue to blow her nose. "She must have to deal with a lot of jerks in that job. It makes me really appreciate our clientele."

"Yeah, like a church where everyone behaves."

159

Jenna flicked a glance at Gracie in the rearview mirror. "You sound disappointed."

"I just think it would be nice if we had a hunk come in now and then." Gracie paused, then added with a hint of mischief, "Like Detective Messina, for instance."

"If you're so hung up on him," Jenna said, "why don't you make a play for him?"

Gracie snorted. "He's too old for me. Besides, he's probably married."

"He is," Jenna said. "He wears a wedding ring."

"He's not married anymore." Still dwelling on the footsteps in the parking lot, Vivian had spoken without thinking. Gracie's gasp of excitement reminded her that Hal had asked her not to tell anyone about Messina's past.

"Well, go on," Gracie said, sounding breathless. "Tell us more!"

"I only know his wife died," Vivian said, wishing she had better control over her tongue. "And that he doesn't like people talking about it, so please, don't say anything about it to anyone. Especially Natalie."

"You don't know what she died of?" Gracie asked.

To Vivian's relief just then, Jenna pulled up outside the tearoom. "Okay if I come in and change my shirt?"

"You can take it home with you," Gracie said. "You'll need it again when we find out how to meet up with the councilmen."

"I'd still rather change back before I go home. I can leave your shirt here until the next time I need it."

Vivian wasn't sure of the logic of that decision, but she answered with a smile. "Of course you can come in."

"And I left my makeup here. Do you have any scones left?" Gracie asked. "That salad wasn't very filling."

Jenna laughed. "You turn your nose up at my burger, yet you stuff yourself with scones."

"Scones don't have dead cows in them," Gracie said, scrambling out of the car.

"Your salad had a dead pig." Jenna climbed out of the car after her. "It had ham in it, didn't it?"

"I didn't eat the ham." Gracie danced up to the door of the tearoom.

Vivian dug into her purse for her keys. "I didn't know you were a vegan."

"Neither did I until a little while ago." Gracie stepped aside to let Vivian unlock the door.

"Is that what your meetings are about?" Jenna asked as Vivian opened the door and switched on the lights.

"Nope." Gracie dove inside, with Jenna following close behind her.

Shutting the door, Vivian asked, "Does anyone want tea?"

They both answered at once with a firm, "No!"

"It's a wonder you don't float away, drinking all that tea," Jenna said as she headed for the bathroom.

"I don't drink it that much," Vivian called out after her. "I'm just in the habit of offering it."

Jenna vanished into the bathroom with Gracie, leaving Vivian alone with the empty tables. After wandering around to inspect everything, she sat down on one of the chairs to wait for them.

Katie's mom had sat at that table the last time she'd come in. Vivian pictured the petite, blond woman, also finding it hard to imagine her with a grown-up daughter. Some women never put on weight, no matter what they ate.

Look at Gracie—thin as a reed, in spite of all the scones she consumed. Katie was skinny too. Probably because she was on her feet half the night. Remembering the harsh voice demanding service, Vivian shook her head. She hadn't noticed who was yelling at Katie.

The only person she had noticed was the guy sitting next to her. In fact, now that she thought about it, he'd seemed vaguely familiar. She was still struggling to remember who he'd reminded her of when Gracie came back, carrying her makeup bag.

"Jenna will be out in a minute," she said. "She's cleaned off her makeup and she's changing her shirt. I think she doesn't want her neighbors to see her all gussied up like that."

"I think you're right." Vivian stared at her as a thought struck her. "Gracie, can you find the pics of those two councilmen on your phone again?"

"Sure." Gracie hauled her phone from her purse and did a little dance with her thumbs on it. "Here."

She thrust the phone at Vivian, who plucked it from her fingers and took a look at the screen. "That's him," she said, with a stab of frustration. "That's Philip Stedman!"

"Yeah," Gracie said slowly. "We already know that."

"No, I mean I saw him." Vivian handed the phone back to Gracie. "He was sitting at the bar when I went back to get my card. He must have come in while we were talking at the table and we didn't notice him."

"Seriously?" Gracie sighed. "What a bummer. We could have had Jenna flirt with him."

"I know. We missed a golden opportunity."

"Who am I supposed to flirt with now?" Jenna demanded, having walked up behind them.

Gracie showed her the phone. "Him. That's Philip Stedman, the councilor. He was at the bar while we were eating dinner. We missed him."

Jenna rolled her eyes. "We have to get better at this."

"We do," Vivian agreed. "We need to be more observant. But there's always tomorrow."

"We're going back to the bar tomorrow?" Jenna plopped down on a chair. "If it wasn't for all the dressing up and the escort thing, I could get used to this."

Vivian grinned. "I've always believed in mixing business with pleasure."

"We don't have to go to the hotel tomorrow night," Gracie said, staring at her phone. "Philip Stedman is giving a speech at the library tomorrow afternoon at three o'clock. We could tackle him there."

"In the middle of our rush hour?" Vivian shook her head. "We can't do that."

"Maybe all of us can't," Jenna said. "But one of us could. I could run over there and have a chat with him. I can get all dolled up again and—"

"No!" Vivian held up her hand. "I'm not going to put you through that again. It was a dumb idea in the first place, and it will take up too much time. I'll go and talk to the councilman. You and Gracie can take care of things until I get back."

Jenna looked uneasy. "No offense, but he's not going to believe you're an escort. You look far too respectable."

Vivian sighed. "If that's a polite way of saying I'm too old, I agree with you. Which is why I'm not going to pretend to be one. I'll just mention the escort service somehow and hope that it puts him off guard enough to blurt out something useful."

"But what if he is Dean's killer?" Gracie's voice rose with anxiety. "He could hurt you."

"I'll be safe enough in the library in the middle of the day. I can always call you at the first sign of trouble. I'm sure you'll both drop everything and come running, right?"

"Absolutely," Jenna assured her.

Vivian leaned forward and laid a hand on her arm. "I'm sorry, Jenna. I should never have made you dress up like that tonight. I don't know what I was thinking."

Jenna laughed. "It's okay. It was worth it for the experience."

"Okay, then, if you're both sure you can handle things without me, I'll go to the library tomorrow and see if I can get something useful out of this guy."

"Great." Jenna stood up. "Then I guess I won't be needing the shirt again, Gracie."

"You can keep it if you like," Gracie said. "I'll never wear it."

"Thanks, but it's not my style." Jenna picked up her purse. "Besides, it belonged to your mom. I'm sure you'd like to keep it."

"It was her favorite shirt, but I only saw it on her a couple of times. She said she didn't want to wear it out."

Vivian smiled. "I can understand that." She got up and followed them both to the door. "Looks like you'll be able to sleep in tomorrow," she said as Jenna stepped out into the street.

"Yeah. I'm looking forward to that."

"See you in the morning," Gracie called out as she jogged over to her car.

Vivian was about to close the door when she heard Jenna's cry of dismay. Opening the door again, she stuck her head out to look. Gracie had halted at the sound and was now slowly retracing her steps back to Jenna's car.

Jenna, meanwhile, stood at the curb, staring down at the front wheel.

Hurrying forward, Vivian followed her friend's gaze to the flattened tire. "Oh no." Peering in the misty glow from the street lamp, she bent down to take a closer look. "How did that happen?"

"We must have run over something," Gracie said, hunching down next to the wheel. "Do you know how to change a tire?"

Jenna didn't answer, and Vivian turned to look at her. Her friend was staring at the car's windscreen with an odd expression on her face.

"What's the matter?" Vivian's nerves tightened as she watched her friend reach over to the windshield.

When she straightened again, she held a slip of paper in her hand. Holding it angled to catch the light, Jenna read out slowly, " 'Next time, it will be your brakes.' "

Gracie uttered a cry of alarm, while a cold hand seemed to squeeze Vivian's stomach.

Jenna looked shaken as she stared at the note. "Who would have done this?"

"Someone who doesn't like us asking questions." Vivian looked at each of them before adding, "Things just got a little more interesting."

Gracie stood up, her face looking drawn in the dim light. "You think the killer is after us now?"

Vivian took a steadying breath. "No. I think this is just a warning. And most likely from someone who doesn't want us poking our noses into the escort service. There are a lot more people involved in that than Dean's murder."

Gracie still didn't look convinced. "So, who do you think wrote it?"

"I can think of someone," Jenna said, carefully folding the note. "The only person we talked to tonight."

"Warren Lester?" Gracie shook her head. "That nerd? He wouldn't have the guts."

"Desperate men take desperate measures." Vivian sighed. "There's probably fingerprints on that note. If either of you wants to let Detective Messina handle this—"

"No!" Jenna waved the note at her. "I'm not going to be intimidated by a few scribbled words."

"And a flat tire," Gracie reminded her. "Just be sure to, like, test your brakes before you go anywhere."

"Vivian's right," Jenna said. "He's just trying to scare us off. I bet if the three of us confronted him, he'd go down like melting butter."

"We don't know that it was Warren," Vivian said. "There's another possibility. Philip Stedman was also at the bar tonight, remember? He could have heard that we were asking questions. He was sitting right next to me when I told Katie my name." She caught her breath. "The footsteps in the parking lot. That could have been him. He could have followed me out of the bar, then followed us here."

Jenna nodded. "It's possible. Maybe Florrie said something to him about us asking questions. She probably knows him if he's a member of the escort service."

"Of course!" Just to be sure, Vivian scanned the street, but apart from a young couple strolling arm in arm past the closed stores, she could see no one lurking around. "That settles it. I'll be at that meeting tomorrow at the library, and I'll let him know he's not going to scare us."

"Good for you." Jenna peered at her in the gloom. "You will be careful, though, right? Maybe we should wait until the three of us can question him."

"I'll be fine." Vivian smiled at her. "Gracie's right. What could happen to me in a library in the middle of the day?"

She hoped she sounded more confident than she felt. Facing a possible murderer on her own was going to be a unique experience. No matter how it turned out.

* * *

The phone on Messina's desk jangled, and he gave it a sour look. He was not in the best of moods this morning. He'd fallen back to sleep after turning off the alarm and hadn't had time to make his usual breakfast of coffee and a toasted bagel. He'd had to make do with the lousy office coffee and a greasy doughnut.

The report on the lipstick Brady had found still hadn't come back, and he was no closer to solving the case. Everyone he'd talked to either swore they didn't know Dean Ramsey or knew little about him. Those who did know him had nothing good to say about him. Apparently the guy didn't have many friends.

He couldn't help wondering why someone like Jenna Ramsey would have married a man like that. She was an attractive woman and must have had her pick of partners when she was younger. He could understand her being a little abrasive when upset, but he liked a woman who could stand up for herself. Sparring with her was actually a stimulating experience.

For a moment or two he allowed his mind to relive the moment he'd taken a sample of DNA from her. She'd seemed vulnerable then, and he'd felt a strong urge to protect her. She probably wouldn't thank him for that.

"Sir?"

He looked up with a start to see Brady staring down at him.

Quickly wiping the smile from his face, Messina cleared his throat. "What is it?"

"I've got the report back from the lab on that lipstick. The prints didn't match any in the system, and Mrs. Ramsey's DNA was a no-match."

He couldn't stop himself from grinning with relief. "Okay. It was a long shot anyway. Get the car. We're going to the Blue Surf."

"Yes, sir." Brady ambled off, and Messina straightened up his desk before getting to his feet. He wasn't too optimistic about his chances of learning something new. He'd already talked to everyone at the hotel who had a connection with Ramsey. The question that kept coming up in his mind was why the man would risk his job for a roll in the hay at the hotel where he worked. Why wouldn't he pick somewhere else to get his thrills? Who was he trying to impress?

It seemed doubtful that he would go to all that trouble and risk for a one-night stand, yet no one seemed to know if Ramsey had a girlfriend. Someone owned the negligee that was found on his body, however, and that someone had probably been with Ramsey when he died. He still couldn't rule out Jenna. Much as he wanted to declare her innocent.

If only they hadn't done such a good job of cleaning that room.

Something clicked in his mind, and he paused, leaning both hands on the desk. Wait a minute. Dean Ramsey died around seven AM. By the time they'd gotten the call and gone out to the beach and then up to the room, it must have been close to eight AM. The room was listed as unoccupied. So why was a housekeeper up there cleaning it at that hour of the morning?

He could understand the killer trying to wipe surfaces clean, but changing the sheets and towels? That was the work of a housekeeper. One who apparently knew about the murder. Someone right there in the hotel.

Wondering why the heck he hadn't thought of it earlier, Messina shoved his gun into its holster and strode across the room to the door. Someone in that hotel knew who Ramsey had slept with that night, and he was going to keep asking questions until that someone made a slip. If it wasn't Jenna—and he was almost sure now that it wasn't—then he was going to find the other woman and get the truth from her. One way or another.

Chapter Ten

Threatening clouds over the ocean suggested an approaching storm, and Vivian arrived at the library wearing a black belted raincoat over one of her favorite outfits—a loose-fitting white sweater with gold trim and black pants. She was out to impress and had dabbed on extra makeup for good measure.

The large turnout for the meeting surprised her when she walked through the door. She wouldn't have thought the councilman would have that many fans.

She had to sit through a largely boring speech about the Fall Beach Cleaning Project and the numerous reasons it was so important to the town. Her ears pricked up when Philip Stedman announced possible future additions to the town, such as a boardwalk along the beach with shops and entertainment.

That was met with hearty boos and groans from the restless audience, and Vivian realized these people weren't fans of Stedman's—they were there to voice their displeasure with the council's plans for Misty Bay. She added her own boos and was rewarded by a smile of approval from a woman she recognized as one of her customers.

Another woman on the other side of the meeting room stood up. Recognizing Natalie Chastain, Vivian slid down on her chair so she wouldn't be seen. The last thing she needed was the meddling woman demanding to know why she wasn't at the tearoom, attending to her customers, and keeping her from intercepting Philip Stedman on his way out.

Natalie asked if the proposed improvements would be put to a vote of the people. The councilman hemmed and hawed for a few moments, then admitted he couldn't be certain on that point and promised he would bring it up for discussion at the next council meeting.

The audience had to be satisfied with that, and the crowd broke up, most of them hurrying out the door. Vivian was relieved to see Natalie disappear into the street and turned her full attention on the councilman, who was talking to Stella, the librarian.

Hovering around the bookshelves, Vivian kept Stedman in her sights until he finally turned to head for the door. She took a deep breath. It was now or never.

She reached him just as he stepped out into the street. Drops of rain had started to spit from the gray sky, and he paused to fasten the top button of his raincoat. He looked up when Vivian edged in front of him.

Smiling at his blank face, she announced, "I'm Vivian Wainwright. I own the Willow Pattern Tearoom on Main Street. I heard your speech, and I was wondering if there were any plans to upgrade Main Street."

"None that I'm aware of, though I can't rule them out completely." He jammed his hands in his pockets. "Upgrades are pretty much essential for small towns if you want to keep them solvent."

Vivian shrugged. "Not necessarily. Misty Bay depends largely on tourism, and most of the visitors come here to get away from the noise and turmoil of city life. We have a reputation for being the quiet, peaceful haven that jaded workers need to recoup and refresh. They're not going to get that with raucous updates to the town. We already have that obnoxious hotel on the beach."

Stedman narrowed his eyes. "You don't like the Blue Surf? I consider it a valuable asset to the town. It's sophisticated, well managed, and caters to the tourists. Isn't that what we want for Misty Bay?"

Vivian raised her chin. "What we don't want is a sleazy escort service operating in there right under our noses."

Stedman's phony smile froze on his face. Seconds ticked by as he stared at her, and she sent a nervous glance down the street to reassure herself that she wasn't alone. She could see at least a dozen bystanders wandering past the shops and made an effort to relax.

"I haven't the faintest idea what you're talking about," Stedman said, apparently finding his voice again. "Now, if you don't mind, I need to get back to the office."

"I believe you knew Dean Ramsey." Vivian looked him straight in the eye. "I'm trying to locate his girlfriend. It would help me a great deal if I knew her name."

She realized the moment the words were out of her mouth that it had sounded like blackmail. *I'll keep quiet about your involvement with the escort service if you give me the name of Dean Ramsey's girlfriend.*

Before she could reassure him, however, he thrust past her, muttering, "I've never met the man. Good afternoon, Ms. Wainwright."

She watched him stride across the street to a parked Lincoln and drag open the door. Obviously, he didn't want to admit he knew about the escort service. But was his hasty departure due to his guilt about his participation with the service, or did he have a more ominous secret to hide?

She mulled over the question as she walked back to the tearoom, but as she arrived at the door, she had to admit she had no answers to give her assistants. They were no closer to solving the puzzle, and Jenna was still a murder suspect. It didn't look as if they were going to find Dean's killer after all.

She didn't have time to talk to either woman right then, in spite of Gracie's attempts to whisper questions. All the tables were occupied and they were running behind, thanks to Vivian's library visit.

After grabbing an apron, she began feverishly making sandwiches, leaving Jenna to wait tables. Gracie helped her out while keeping an eye on the store shelves for potential customers. By the time they were able to shut the door and turn the sign to CLOSED, Vivian was feeling exhausted.

"All this excitement is getting to me," she announced as she slumped down on a chair in the kitchen. "I think I'm going to have a quiet evening at home to recuperate."

Jenna sat down opposite her. "I take it you didn't get any answers from Philip Stedman."

Vivian sighed. "I'm sorry. Jenna. I brought up the escort service, but he just froze up." She considered telling them that she'd practically threatened him with blackmail, then decided she didn't need to worry them without good cause. "I asked him if he knew Dean's girlfriend, but he said he never met Dean."

"Well, he has to be lying," Jenna said. "If he's using the escort service, he has to have known him."

"Well, of course he was lying." Vivian stretched her aching back. "He's not going to admit he's involved in any of that."

"That doesn't get us any closer to finding Dean's girlfriend." Jenna frowned. "It's odd that no one seems to know anything about her. They must have gone to great lengths to keep their relationship a secret."

"She's probably married," Gracie said, munching on a scone.

Vivian stared at her. "That's a good point. It gives us another motive. What if the girlfriend's husband found out about their affair and killed Dean in a fit of jealousy?"

Jenna nodded. "That would make sense. Messina must be looking for her too. He has to know some woman was with Dean that night." She gave Vivian a bleak look. "Unless he's still convinced it was me and is just looking for a way to prove it."

"Well, he hasn't come to arrest you yet, so that's a good sign." Vivian leaned back on her chair. "So far, all we know is that a woman was probably with Dean either when or shortly before he was killed." She mulled on that for a moment, then added, "The way I see it, if the girlfriend didn't kill Dean, then she most likely knows who did and is in danger herself. Which is probably why she's in hiding. Which will make it all the more difficult to find her."

"Someone must have seen them together. We know at least one woman did." Jenna yawned, covering her mouth with her hand, then added, "I hope Natalie remembers to ask her hairdresser for that woman's name."

"Well, we still have to talk to the other men on Florrie's list," Vivian reminded her. "I think the blackmail motive is a lot stronger than a jealous husband."

"I think you're right." Jenna yawned again and stood up. "I'm just happy I don't have to play a lady of the night again. Warren Lester might be fooled by it, but the rest of them are not dumb. They would have seen right through me."

"What's the time?" Gracie stared at her watch, then jumped to her feet. "I'm going to be late for my meeting. See you tomorrow!" She dashed out the kitchen door, and a moment later the shop doorbell dinged, signaling her flight to the street.

Jenna shook her head. "Whatever that meeting is, it's important to her."

"Yes, it certainly looks that way." Vivian sighed. "Drive carefully, Jenna. Check your brakes before you go up that hill."

"My brakes are fine." Jenna retrieved her purse from the closet and slung it over her shoulder. "Don't worry about me. Get some rest. You look tired."

"What every woman is dying to hear," Vivian murmured as she followed her friend to the shop door.

Jenna laughed. "Don't worry. You look years younger than your age." With a quick wave, she vanished into the street.

With thoughts of a glass of wine enticing her upstairs, Vivian took a quick survey of the tearoom. Jenna had cleaned up nicely, as usual. Dazzling white tablecloths covered the tables, and fresh daisy sprigs nestled in the vases. All was well for the night.

Now all she had to worry about, Vivian told herself as she climbed the stairs, was what to have for supper. An omelet, maybe? Or a salad with a ham-and-cheese sandwich? It was the most ambitious she wanted to be right now.

She settled on the salad and sandwich and spent a relaxing evening watching an old mystery movie that she'd seen before but had mostly forgotten. Just as the news began, her phone's jingle announced a call.

Hearing Natalie's voice gave her a spark of hope, but it was soon dashed as the woman went on talking.

"I asked Carol for the name of that customer who sat next to me," Natalie said, "but she couldn't remember who it was."

Couldn't or wouldn't? Vivian wondered. She had long suspected that most hair stylists had a code of secrecy when it came to their customers. "That's okay, Natalie," she said. "Thanks for trying."

"Sure. I guess Jenna hasn't been arrested yet?"

She sounded disappointed, and Vivian rolled her eyes as she answered. "No, and we don't expect her to be. We're confident that Detective Messina will find Dean's killer and arrest him soon."

"I hope you're right. Let me know if there's anything else I can do to help."

The click in her ear told Vivian that Natalie had hung up. Sighing, she put down the phone. The woman meant well, but she was a little too eager to broadcast any juicy tidbits she came across. Which would be a great help to the investigation but not so good for Jenna's well-being.

After watching the news, she turned off the TV, relieved that the anchor had made no mention of the murder. Though she had no doubt it was still a hot topic in Misty Bay.

Later that night she awoke suddenly out of a dream. She'd been on the beach, searching for her phone that was buried in the sand.

For a few seconds she lay there, listening for a repeat of the sound that had woken her. She wasn't even sure it had been a sound, but she seemed to remember hearing a tinkling noise as she opened her eyes.

She could hear nothing but silence now, and deciding that it must have been her imagination, she turned onto her side and closed her eyes. It took her some time to go back to sleep, and when she finally woke up again, the sun was already peeking through the blinds.

Annoyed with herself for oversleeping, she scrambled to get showered and dressed. She had pastries and scones to bake and she needed more supplies, which meant she would have to get them delivered now, since she didn't have time to go to the store.

Hurrying down the stairs to the kitchen, she promised herself she would set the alarm again at night. She'd stopped doing that because lately she'd been waking up shortly before six every morning. She couldn't believe she'd slept until seven thirty. She must have been exhausted last night.

Chiding herself, she pushed open the kitchen door, then came to an abrupt halt just inside the room as a blast of cold air greeted her.

It took only one glance to see the reason. The kitchen window behind the sink afforded a glimpse of the ocean between the buildings behind the shop. Every morning she made a beeline for that window to check the weather. She could usually tell from the small strip of horizon in her view if a storm was on the way or if the day would be bright and sunny.

This morning, however, the sun couldn't warm the window. The breeze from the ocean swept throughout the kitchen instead, filling it with the smell she loved so much—seaweed and sand. Only she'd rather not smell it right here in her kitchen, she thought as she stared at the large, gaping hole in the glass.

Hurrying over to the counter, she winced at the sight of broken glass scattered across the surface. At first, she thought a sea gull might have crashed into the window. She'd heard of them doing that. But then she saw the words scrawled across the remaining glass in black letters. She peered at them, blinking hard as she tried to read the backward message. Finally, she interpreted it.

STAY OUT OF IT, OR DIE!

She smothered a whimper of dismay as she stared at the ominous message. With numb fingers she scrambled for her phone. Her first instinct was to dial 911, but she paused just long enough to think things through.

Jenna could easily have broken the window and left the message. She hadn't, of course, but with Detective Messina convinced that Jenna had killed her ex-husband, was it really wise to give him more reason to suspect her?

Her knees felt weak and she sat down at the table. A vision of Philip Stedman's face when she'd mentioned Dean turned her blood cold. If he'd murdered once to get rid of a black-mailer, what was to stop him from doing so again?

One thing was certain. Whoever Dean's killer was, he could kill again. Though that person had to know that Jenna and Gracie were involved in the hunt for his identity. Was he prepared to kill all three of them?

She needed to talk to someone. Her first thought was Hal, but she had no doubt that if she told him about the threat, he'd insist on calling in the police. After another moment's hesitation, she called Jenna.

The drowsy voice that answered warned her that she'd woken her friend out of a deep sleep. "I'm sorry," she said, "but we need to talk. Can you get here early?"

Jenna's voice sharpened at once. "What's up? Are you okay?"

"I'm fine." Vivian wished that were true. "I'll tell you more when you get here."

"I'll be there as soon as I can."

Gracie sounded a lot brighter than Jenna when she answered. "I'm on my way," she sang out when Vivian asked her to come in early. "Can I have a scone when I get there?"

In spite of her anxiety, Vivian had to smile. "Of course. I'll have to bake while we talk, so you can have one fresh from the oven."

"I can't wait."

Putting down the phone, Vivian checked her watch. She needed to call in the order for supplies, then start baking right away. Tea and breakfast would have to wait.

Gracie arrived while Vivian was still in the kitchen mixing the dough for the scones. "I didn't have time for breakfast," she said as she flung off her jacket and draped it over a chair. "So I guess a scone will have to do."

"I have a couple of eggs left in the fridge," Vivian said, starting to knead the dough. "You're welcome to fix yourself breakfast."

"Thanks, but I'd rather have a scone. Maybe two." Gracie looked around. "What can I do to help? Is Jenna coming in too? Are you sick or something? Why is it so cold in here?"

Vivian threw her a look over her shoulder. "Look at the window."

"Oh no!" Gracie trotted over to the sink and stared at the hole. "What happened?"

"Someone broke in last night. It woke me up, but I thought I'd imagined it and went back to sleep. That's why I overslept this morning." She pummeled the dough with her knuckles. "I'd like to get my hands on the miserable blighter who did it."

Gracie walked back to the table. "Miserable what?"

"Blighter. One of my English mother's expressions."

"Oh, bummer! Who'd do something like that?"

"The same person who left the note on Jenna's car, I guess. He left a message on the glass."

"I didn't see a message."

"That's because I washed it off. I didn't want anyone else to see it."

"So, what'd it say?"

Vivian told her, and Gracie sat down hard on a chair. "Shouldn't you have left it for the cops to see?" She caught her breath. "You think Philip Stedman did it?"

"I think it's a possibility. Especially since I sounded like I was blackmailing him. But I can't call the cops." Vivian reached for her rolling pin. "I've beaten the heck out of this dough. The scones will be as hard as rocks."

"Why can't you call the cops?" Gracie got up again. "That was a death threat."

"The first thing that detective is going to do is arrest Jenna. I'm not going to put her through that again."

"So, you're going to risk your life instead?"

Vivian finished rolling out the dough and put down the rolling pin. "Look, we don't know for sure that it was Stedman. In any case, I still think this is an empty threat designed to scare us into dropping our investigation. There are three of us. Whoever is doing this isn't going to kill all three of us. That's a sure way of getting caught."

"He could make it look like an accident." Gracie sent a nervous glance at the door to the tearoom. "Like set fire to this place with the three of us locked inside."

Vivian picked up her pastry cutter and started cutting circles out of the dough. "The doors lock from the inside."

"Oh yeah. I forgot that."

She still sounded scared, and Vivian tried to reassure her. "As long as we stick together, I feel confident that nothing's going to happen to us, but we'll talk to Jenna and see what she wants to do. She should be here soon. Meanwhile, I cleaned up the broken glass in a hurry to get it done. Can you check and make sure I didn't miss any?"

"Sure." Gracie walked over to the closet and pulled out the dustpan and brush.

Vivian carefully laid out the circles of dough on baking sheets, her mind still churning with indecision. She'd washed off the message on impulse, worried that someone would see it and broadcast it all over town.

If Jenna wanted to report it to Detective Messina, he wasn't going to be too thrilled that the message, and probably all hope of identifying the writer, was gone forever. Then again, if they called this in, they should probably tell him about the note on Jenna's car, and that would lead to the escort service, and they would be opening up the biggest can of worms this town had ever seen.

Would that be bad or good for business? She couldn't make up her mind. Then, ashamed that she was actually worrying about the business when Jenna's freedom was at stake, she shoved the trays into the ovens, vowing that she would do whatever Jenna wanted to do.

When Jenna finally arrived, she took one look at the window and declared, "Messina's going to say I did it."

"That's what I was afraid of, which is why I washed off the message." Vivian opened an oven door and pulled out a tray. The smell of freshly baked scones wafted across the kitchen, then disappeared in another fresh blast of sea air. "I need to cover up that hole until I can get it repaired." She looked at Gracie. "Empty one of the cartons in the storeroom, please, and bring it to me."

"Sure." Gracie eyed the scones with a look of pure longing, then darted over to the storeroom.

"What are we going to do?" Jenna slipped off her jacket, shivered, and pulled the jacket back on again.

"Well, the cardboard will make it dark in here, but we'll keep the light on until I get the window fixed."

"I mean about the message. We should tell Messina about this."

"Yes, we should." Vivian gave her a long look. "I'm willing to keep quiet about it for now if you are."

"But that's putting your life in danger."

"All three of us, possibly."

"Yeah." Jenna dug her hands into the pockets of her jacket. "We should tell him."

"Is that what you want?"

"No, it's not. I'm afraid he'll arrest me. But I don't want to be responsible for something bad happening to you and Gracie."

Vivian pulled another tray from the oven. "If it's any help, I don't think this person is going to risk harming all three of us. It's hard enough to get away with one murder."

"You still think he's trying to frighten us?"

"Yes, I do." Vivian laid the tray on the counter and opened the second oven door. "But the decision to tell the detective is up to you."

"What about Gracie? How does she feel about it?"

"Gracie's scared, but she'll do whatever we decide."

"No, that's not enough." Jenna walked over to the stove and picked up the kettle. "She has to do what's best for her. If she's scared, then I'll take my chances with Messina."

She swung around as Gracie spoke from the doorway. "I'm not scared, and you're not taking any chances with the cops." She walked into the room, holding the empty carton like a shield in front of her. "We're going to find this creep ourselves and hand him over to your detective." She looked at Vivian. "Right?"

Vivian smiled. It was the answer she'd expected. "Right."

Jenna turned around, the kettle still in her hand. "You guys. I don't know what I'd do without you two."

She sounded choked. Gracie dropped the carton and rushed over to her to give her a hug. "We'll always have your back. The three rookies, remember? All for one and one for all."

Vivian cleared her throat. "This is all very inspiring, but I could really use some help here. I got up late, and now I'm running behind with all this excitement."

"I'll fix the window." Jenna picked up the carton.

Gracie leapt over to Vivian's side. "What do you need me to do?"

"Well, I've got supplies being delivered, but I need some more eggs and milk right now. Can you run to the store and pick some up for me?"

"Sure." Gracie grabbed her jacket. "Can I take a scone with me?"

Vivian handed her one, and she rushed out the door.

"By the way," Jenna called out after her. "He's not *my* detective!"

Gracie's voice floated back from the tearoom. "Yeah, yeah." Seconds later the store doorbell dinged.

"She's a good kid," Jenna said, as she opened a drawer. "But she needs to grow up. Do you have masking tape?"

"In the storeroom. Second shelf up on the right." Vivian glanced at the broken window. All she could hope was that her theory was right and that whoever was threatening them was just trying to frighten them. If she was wrong, she'd regret it the rest of her life.

It was well into the afternoon before she finally had a chance to call Hal and ask him if he knew someone who could fix her window. "I think a sea gull flew into it," she told him, when he responded with shocked concern.

"Are you okay?"

"I'm fine. I've got the window covered with cardboard at the moment, but that won't hold up for long in the wind."

"I'll call around and see what can I do." Hal paused, then added, "What about the bird? Is it dead?"

"What?" She had to think for a minute. "Oh, no. There was no sign of it, so it must have flown away."

"Oh, good. I hate to think of the poor thing wandering around wounded."

Feeling bad for lying to him, she answered him in a rush of words. "I'm sorry, Hal. I have to go. I overslept this morning, and it's been a madhouse in here ever since. Thanks for the help."

"I'll stop by after closing and check it out. Maybe there's something I can do until you can get it fixed."

"Oh, you don't have to do that. It'll be fine." The last thing she wanted was to have to keep up the pretense face-to-face.

"You don't want me to stop by?"

Now he sounded hurt, and she sighed. "Of course I'd love to see you. I just didn't want to put you out."

"You're not putting me out. That's what friends do. They help each other when needed. Right?"

"Right. See you later, then." She was actually smiling when she hung up. It never failed to surprise her how much better he could make her feel when she was down. He was a good friend.

Her smile faded when she wondered how he would feel when he found out she hadn't been truthful about the window. Hurt, probably, that she hadn't trusted him. But she couldn't take that chance. Not as long as there was the slightest possibility of Jenna getting arrested.

By closing time, her anxiety was giving her a headache. She wasn't sure if it was the prospect of having to lie to Hal again or the thought of having to spend the night alone, not knowing if she was going to be attacked in her bed.

She tried to convince herself that her gut instinct was reliable and that the messages were empty threats, but as the sun began its slow descent into the ocean's horizon, her nerves tightened.

It didn't help when, just before Gracie left for her meeting, she warned Vivian to be careful. "If you hear the slightest noise," she said, "don't hesitate to call the cops."

Jenna seconded that. "Absolutely. After all, I'll have an alibi, so they can't accuse me."

"You won't be able to prove you were home," Gracie reminded her. "Unless you can get Misty to talk."

Jenna rolled her eyes. "I'll think of something."

The exchange left Vivian with a fluttery stomach and a dull throb behind her eyes. Things were getting complicated. She hated the feeling that her life was out of control. She needed to get her act together and get something concrete done. If only she knew how to do that.

Chapter Eleven

Hal arrived about an hour after she'd closed up shop. She was halfheartedly swallowing down a plate of spaghetti when she heard the shop doorbell announce his arrival.

She quickly scraped the remains of her meal into the sink and ran the garbage disposal before hurrying down the stairs to the tearoom.

After unlocking the door, she pulled it open and felt better already at the sight of his smiling face.

"I thought you might need a drink," he said, holding up a bottle of wine. "You sounded jittery this afternoon."

She opened the door wider. "Come on in, friend. You know me well."

Grinning, he stepped into the tearoom and looked around. "I always feel as if I've gone back in time when I come in here. It looks like something out of *Downton Abbey*."

She laughed. "Exactly what I'm going for. Come along, I'll show you the window."

He followed her into the kitchen, where he put the wine down on the table and walked over to the sink. "It looks as if you've got it well covered." He reached up and pulled one side of the cardboard away to peer at the hole. "Not too big. Just big enough to be a nuisance."

"Especially with the wind blowing directly off the ocean. It was like a freezer in here this morning."

"Why didn't you call me this morning? I maybe could have had a guy out here this afternoon."

She floundered around in her mind for an excuse. "Like I told you, I overslept this morning and had to call in the girls early to help out. We all had to scramble to get ready to open, and I didn't even have time to think until this afternoon."

To her relief, he seemed to accept that. "Well, I talked to a guy I know. He's going to try and get over here tomorrow afternoon. His name's Ben Guinto. He's from the Philippines, and his accent is a little strong, but his English is good. He's a good guy. You'll like him."

"If he's a friend of yours, I'm sure I'll like him." She looked at the wine bottle. "You want to come upstairs to drink that?"

"I thought you'd never ask." He grabbed the bottle and waved his hand at the door. "After you, fair maiden."

She wrinkled her nose at him. "You really need to modernize your reading habits."

"And what's wrong with reading historical novels?"

She was halfway to the door as he said it, and she stopped short to turn around to look at him. "You read romance novels?"

He looked a little sheepish as he shrugged. "I have to do something to occupy the time."

She stared at him for another ten seconds or so before saying softly, "Hal Douglass, I really like you."

"I'm glad." His smile spread over his face. "Because I really like you."

For just a second longer she allowed herself to enjoy the look in his eyes, and then common sense prevailed. Turning back to head for the door, she muttered, "I hope you've eaten, because I've already had dinner."

He followed her up the stairs without saying a word, and she worried that she might have upset him with her abrupt dismissal of what could have been a significant moment.

Once inside her apartment, however, he seemed fine as he walked into her kitchen, opened a cabinet, and took down two wineglasses.

Still uneasy about her rather ungracious response, she tried to sound casual. "I can soon fix you something to eat if you're hungry."

He pulled open a drawer and took out her corkscrew before answering her. "I'm fine. I grabbed a bite before I came over here." He looked up at her, and she could see no resentment in his eyes when he added, "I hope you don't mind me helping myself here."

She smiled. "Of course not. That's what friends do, right?"

"Right. That's what friends do." He dropped his gaze to the bottle as he deftly twisted the corkscrew to open it. "So, tell me, how's your investigation going? Find any more clues to who might have killed Dean?"

"No." She took the glass he offered her and led him out into the living room. "We talked to one of the escorts. Did you know that Dean owned the service?"

"No way." Hal sunk down on the couch and put his glass on the coffee table. "Then what was he doing working maintenance at the Blue Surf?"

"We don't know. We did get the names of some clients." She hesitated, wondering how safe it would be for Florrie if she told him. She was dying to let him know that among the prominent men involved was the town's chief of police.

Hal, however, seemed uninterested in knowing who was patronizing an escort service. "I haven't seen anything in the news about the murder. The cops must not be making any progress."

Vivian sat down next to him, still holding her glass. "Detective Messina took a sample of Jenna's DNA, but so far we haven't heard anything from him."

"You probably won't." Hal leaned back on the couch. "From what Ken told me, the bridal suite had been thoroughly cleaned up before they got to it, and the only traces of DNA they found on the nightgown belonged to Dean."

"Really." Vivian took a sip of her wine and set down the glass. "I wonder why Messina bothered to get DNA from Jenna, then."

Hal shrugged. "Maybe he found DNA somewhere else."

"Well, whatever it is, it won't prove Jenna killed her ex, because she didn't. I'd stake my life on that."

Hal met her gaze, unsettling her again. "I hope you never have to do that."

"Do what?"

"Stake your life on it."

"So do I." She made light of the moment with a laugh and reached for her glass again. "So, how's the business going?

Are you still getting plenty of customers? I thought things would start to die down now that the summer is over, but the town still seems to have a fair share of visitors. I was talking to Councilman Stedman yesterday, and he said the council members were talking about adding a boardwalk to the beach with shops and entertainment."

For a moment he didn't answer, and again she thought she might have upset him with her abrupt change of conversation, but then he said quietly, "That, in my humble opinion, would be a ghastly mistake."

Relieved, she smiled. "That's pretty much what I told him."

Hal raised his eyebrows. "What did he say to that?"

"I don't think he appreciated my opinion."

He laughed, and pleased that she'd evaded another awkward moment, she led him into a discussion on the results of changing the face of Misty Bay.

Long after he'd left, she lay in bed, wondering when and how things had become so complicated between them. She'd always had an easy relationship with Hal, without all the confusion of a more intimate connection. Much as she enjoyed his company, she wasn't looking for anything more than a casual friendship.

Lately, however, she'd gotten the distinct feeling that Hal wanted more. She knew that both Jenna and Gracie thought the same thing. She hoped with all her heart that it wouldn't wreck what had been, up until now, an enjoyable bond between them. She would miss that.

It surprised her to realize just how much she would miss it.

Embroiled in her thoughts, she drifted off to an uneasy sleep, punctured by disturbing dreams of armed assassins hunting her down. She awoke the next morning with the firm conviction that she needed to get a dog. A big one.

She arrived downstairs in the kitchen half afraid to open the door, wondering if some other disaster awaited her. To her relief, nothing was out of place, and she was able to spend a normal morning baking Eccles cakes, Bakewell tarts, and cream horns.

Gracie arrived at the tearoom first, shortly before noon. By the time Jenna arrived fifteen minutes later, Gracie had unpacked a carton of English tea and two cartons of assorted British candy.

"Sorry I'm late," Jenna called out as she sailed across the room. "I lost Misty and had to go look for her."

Standing in front of one of the tables, Vivian paused in the act of placing the delicate china cups upside down in their saucers and stared at Jenna in concern. "Did you find her?"

Jenna had reached the door of the kitchen and stopped to look back at her. "Yes, I did. She was hiding under a rosebush in the backyard. I think she was stalking a robin. I was worried she'd wandered off again, which is how she probably got lost in the first place."

She vanished into the kitchen and moments later emerged again, wearing her apron and carrying a tray of cups and saucers. "That's my job," she told Vivian. "Get back in the kitchen."

Vivian smiled. "Yes, mom." She headed for the kitchen, reminding herself as she had so often done that she was lucky to have such reliable and competent assistants to help her live her dream.

It was almost closing time before she had a chance to talk to them. The last of the tea customers had already left, and only one visitor was browsing the shelves when Vivian took off her apron and sank onto a chair at the kitchen table.

"You want tea?" Jenna asked as she headed for the stove. "I'll make it for you."

"What I want is a tall glass of wine." Vivian wriggled her aching toes. "But I guess tea will do for now."

"I can run down to Natalie's and get a bottle for you if you want."

"Thanks, but I have a couple of bottles upstairs in the fridge. I'll wait until I get up there." She gave Jenna a tired smile. "But tea would be nice right now."

"You got it." Jenna took hold of the kettle and filled it. "Did you find someone to fix the window?"

"Oh!" Vivian sat up straight. "I forgot. Hal said a friend of his would come over this afternoon to look at it. He's probably held up somewhere. Just as well, I guess. We really don't need someone pounding away in the kitchen while our guests are trying to enjoy a peaceful afternoon tea."

"Yeah. Maybe you should ask him to get here in the morning."

"Well, Hal was kind of doing me a favor, so I didn't want to get picky."

"Did you tell him about the note?"

Vivian shook her head. "No. I know Hal. He would have immediately called the cops."

"He's very protective of you."

For some reason, the comment made Vivian uncomfortable. "He's a protective kind of guy. You should see him when he's serving customers at his store. He's always asking questions about the pets, wanting to know if they have any allergies or problems before he lets them leave with the food."

Jenna turned around and smiled. "He's a good guy."

"Yes," Vivian said, returning the smile. "He really is."

The shop doorbell dinged at that moment, and seconds later Gracie appeared in the doorway. "The last customer just left. Do you want me to switch the sign?"

Vivian smiled at her. "Yes, please. Make sure you lock up too."

"Copy that." Gracie disappeared again, while Jenna took down a mug from the cabinet.

"I told Hal about Detective Messina taking a sample of your DNA," Vivian said. "Hal said he heard that the bridal suite had been cleaned up before Messina got there and that the only DNA on the nightgown belonged to Dean."

Jenna swung around to stare at her. "That means I'm in the clear?"

"It means that Messina can't prove you're guilty," Vivian said carefully.

"But she's still a suspect?" Gracie stood in the doorway, her face a mask of dismay.

Jenna groaned. "Wonderful."

"I don't know." Vivian slumped back in her chair. "The fact that he hasn't charged you means he's not totally convinced you killed Dean." She looked at her friend, wary of raising her hopes too much. "On the other hand, he could still be looking for evidence to convict you."

"Yeah, I figured that." Jenna turned her back on them as the kettle began to screech. "He's not going to give up."

"Nor are we." Vivian stared at Jenna's back as a thought struck her. "Wait a minute. Hal said that the only DNA on the nightgown belonged to Dean. Which probably means that whoever was with him that night never wore it."

"She probably intended to wear it but never got around to it," Jenna said. "It must have been lying on the bed when Dean got woken up, which is why he grabbed it."

"What if it was new? If she's local, she probably bought it here. The news said it was a bright-pink, lace-trimmed negligee. Surely if someone bought a nightgown like that, the person who sold it to her would remember her? We might be able to get her name."

"There's only a couple of clothing shops in Misty Bay," Gracie said as she flopped down on a chair. "One sells old-lady stuff, and the other one sells beach gear. If that woman did buy it locally, I'm betting she bought it in Newport."

"Tomorrow's Saturday. Our busy day. I'll go early on Monday. That's our quietest day in the tearoom."

"I'll come too. I know where all the best shops are." Gracie peered across the room at the shelves. "Were there any scones left?"

"Sorry. They're all gone." Vivian waved a hand at the shelves. "There's some Bakewell tarts and a couple of cream horns, though you'd have to fill it yourself."

"Okay. Thanks." Gracie jumped up again and darted over to the shelves.

"I'll come with you too," Jenna said as she poured tea into the mug. "I haven't been into Newport for a while." She glanced at Gracie, who had plucked a tart from a tray and was looking at it as if she'd discovered gold. "You want tea?"

"No, thanks. I have to get to my meeting." She looked over at Vivian. "What time do you want to meet Monday?"

"I don't know. Meet here around ten? That's usually when the shops open."

"We could go early and have breakfast there." Gracie took a bite out of the tart. "I know an awesome place right on the beach. You'll love it."

"We should probably meet here around eight thirty, then."

Jenna rolled her eyes. "Always thinking of her stomach." Carrying the mug of tea, she walked over to the table and set it down in front of Vivian.

"Better than thinking about the bad stuff." Gracie looked at her watch. "I gotta run." With that, she grabbed her jacket and purse from the closet and dashed out the door.

As the shop doorbell chimed, Jenna sighed. "What kind of mess can she be in to have a meeting every single night?"

"It doesn't have to be a mess. She could be learning something new."

"Like what?"

Vivian shrugged. "I don't know. Maybe she's studying for something."

"To get a better job, you mean?"

A pang of dismay made Vivian gasp. "I hadn't thought of that."

Jenna shook her head. "She's more likely meeting a new boyfriend and doesn't want to tell us. Anyway, I'm leaving too. I'll see you tomorrow."

"Right." Vivian started to reach for the mug, then swung around, her nerves jumping, as a raspy voice spoke from the doorway.

"Please excuse? I come to fix the window."

Catching her breath, Vivian stood up.

"My name is Ben. The young lady told me to come in." The frail-looking man shuffled forward, his scrawny face wreathed in smiles. "You are Mrs. Wainwright?"

Vivian relaxed. "I'm Vivian, yes. And this is Jenna."

"Hi! Nice to meet you." Jenna switched her gaze to Vivian, clearly questioning if it was okay for her to leave.

"You also." Ben slowly advanced to the sink and leaned across it to lift a corner of the cardboard away from the window. "Ah, yes," he said. "I will replace this. I go outside to take measurements."

"You can go out the back way." Vivian showed him the door, and nodding his head, he stepped outside.

After closing the door behind him, Vivian turned to see Jenna staring at her.

"Are you sure he's Hal's friend? He could be the one who broke the window in the first place and left that note."

Vivian laughed. "Don't worry. He's fine. He looks and sounds exactly as Hal described him. I'm sure he's the guy."

"Well, I could stay, just in case."

"No, you get home to your Misty. She's probably waiting for her supper."

"Okay, if you're sure." Jenna pulled on her jacket and gathered up her purse. "Call me if you need me, okay?"

"I promise." Vivian gave her arm a little push. "Now go."

Left alone, she took a few moments to sip her tea and relax her tired muscles. She could hear Ben rustling around outside, and minutes later he opened the back door and poked his head around it. "Okay if I come in?"

"Of course!" She smiled at him. "Would you like some tea?" She raised her mug at him. "It's still hot."

"Thank you, no. I must get home." He hobbled over to the door with an obvious limp. "I come back Monday morning with new window, yes?"

"Thank you, yes. How much will it cost me?"

He gave her a figure that seemed reasonable and took off.

She sat for a while longer to finish her tea, then cleaned up the kitchen, turned out the light, and climbed the stairs to her apartment.

Saturday passed swiftly for Vivian, with a surge of customers that kept all three women busy for most of the day. She had little time to dwell on the disturbing message on her window, but lying in bed that night, she thought about Ben Guinto, wondering what caused his bad posture and limp. If he was in pain, it must be hard for him to work. Some people had to suffer so much just to make a living.

Jenna's life was like that. She'd always had to struggle to make a living. Vivian sighed, wishing she could pay both assistants a bigger salary. Since they both worked part-time, what she paid them was fair, but it certainly wasn't making them rich.

One thing was certain, Dean Ramsey sure hadn't been making big money while Jenna was married to him. Which meant that his ownership of the escort service must have happened in the last year or so.

Since he'd started working at the Blue Surf.

Vivian flicked open her eyes. There could be a connection there somewhere. More than just using the rooms. Someone Dean had met while working there who'd gotten him involved in the escort service. They needed to talk to Paula Lambert again. She handled all the staff. She had to know who spent time with Dean.

Except she didn't want to talk to them. What was she hiding? Did she know about the service after all? Did Reggie know?

Vivian sat up and ran a hand through her hair. There had to be a way to find out. She wrestled with the problem for a moment, then let out her breath. Gracie could talk to Paula. They'd never met. Paula wouldn't know she was helping with the investigation. Maybe Gracie could apply for a job there. It would get her in the door and give her a chance to talk to Paula.

Having settled that in her mind, she did her best to go to sleep.

She'd never noticed before how many odd noises the building made at night. Like creaks and whispers, and a soft rattling that she couldn't identify.

She sat up again, her ears straining to make sense of each sound. The rattling unnerved her. Her cell phone lay next to her on the bedside table, and she reached for it, ready to dial at the first sign of danger. Maybe she should go downstairs and investigate. If someone was trying to break in, she could catch them red-handed.

She didn't want to go downstairs. She didn't want to be alone right now. What she wanted to do was call Hal and hear his reassuring voice tell her everything was okay. Or better yet, that he'd be right over.

A quick glance at her alarm clock warned her that it was far too late to call him now. Too late to call anyone just to find out that it was a false alarm.

She wasn't going to get any sleep unless she checked things out downstairs. The rattling sounded louder now. She had to know what was going on down there. She flicked on her bedside lamp, drew a deep breath, and slid her legs out of the bed.

Drawing on her robe, she crept toward the bedroom door. She needed a weapon. Not anything lethal—just enough to fight off an attacker. The thought made her stomach churn. Again she thought about calling Hal. But then she'd look like a prize idiot if she was panicking over nothing.

Worse, he might take it as an invitation or something. Calling him in the middle of the night, dressed only in shorty pajamas, with a fake excuse that she'd heard an intruder? Yeah, right.

She trod lightly over to the closet and opened the door. The heavy walking stick Martin had used when his sciatica flared up lay on the shelf, and she grabbed it. It would deliver a nasty blow if she had to use it.

As she turned back, a floorboard creaked beneath her foot, and she froze, wondering if she'd alerted the intruder. If there was one. She could still hear the rattling sound, however, and she cautiously opened the door and tiptoed across the living room to the main door.

There was a small window in the side of the building, and the faint glow from the streetlamp outside gave her just enough light to see the stairs. She would have loved to turn on the overhead light, but if there was someone downstairs, he could be warned before she got a look at him. And she badly wanted to know who was behind the threats.

As she stole down the stairs, holding the walking stick aloft, it occurred to her that she should probably call the cops. Then again, if all this was her overactive imagination, she would be drawing the attention of the very people she was trying to avoid, all for nothing.

No, first she needed to make sure there was actually a crime going on before she reported one.

She'd reached the door to the kitchen. The rattling sounded more like a vibration now. She frowned. If it was someone breaking in, he was making a lot of noise. Very carefully, she inched open the door and peered through the crack.

Seconds later, realization hit her. She threw open the door, switched on the light, and marched over to the sink. Leaning forward, she pressed the tape on the corner of the cardboard tighter to the window. The rattling stopped. Ben hadn't fastened the cardboard down again after checking the hole, and it was vibrating in the force of the wind.

Just to make sure, she opened the drawer and pulled out the tape. After making certain the cardboard was securely attached to the window, she left the kitchen and returned to her bed.

She couldn't believe how close she'd come to calling Hal. Or worse, the cops. As she snuggled back down under the comforter, once again she promised herself that as soon as she had time, she would visit the animal shelter in Newport and pick out a dog. With that in mind, she finally drifted off to sleep.

She spent most of Sunday morning cleaning the apartment and going over her orders for the week. That afternoon she went down to the kitchen and took down a bag of flour from the cabinet. If she wanted to go into Newport tomorrow, the baking would have to be done before then.

After placing sugar, baking powder, almond extract, and raspberry jam on the worktable, she walked over to the fridge to get the eggs and butter. Next to the scones, her Bakewell tarts were a customer favorite. She had to make sure she had enough to satisfy her clients.

Baking always relaxed her, and she tried not to think about the murder case as she worked. Instead she focused on the mixing, whisking, and folding until she had trays of pastries waiting for her appreciative customers.

Then, with a sigh of satisfaction, she turned out the light and went back upstairs to enjoy an evening of TV entertainment.

Gracie laughed the next morning when Vivian recounted her Saturday nighttime adventure. Jenna, however, was more cautious. "Supposing it had been someone breaking in," she said as they took off in her car, heading for Newport. "You could have been killed."

"I guess I knew in the back of my mind it couldn't be an intruder," Vivian said. "There was too much noise."

"You should have called me." Jenna turned onto the coast road, and the car surged forward. "I could have come over."

"Me too," Gracie said, leaning forward to give Vivian's shoulder a light shove. "We told you to call us if you were in trouble."

"I wanted to make sure I was really in trouble first." Vivian sighed. "I think I'm letting all this get to me."

"Someone threatened to kill you," Jenna said, her voice subdued. "That's enough to make anyone edgy."

"I know, but usually when someone really wants to kill you, they don't warn you ahead of time. Like I said, I believe it's just a threat to get us to stop asking questions."

"But someone did kill Dean," Gracie reminded her.

"That could have been an accident."

"Then why is the guy in hiding? You can't be convicted for an accident."

"Unless your actions cause a death." Vivian let her gaze rest on the ocean for a moment, trying to relax her troubled mind. "Until we find the woman who was with Dean that night, we may never know how all this happened."

"We'll find her." The car sped up even more as Jenna's foot leaned on the accelerator. "We have to, or I'll be a murder suspect the rest of my life."

"I can't believe Mighty Messina hasn't found her yet," Gracie said from the back seat. "Surely someone must have seen her with Dean."

Vivian shrugged. "If Dean was running an escort service, he was probably seen with a lot of different women. Unless it was someone who knew him well, it would be hard to tell if he was personally involved with any of them."

"Or if he was personally involved with more than one," Jenna said dryly.

Vivian clutched the door handle as the car sped around a curve. "You might want to slow down a little. I don't think you want any more confrontations with a cop."

"Sorry." Jenna gave her a rueful smile and eased off the gas. "That was Dean's face under my foot." She sighed. "I shouldn't speak ill of the dead. He wasn't all bad, and he didn't deserve to die that way."

"No, he didn't." Vivian relaxed again as the car reached a more comfortable speed. "And whoever killed him deserves to be punished."

They were entering the town of Newport now. As they crossed the Yaquina Bay Bridge, they had a breathtaking view of the harbor. Rows of white crab boats waited for eager fishermen, small yachts dotted the shoreline, and a majestic lighthouse stood watch over the treacherous waters of the Pacific Ocean.

The town nestled between the ocean and the bay, sheltered by the rugged coastal mountains. It's quaint inns, colorful antique stores, and restaurants made Vivian feel as if she'd stepped back in time to an age where the problems of the world were far removed and peace and tranquility prevailed.

Maybe there had never been any such time, she thought as she walked with her two friends to Gracie's recommended Pig 'N Pancake restaurant, but if there had been, it would feel like this morning, with the quiet streets, the sun gleaming on the heaving ocean, and the salty smell of sea air.

The breakfast was as gratifying as Gracie had promised. Vivian ordered the strawberry blintzes and tried not to think about all the fat and sugar she was consuming as she devoured the delicious crepes. She was thankful for the walk through the town afterward, hoping that would reduce some of the calories.

Gracie took them to two clothing stores before they found the most promising one.

The wooden-planking sign that hung above the door bore the name *Belle's Boutique*. The letters were painted in bright pink, with red hearts and pink rosebuds scattered around them. Two mannequins stood poised in the window. One of them wore a skimpy bikini. A black negligee, trimmed in black lace, draped the second one.

Vivian felt a stab of excitement when she saw them. "This could be the place," she said, grabbing Jenna's arm. She could tell by her friend's expression that Jenna was also trying to hold down her hopes.

"It's worth a shot, I guess." Jenna pushed open the door and was immediately greeted with a tinkling melody that Vivian didn't recognize.

The whole place smelled like roses. The sight of the lingerie hanging from the racks raised Vivian's eyebrows. She had to wonder why a woman would bother wearing anything whatsoever if all she had to cover herself with were a couple of strings and mere inches of transparent cloth. Styles had drastically changed since the days when she'd gone shopping for captivating underwear.

Both Jenna and Gracie seemed entranced by the items, however, and she left them to explore while she hurried over to the counter.

A dark-haired, dark-eyed young woman with thick black eyebrows watched her approach, no doubt wondering what an old hag like her was doing in a store like this.

Deciding to come straight to the point, Vivian gave the woman a broad smile. "Hi. I'm sorry to bother you, but I was hoping you could tell me if you recently sold a pink, lace-trimmed negligee?" She remembered just then that the news anchor had described the negligee exactly the same way when announcing the murder.

Fortunately, the saleswoman appeared not to have paid attention to the news. "We sell a lot of negligees," she said, without a flicker of a change in her bored expression. "When was it sold?"

"I don't know." Vivian sighed. It had been a faint hope at best. "I think it must have been recently, but I'm not sure."

The woman must have recognized the sound of defeat in her voice. "Wait. Let me look." She turned to the computer next to her and began tapping away on the keyboard. "We sold three negligees last week. I can't tell what color they were."

"Can you tell me who bought them?"

For the first time, a wary look crept into the woman's eyes. "I don't think—"

"Someone sent me one as a gift," Vivian said quickly, trying not to envision herself wearing one. "They didn't sign the card, and I'd really like to know who it is."

The woman stared at her for a moment, and Vivian could tell her thoughts were echoing her own. No woman her age should be wearing something so frivolous.

In Hot Water

To her relief, the saleswoman looked back at the computer. "The names are Chesterton, Forsyth, and Ramsey. Does that ring a bell?"

Vivian stared at her. "Ramsey? Jenna Ramsey?" She could hear a roaring in her ears as she held her breath, waiting for the woman to answer.

Chapter Twelve

The saleswoman looked up at Vivian, apparently startled by the tension in her voice. "Actually, it says Dean Ramsey."

Shock rippled through Vivian once more. She kept staring at the woman, trying to make sense of the confusion in her mind.

Finally, the saleswoman said, with an edge of impatience, "Well? You know him?"

Vivian swallowed. "Yes, I do."

The woman's mouth twitched. "He must like you."

Before she could answer, Jenna spoke from behind her. "He liked a lot of women."

Vivian turned her head to look at her and saw disbelief in her friend's eyes. Turning back to the saleswoman, she smiled. "Thank you. I appreciate the help."

The woman nodded and looked at Jenna. "Can I help you with something?"

"No, thanks." Jenna swept a glance around the store. "Nice things, just not me."

The woman nodded again, as if agreeing with her.

Before they could leave, they had to drag Gracie away from a rack of sleepwear that left nothing to the imagination.

Once outside in the street, Jenna couldn't contain her disgust. "I don't believe it. The Dean I knew wouldn't have been caught dead in a place like that, much less actually buy something there. Whatever happened to that guy?"

"Maybe it was a business deal," Gracie said. "You know, for the escort service."

Jenna stared at her. "If that were so, he'd be buying it online or sending someone else to buy it. No, this was personal. He was buying it for his girlfriend. He was really into her, to buy her something like that."

"Or he was buying it for himself," Vivian said, feeling compelled to return to her theory.

Jenna shook her head. "I'll never believe that. He wasn't into cross-dressing. I'm as sure of that as I am of my own name."

"Okay, then. I guess we're back to finding the girlfriend."

"I still can't believe he's dead," Jenna said, as they headed back to the car. "He must have really pissed someone off to get himself killed like that."

"That's what makes this so difficult." Vivian stopped to pat a large, shaggy dog tied up outside a bakery. "We don't know the motive. It could be one of so many things."

Jenna was silent for several long seconds before saying, "It wasn't all bad. There were some good times, especially at the beginning."

Straightening, Vivian laid a hand on her arm. "I'm sorry, Jenna. This must be so hard on you, for many reasons."

Jenna flicked her a brief glance. "I just want it to be over with and done."

"I know." Vivian sighed. "Right now, we seem to be running around in circles. The only thing I'm certain of is that someone in that hotel knows something that would help us find the truth. We have to find that person and make them talk." She shook her head. "This isn't as easy or logical as it seems in the books."

Jenna laughed. "Isn't that the point in fiction? To emphasize the good over evil? No matter how fierce the struggle, the hero overcomes all obstacles to win?"

"If only real life were like that." Vivian glanced down the street. "We'd better catch up with Gracie before we lose sight of her."

"Don't worry. I know how to find the parking lot." Jenna started off at a brisk pace, and Vivian hurried to keep up with her.

She waited until they were in the car, heading back to Misty Bay, before bringing up her next suggestion. "I've been wondering how Dean got involved in the escort business. It must have happened since he started working at the hotel."

"And after our divorce," Jenna said. "I'm sure I would have known if he'd been doing it before that."

"So, if he had a partner, whoever that is could be connected to the hotel."

"Maybe he was a guest there," Gracie said.

"If so, he would most likely have been a regular guest for Dean to get to know him well enough to go into partnership with him."

Jenna sent her a quick glance. "You want to find Dean's partner?"

"I'd like to know who it is, yes. But finding Dean's girlfriend is more important right now." Vivian twisted her head to look at her. "There's one person at that hotel who knows everyone who comes in and out of it. Paula Lambert."

"But we already tried that. She wouldn't talk to us," Jenna reminded her.

"She wouldn't talk to *us*." Vivian switched her gaze back to the rear seat. "But she's never met Gracie."

Jenna chuckled. "You're right. She hasn't."

Gracie sat up straight. "You want me to talk to Paula?"

"I thought you might apply for a job at the hotel. Paula would be the one interviewing you, and you'd get a chance to talk to her."

"Awesome!" Gracie leaned forward. "How do I find out about Dean's girlfriend?"

"We'll figure that out later. First, we have to get you an interview." Vivian checked her watch. "We just have time to stop by the hotel and pick up an application. Okay, Jenna?"

"Don't people usually apply for those jobs online?" Jenna switched her gaze briefly to the rearview mirror. "Right, Gracie?"

"Right." Gracie sounded excited. "I can do that."

Vivian sighed. "I really do need to get with it. It's been decades since I applied for a job. Applying online is so much simpler." She glanced out the window. Little white horses were dancing on the waves far out from shore. A thick ridge of dark gray lined the horizon, though the sky above was still sparklingly clear. "There's a storm coming in," she added. "I hope Ben keeps his word and puts my new window in today."

"Are you going to claim it on your insurance?" Gracie asked.

"I am. I'm going to tell them a sea gull flew into it."

"Good idea," Jenna said. "It's probably not a good idea to tell them someone left it as a death threat."

Vivian felt a twinge of uneasiness at her words and quickly smothered it before it could develop into panic. "I'm thinking of getting a dog," she said, and was faintly surprised that she'd said the words out loud.

"You are?" Jenna sent her a swift look of surprise.

"Cool!" Gracie was practically bouncing around on the back seat. "When? What kind of dog? Where are you going to get it?"

"I don't know when or what kind, but I thought I might go to the shelter in Newport."

"We should have gone while we were there." Gracie leaned forward. "Can I come with you when you go? I love dogs."

"Sure you can." Vivian smiled at her. "I don't know when I'll have time to go, though. Those places usually have office hours."

"You can go in the morning, like we did today," Jenna said. "Things are usually quiet in the shop the first couple of hours anyway. Gracie and I can handle things if you're late getting back."

"You bet we can." Gracie sounded disappointed at missing the visit to the shelter. Vivian turned again to smile at her. "I don't know what I'd do without you two. Bless you both."

Gracie's grin reassured her. "The three rookies, remember?"

"How could I possibly forget?"

To Vivian relief, they arrived back at the tearoom to find Ben loading up his truck, having finished installing the window. After giving him a check, Vivian invited him to come in for tea and a scone.

He looked tempted but shook his head, regret written all over his face. "Thank you, but I have more work to do. It was a pleasure doing business with you, Ms. Wainwright."

"You too, Ben. Thank you." She watched him leave, reminding herself to thank Hal for sending him along. Returning to the kitchen, she found Jenna admiring the new window while Gracie sat at the table, munching on a scone as usual.

"I helped myself," she said, when Vivian looked at her. "I'm starving. I hope that's okay."

"Perfectly," Vivian assured her. "But you should be eating something a little more substantial for lunch. I'll make us some sandwiches."

"I'll make them." Jenna walked over to the fridge and opened one of the three doors.

"There's ham and cheese in there," Vivian told her, "and some slices of turkey."

"We should be paying you for these," Jenna said, pulling a plate of ham slices from the shelf. "We're eating into your profits."

Vivian laughed. "What profits? I barely cover my expenses. If it weren't for the products we sell in the shop, I'd be running at a loss."

Jenna turned to look at her. "Then let us pay for what we eat here."

"Nonsense." Vivian hurried to reassure her, cursing herself for her thoughtless comments. "Martin, bless his soul, left me a decent inheritance, and with the sale of our house in Portland, I'm doing fine. So, please, don't worry about a couple of ham sandwiches and a few scones."

Jenna raised her eyebrows. "Then why do you work so hard running this place? Why not just take off and travel? See the world?"

"Because, for one thing, I don't like to travel alone."

"Then take Hal with you," Gracie suggested, her voice muffled by a mouthful of scone.

Vivian sighed. "I wish you two would quit it with the matchmaking. Hal and I are just friends, that's all."

Busy making sandwiches at the counter, Jenna spoke with her back to them. "Are you sure about that?"

"As sure as I can be." Beginning to feel unsettled, Vivian hurried over to her. "Let me help with those." To her relief, Jenna let the matter drop, though her friend's words haunted her for the rest of the afternoon. Thinking back, she realized that for the first time, she had mentioned Martin without feeling the stab of pain that normally hit her when she spoke his name.

The knowledge made her feel guilty. Surely she couldn't be forgetting him already? All those years of marriage, just vanishing into a fog of lost memories? No, she wouldn't let that happen. She'd loved Martin and had been secure in his love for her. The thought of replacing him with someone else was unthinkable. Even if that someone else was kind, and thoughtful, and so easy to get along with, as if she'd known him her entire life.

Much easier than Martin, who had seemed to live in a different world than her. At times it had been difficult to communicate with him. She rarely knew what he was thinking, and had put it down to his reluctance to involve her in the more lurid details of his profession.

Although she'd never doubted his love for her, she had to admit that they'd never had the companionship she had with Hal.

The sudden realization of that fact left her confused and restless, and she was thankful when the last of the customers had left the shop and she could finally close up. Gracie, as usual, tore off to her meeting, while Jenna stayed behind to help clean up the kitchen.

"Are you okay?" she asked, when Vivian sat down at the table and buried her face in her hands. "You've been kind of quiet all afternoon."

"I'm just tired." Vivian dropped her hands and smiled at her. "I didn't sleep well last night."

"Yeah, I know. You were creeping around the house half the night." She walked over to the table and sat down. "I could stay here tonight with you, if that would help."

"What? No!" Vivian gave her an emphatic shake of her head. "I'm perfectly fine. You go on home. It's been a long day for all of us."

"Why don't you come home with me? Misty would love to see another face in the house. I can make dinner, and we can have a nice, relaxing evening. You can stay the night, and we'll come back together in the morning."

"Sounds wonderful." Vivian yawned. "But you'd have to get up at the crack of dawn, and I know how you hate that.

I think I'll just grab something from the fridge and have an early night."

"Okay." Jenna got up again. "But the invitation is always there. Anytime."

"Thanks. You're a good friend." Vivian stood up too and followed Jenna out to the shop door. "Give Misty a hug from me."

"Sure thing." With a wave of her hand, Jenna crossed the street and climbed into her car.

Vivian closed the door and locked it, then took a last look around the tearoom before walking back into the kitchen. Jenna, as usual, had cleaned up nicely, and there was little to do before she could finally go upstairs to her apartment.

She had just settled down in front of the TV with a plate of spaghetti on a tray table in front of her when her cell phone played its tune. Seeing Hal's name on the screen, she almost didn't answer it. She still hadn't sorted out her feelings about their relationship.

After a moment's hesitation, however, she picked up the phone and held it to her ear.

Hal's husky voice answered her. "Hi! How did things go with the window?"

"Fine!" She gripped the phone. This new awareness of him made her tense, and she did her best to relax. "Ben is a very nice man. He did a great job and didn't overcharge me, so I'm happy. Thanks so much for sending him over."

"Sure. Anytime." He paused for a moment. "I have a bottle of wine here that's begging to be shared. I was wondering if you'd like to help me out."

She smiled at that, but the grin quickly vanished as she envisioned herself in his apartment. "Thanks, Hal, but I think I'll pass for tonight. Maybe another time?"

"Sure." He paused again before asking, "Are you okay? You sound a little edgy."

"I'm fine." She managed a shaky laugh. "Just tired. It's been a long day."

"Oh, okay. Then I guess I'll talk to you later."

"Good night, Hal." The second she hung up, she regretted turning down his invitation. He'd sounded deflated, and she hoped she hadn't upset him. The last thing she wanted to do was wreck her friendship with him.

She should have just gone over there. Spending time with Hal always made her feel better. Angry at herself now, she pushed the spaghetti away from her. She had no appetite to eat it. What in heaven's name was the matter with her? She was acting like an immature teenager.

The temptation to just go and surprise him was hard to resist, but common sense got the better of her as she took the food back to the kitchen. She needed time. This wasn't something to rush into and regret later.

She'd been lonely since Martin died. At first the emptiness had overwhelmed her, but she was gradually getting used to being alone. She had to be sure that her developing affection for Hal wasn't just a need to fill that hole in her life. She valued their friendship and would hate to ruin it by pursuing something more, only to find out she'd made a mistake.

She opened the fridge door and studied the contents for a moment before pulling out some cheese and the last of the grapes she'd bought a few days ago. She half closed the door, then pulled it open again and took the opened bottle of wine from the shelf.

It needed using up anyway, she told herself as she carried it back to the TV. Munching on cheese and crackers, she watched the news, and again heard nothing more about Dean's murder. She wasn't really surprised. On a Portland station, Misty Bay wasn't high on the list of newsworthy towns.

She slept better that night and got up feeling refreshed. She was putting lemon curd tarts in the ovens to bake when she heard knocking on the shop door. Hurrying across the tearoom, she wondered if Jenna had woken up early and decided to come in to lend a hand with the baking. When she opened the door, however, she was surprised to see Natalie standing there holding an umbrella over her head.

"I saw your light," Natalie said, shivering as a gust of damp wind ruffled her hair. "I was wondering if Jenna is still a murder suspect."

"Nothing's changed so far." Vivian opened the door wider. "Do you want to come in? I was just going to make myself a cup of tea."

Natalie wrinkled her nose. "Don't you ever drink coffee?"

"Sometimes. I have that, too, if you like."

"I'd like." Natalie folded her umbrella, shook it, and stepped into the tearoom. "It's raining in torrents out there." She hooked the umbrella over the back of a chair. "I woke up early this morning and thought I'd check some inventory before I opened up the store." She swept a glance around the room. "It always looks so elegant in here. I remember when it was the Beach Bums Café. So tacky."

Vivian laughed. "To each his own. I have to admit, I prefer it this way."

Natalie followed her into the kitchen and sat down at the table. "Something smells good."

"Lemon curd tarts. And scones. I just finished baking those. Would you like one with your coffee?"

Natalie sent a look full of longing at the shelves of scones. "Well, I shouldn't. I have to watch my weight."

"I don't think one is going to hurt you." Vivian slid a scone onto a plate, cut it in half, spread cream and strawberry jam on it, and handed it to her. "The coffee will be ready in a minute."

Natalie stared at the scone as if were about to bite her, then broke off a small piece and cautiously nibbled at it. "This is actually quite good!"

"Thank you." Vivian sat down to wait for the coffee to percolate. "So, how's your business doing?"

"Pretty well." Natalie took a larger bite out of the scone. "Oregon folk are big wine drinkers."

"And wine makers. Last night I enjoyed that very good Oregon Pinot you sold me."

Natalie nodded. "That's a nice one. One of my favorites." She took another bite of the scone. "Do you do takeout?"

Vivian laughed. "Not as a rule. I'll give you a couple to take home with you."

"Thanks!" Natalie's face lit up. "I'll bring a bottle of the Pinot for you the next time I stop by."

"Done." Noticing that the coffee had finished percolating, Vivian got up and walked over to the counter.

"I had a scone in the Blue Surf's cafeteria the other day," Natalie said, "and it was awful. Dry and stodgy. And the omelet was ghastly. I actually complained to the manager about it. At their prices, they should at least be serving decent food."

Carrying two steaming mugs of coffee back to the table, Vivian asked lightly, "Did he refund your money?"

Natalie nodded. "Yes, he did. He was quite charming, actually. He said he would speak to the chef about it and gave me a free ticket for the Sunday buffet. Nice man."

"I've met Mr. Lambert," Vivian said, as she poured cream into her coffee. "He seems pleasant enough."

Natalie finished her scone and dabbed at her mouth with the paper napkin Vivian had given her. "A friend of mine is really mad at him right now. She's the manager of the Bellemer restaurant in Newport." She picked up her coffee mug. "Do you know it?"

"Not personally, but I've heard of it. It's a bit expensive, so I've heard."

"Not just a bit." Natalie sipped at her coffee and put down the mug. "Extremely expensive, but worth every penny. The decor is pure class, and the food is superb. It's the kind of place you go to celebrate a special occasion." She nodded at Vivian. "You should go there sometime. You'd absolutely love it."

"I'm sure I would." Vivian wrapped her fingers around her mug. "So, why is your friend mad at Reggie Lambert?"

"Oh, well, apparently he made reservations for Friday night before last, then just didn't turn up. Didn't bother to call and cancel, and she was left with an empty table that she could have filled. They're always booked solid on a Friday night. When you consider that a table often brings in around three or four hundred dollars, that's a big loss. She'll bill him seventy-five for not showing up, but it's the inconsideration that got to her."

Vivian stared at her. "He must be well off to afford that kind of money for dinner. Does he go there often?"

Natalie shook her head. "I don't think so. Sharon didn't remember having met him. She said she won't take reservations from him again, so he's missing out on a good thing."

"He must have intended to celebrate something. I wonder why he didn't go. Did your friend say how many people were booked for the table?"

"Just two, if I remember." Natalie frowned. "You seem awfully interested in him. Am I missing something?"

Vivian uttered a weak laugh. "No, I'm just wondering why someone would make reservations at a place like that and then just not turn up. I mean, it's not like you'd just forget . . ."

She broke off as her mind prodded her with a memory. She closed her eyes for a moment, envisioning Reggie Lambert in the lobby of the Blue Surf. She'd asked him what he knew about the murder. Not much, he'd told her. She could hear his voice in her mind as clearly as if he were there in her kitchen. *I was on my way back from LA when it happened.*

But the murder had happened on Saturday morning. Why would Reggie Lambert make reservations at an expensive hotel for Friday night if he knew he would be out of town until Saturday?

If she knew the answer to that, she told herself, she might be closer to finding out exactly what went on in that hotel room the morning Dean Ramsey was killed.

Natalie left soon after that, and Vivian went back to her baking. She was carving thin slices of ham for the sandwiches when Gracie arrived at the shop, obviously bursting with news.

She bounced into the tearoom when Vivian opened the door to her, words gushing from her mouth. "I applied for a job at the Blue Surf last night, and they answered me this morning. I have an interview this afternoon at three. Is that okay? I know that's our busy time, but I thought it was important. We need to sit down and, like, work out what I'm going to ask Paula Lambert, because I haven't the slightest idea and I don't want to mess this up, so—"

"Whoa, slow down!" Vivian held up her hands as if warding off an angry bee. "Let's go into the kitchen and talk about this."

"Okay. Can I have a scone?" She skipped over to the door, while Vivian followed more slowly, deciding that it was Gracie's energy that kept the pounds off her slim figure, in spite of the scones.

They had barely sat down before Jenna knocked on the door. She greeted Vivian with a smile that quickly faded as she stepped inside.

Vivian studied her friend's face before closing the door. "Is something wrong?"

"Reporter," Jenna said, dragging her raincoat off her shoulders. "Waiting in the rain outside my house when I left this morning."

"Rita Mozell again?" Vivian led the way back to the kitchen.

"No, it was some guy. Said he was a reporter for the local newspaper. I told him no comment, but he followed me to my car, saying he wanted to tell my side of the story. I told him I didn't kill my ex-husband and that's my side of the story. Then he asked me if I was going to the funeral. Apparently, Dean's family is in town and they want to bury him here."

"Oh my."

Vivian walked into the kitchen, followed by Jenna, who was immediately greeted by Gracie waving a scone at her.

"I got an interview today at the Blue Surf," she announced to Jenna, "and I haven't a clue what I'm going to say."

"We were just going to work out something," Vivian said, as Jenna sat down at the table.

"Is that coffee I can smell?" Jenna sniffed the air. "Don't tell me you've given up your morning tea."

"Natalie stopped by earlier, and she doesn't drink tea." Vivian walked over to the coffeepot. "There's still some left, or I can make you some fresh coffee, if you'd like."

"I'll have whatever everyone else is having."

"Then tea it is." Vivian filled the kettle with water and set it on the stove. "So, what did you tell this reporter?"

Gracie stared at Jenna. "What reporter? Is that gussied-up moron still following you around?"

"No, this is a different reporter, from the local newspaper."

"Have you met Dean's family?" Vivian sat down at the table.

"No, and I don't want to. I didn't think he had any contact with them. I know his father is dead; he actually died in prison." She uttered a cynical laugh. "It's one of the few things we had in common."

Gracie's eyes filled with tears as she stared at Jenna. "I'm so sorry, Jenna. That must have been awful."

Afraid that Gracie was about to let on that she knew about Jenna's past, Vivian said loudly, "I didn't know that Dean's father was in prison. That must have been hard on Dean."

"It was. He never talked about it to anyone. In fact, we'd been married almost a year when he finally told me. He'd had a few drinks that night and I mentioned my father, and that's when it came out. He made me swear I wouldn't tell anyone, but I guess it doesn't matter now that he's dead as well."

Vivian broke the awkward silence that followed. "So, you won't be going to the funeral, then."

Jenna shrugged. "I didn't know there was going to be a funeral, or when and where it's being held. I don't think I'm going to the trouble of finding out either. After the way we parted, I doubt Dean would want me there. Anyway, his new girlfriend will probably be there." She uttered a soft gasp. "Maybe if we went there, we'd find her."

Vivian got up again as the teakettle whistled. "I doubt it. She hasn't shown up so far, or we would have heard about her. If she's in hiding, she's not going to risk going to a funeral."

Jenna sighed. "I think you're right. I'm going to be a murder suspect for life."

"Oh, that reminds me," Gracie said. "I checked up on Philip Stedman last night. He couldn't be Dean's killer. He was in Portland weekend before last for his son's wedding."

Vivian swung around to look at her. "All weekend?"

Gracie nodded, her mouth full of scone. "Left here Friday, got back here Monday."

"Well, then, I guess that takes him off the list." Vivian swished a trickle of boiling water inside the teapot to warm it. "Actually, I found out something interesting this morning." She popped three tea bags into the pot and poured the rest of the boiling water on top of them. "Natalie told me that Reggie Lambert made reservations at the Bellemer restaurant for Friday night but never turned up."

She added milk to the mugs, then turned to find both women looking confused.

"He's all right, isn't he?" Gracie asked. "I mean, he's not dead?"

Vivian laughed. "Of course not. We saw him Sunday morning, remember?"

"And the other night when we came out of the hotel bar," Jenna reminded her.

"That's right," Vivian said, feeling a flash of enlightenment. "I'd forgotten that."

Jenna stared at her. "Are you trying to tell us something?"

Vivian turned back to the counter, stirred the tea in the teapot, and filled the mugs. "Reggie Lambert told me he was on his way back from LA when the murder happened." She picked up two of the mugs and carried them over to the table. "I may have read too many mystery novels, but I got to thinking. Why would Reggie make reservations at a very expensive restaurant if he knew he wasn't going to be in town?"

Gracie took a mug from her. "Thank you." She put the tea down in front of her. "Maybe he forgot."

"That lack of memory is going to cost him seventy-five dollars. He didn't come across as someone who would be that careless with his money."

"Maybe he planned on coming home Friday but then got delayed," Jenna said, taking the mug from her with a nod of thanks.

"Then wouldn't he have called his wife to cancel the reservations?"

Jenna paused in the act of bringing the mug to her lips. "Maybe."

Vivian walked over to the counter, picked up her mug of tea and returned to the table. "There's just something about it that seems odd to me. What if Reggie actually did come home on Friday, planning to go the restaurant, but then something happened to prevent him from going there?"

Jenna frowned. "Like what?"

"I don't know. But if so, it had to be something that he didn't want anyone to know about. Which is why he had to lie about coming back from LA after the murder. A bit of a coincidence, wouldn't you say?"

Gracie gasped. "You think he killed Dean?"

Vivian shrugged. "No, I don't. But I think it's possible he knows more about it than he's telling anyone."

Jenna shook her head. "And maybe the man is a complete moron who simply forgot he made reservations for dinner. He could have made them months ago."

"He could have," Vivian said. "There's one way to find out when he actually arrived back in town, but I doubt very much that the airlines will give us that information."

"They'd have to give it to the cops, though, right?"

"Right." Vivian looked at her. "You want to tell Detective Messina about this? I could easily be wrong, like you said."

Jenna thought about it. "No. There's no real proof of anything, and it will fire up Messina if he finds out we're interfering in his investigation. We've come this far; let's go with it until we're sure."

"Which is why we really need to talk to his wife. Maybe we can find out from her if Reggie was lying." She looked at Gracie. "Okay, kiddo. I guess now it's all up to you."

Chapter Thirteen

"Oh, crap." Gracie stared at what was left of her scone. "I was afraid you were going to say that."

Vivian laid a hand on her arm. "Don't worry, sweetie. We'll rehearse what you need to ask, and you'll be fine. I doubt very much if Paula Lambert knows anything about any of this, but she could let slip something useful."

Gracie seemed unconvinced and didn't appear to feel any better as Vivian suggested some leading questions to ask.

"Mention that you'd heard about the murder," Vivian said, getting up to put another scone in front of Gracie. "Act like you're nervous about working in a place where someone has been killed."

"Won't that hurt my chances of getting the job?" Gracie picked up the scone and took a bite.

Jenna heaved a sigh. "You're not actually applying for the job, dummy. You're just there to get some information."

"Oh, right." Gracie frowned. "I had to put on the application where I'd worked before. I just said a small restaurant and retail. I didn't put down any names. What will I say if Paula asks me for names?"

Vivian thought about it. "Tell her where you worked before you came to me. At McDonald's."

"Okay, so then what?"

"I imagine Paula will try to convince you that you'll be safe working there," Vivian said, sitting down again. "They must be looking for workers if they answered your application so quickly. Then you can mention that you met Dean a couple of times. Tell her that he seemed like a nice man."

Gracie pulled a face. "Well, half of that is true."

"Just don't tell her you know Jenna. Tell her that the last time you saw Dean was at the Bellemer restaurant in Newport. Ask her if she's been there and see what she says."

"I know where it is," Gracie said, "but I've never been inside. It cost a fortune to eat there."

"It doesn't matter. Just tell her that you saw Dean in there with the woman he was always hanging out with, mention that you met her once, then act like you're trying to remember her name. There's a chance Paula will supply the name for you."

"Wow." Gracie looked at her in awe. "That's clever."

Vivian shrugged. "Thanks, but it's not my idea. It's been used a thousand times in mystery novels."

"Well, then," Jenna said, as she picked up her mug. "Let's hope Paula Lambert doesn't read mysteries."

Vivian drained her mug and stood up. "This might not help us at all, but it's worth a shot. Now, ladies, we have to get moving if we're going to serve our customers."

"It's raining really hard out there," Jenna said as she got up. "We probably won't be all that busy today."

"We have three reservations for tea." Vivian walked over to the counter and stood her mug in the sink. "Hopefully we'll get some walk-ins."

Gracie jumped up from the table. "I have to stock my shelves before I go to my interview." She took off for the storeroom, leaving Jenna gazing after her.

"Do you think she'll be okay with this?"

Jenna sounded worried, and Vivian hurried to reassure her. "She'll be fine. All she's doing is asking a couple of questions. She's only going to talk to Paula."

"Maybe, but Dean's killer could be someone in that hotel." Jenna hunched her shoulders. "I just wish I could go with her."

"You wouldn't be able to go into the interview with her." Vivian opened the dishwasher and stacked the empty mugs inside. "If you're that worried, you could go with her and wait in the lobby for her."

"No." Jenna took a clean apron from the closet and tied it around her waist. "You need me here, and you're right. She's a big girl. She can take care of herself."

Vivian smiled. "Keep convincing yourself of that or you'll have gray hairs by this evening."

"I've already got gray hairs." She peered at Vivian. "How come you don't?"

"Lucky, I guess. I do have them. Just not that many."

"Well, if I get too many more, I'll be buying bottles of hair dye."

Laughing, Vivian walked over to the fridge and pulled it open. "You have a way to go before you need that." She tried to imagine herself with gray hair and didn't like the vision it presented. Hal had white hair, though, and it looked good on him. But then, everything looked good on him.

Startled by the thought, she snatched a bowl of hard-boiled eggs from the shelf and slammed the fridge door shut. One of the eggs slid off the pile and landed with a smack on the floor. Bending over to pick it up, Vivian uttered a word she rarely used. "*Shit.*"

Luckily, Jenna was already out in the tearoom, setting up the tables, and wasn't there to comment on her boss's odd behavior.

Muttering to herself about her juvenile reaction, Vivian carried the smashed egg over to the trash bin. She had to stop thinking about Hal this way, she told herself. It was going to ruin everything.

She had managed to put her concerns about him out of her mind by the time Gracie left for her interview. She had something else to worry about by then. Jenna's words kept coming back to haunt her. Had she really sent Gracie into danger? If something happened to that girl, she wouldn't be able to live with herself.

She tried to concentrate on the egg-and-tomato sandwiches she was making, but it was hard. She kept imagining Gracie in the clutches of a devious monster, or being chased down by an unknown assailant bent on silencing her.

She was tempted to call Gracie and make sure she was okay, but the girl was probably in the middle of the interview and wouldn't answer her phone.

Annoyed with herself for letting her anxieties get the better of her, Vivian slapped the sandwiches on the plate and began spreading fish paste on slices of white bread. She was laying sprigs of mustard and cress on the paste when she heard a voice from the doorway.

"Hi! I'm back!"

Vivian's chin shot up, and she stared at Gracie. "Already?" Relief had made her voice shrill, and she cleared her throat. "That was quick."

"Yeah, it was a short interview." Gracie slid out of her jacket and hung it in the closet. "I didn't see anyone looking in the shelves. Have we been busy?"

"Nothing Jenna and I couldn't handle." Vivian walked over to the sink and washed her hands. "How did the interview go?"

"Okay, but I didn't find out anything. I tried, but Paula kind of cut me off. Sorry."

Vivian sighed. Another dead end. "It's okay. Get out there and give Jenna a hand. You can tell us about it later."

"Okay." Gracie grabbed an apron from the closet. "I saw Warren Lester when I was going into the hotel. He was acting kind of weird."

In the act of taking down a cake stand from the shelf, Vivian swiveled her head to look at Gracie. "Weird? What do you mean?"

"Well, he was coming out of the elevator. I think he saw me, but he turned around and, like, went back into the elevator, like he was trying to avoid me."

Vivian frowned. "That's odd." She carried the cake stand over to the table. "I wonder what he was doing in the hotel."

"I saw Reggie Lambert, too, just as I was leaving." Gracie shook out the apron and took hold of the strings. "I pretended like I didn't see him, but I could feel him staring at me as I went out the door."

"He was probably wondering why you were there."

"Yeah. If Paula tells him I was, like, interviewing for a job, he's going to think I'm not happy working here." She grinned at Vivian. "He'd be so wrong." She left, tying the apron strings as she went.

Smiling, Vivian took down a three-tiered cake stand from the shelf and arranged sandwiches around the bottom layer, then carefully placed Eccles cakes, lemon curd tarts, maids of honor tarts, and shortbread on the next layer of the cake stand.

She had just started laying scones on the top level when Jenna hurried into the kitchen. "We've just had four walk-ins."

Vivian looked up at her. "Are they all together?"

"Yes. I put them at table six."

"Okay, I'll get another stand ready. Can you put the kettles on for more tea?"

"Sure." Jenna headed for the sink. "I guess Gracie made it back okay."

"Yes, thank goodness."

"Did she say how it went?"

"Not much. She said she didn't learn anything new."

"Oh." Jenna paused, then added, "Well, at least we tried."

Vivian walked over to the fridge and opened the door. "And we're going to go on trying."

"How? No one wants to talk about it, and we're getting nowhere."

"We've learned a lot in the past few days." Vivian pulled out the fish paste and the bowl of eggs. Nudging the fridge door closed with her hip, she added, "We just have to ask the right people the right questions."

"We're running out of people. Unless you feel like tackling the police chief," Jenna said, as she hefted two kettles onto the stove.

Vera groaned. "I don't think that would be very productive."

"It could get us thrown in jail." Jenna reached for another kettle and ran cold water into it. "The point is, if Dean was blackmailing someone who eventually killed him, it could be any one of a number of people. Florrie just gave us the names she knew. There has to be a lot more men who don't want people to know they're using an escort service."

"Not many people can afford one." Vivian started spreading the fish paste. "Anyway, I'm beginning to lose faith in the blackmail theory. I think this all has something to do with Dean's girlfriend. Which is why we really need to find her. It's too bad Gracie couldn't get her name, but we'll keep looking."

"Maybe Messina has found her by now," Jenna said, as she came back to the table.

"I think we would know if he had. It seems the local reporters are still on the story, even if the city ones have lost interest."

Jenna picked up the filled cake stand. "I don't think anyone is ever going to find her. I'll take this to table six." She left, leaving Vivian shaking her head.

She could understand how Jenna felt. It had to be miserable to be under suspicion for a crime, knowing you were innocent and helpless to prove it. This was turning out to be a lot tougher than she'd imagined.

She was still struggling with the question of what to do next when the last customer left and she could turn the sign to CLOSED. Gracie was already in the kitchen, studying the shelves to see what was left to eat.

Vivian waited until Jenna was finished cleaning up the tables before asking, "Tell us about the interview, Gracie. Try and remember everything Paula said."

Gracie pointed to an Eccles cake. "Can I have that?"

"Sure." Vivian sat down at the table and waited for both women to join her.

"You're not going to make tea?' Jenna asked, as she sat down.

"I'm all teaed out today. I'm going to enjoy a glass of wine when I go upstairs." Vivian looked at her. "I'll make tea for you, if you like?"

"No, thanks. I'm going home to a beer."

Gracie plopped down on the chair. "So, what do you want to know?"

"Everything." Vivian focused on Gracie's face. "Start at the beginning—what you said, what she said, everything."

Gracie sighed. "I should have recorded it. I don't know if I can remember everything word for word."

Vivian stared at her. "You had a tape recorder with you?"

"No, I meant on my phone."

"I didn't know you could record on your phone."

Gracie pulled her phone from her pocket, swiped it, and held it out for Vivian to see. "You have to download the app, but after that it works just like a camera. You hit the red button and there you go."

Vivian shook her head. "Technology today never fails to amaze me. Anyway, just do the best you can with what Paula said. Shut your eyes and imagine yourself back there."

Gracie shut her eyes, then opened them again. "That just blanks me out."

"Okay, what was the first thing Paula said to you?"

"She told me to sit down."

Vivian sighed. "Then what?"

Gracie frowned in concentration. "She looked at the computer and goes, 'How long did you work at McDonald's?' and I go, 'Two years.' " She frowned. "That was stretching it a bit. I hope she doesn't check it out."

"It won't matter." Jenna smothered a yawn, then added, "It's not like you're trying to get hired."

"Oh, yeah." Gracie's face relaxed. "I keep forgetting that."

"So, what did she say next?" Hearing the impatience in her own voice, Vivian made an effort to curb it. "Did you ask about the murder?"

Gracie took a bite of the Eccles cake, chewed it, then swallowed. "I did. I told her I'd heard about the murder, and I asked her if the killer had been caught. I was a bit edgy about being interviewed anyway, and I think she thought I was scared about the murder. She goes, 'The police are all over it, and you'll be perfectly safe in the hotel.' Or something like that."

Vivian nodded. "Good. Go on."

"Well, then I go, 'I met Dean a few times, and he seemed like a nice man.'" Gracie stared at the cake in her hand. "I don't know why I said that."

"Nor do I," Jenna muttered.

Ignoring her, Vivian leaned forward. "So, what did Paula say to that?"

"She said he was a very nice man, considering the life he'd had, what with a father in prison and all, and a mother who deserted him."

Jenna made an odd sound, and Vivian looked at her. Jenna was staring at Gracie as if she'd turned into a toad.

"What?" Jenna's voice had risen at least an octave.

Worried now, Vivian leaned toward her. "What's the matter?"

Jenna looked at her with eyes brimming with disbelief. "Dean would never have told her all that unless . . ."

Her voice trailed off, and Vivian studied her face, until realization dawned. "Unless he was really close to her."

"Right." Jenna let out her breath. "Dean's girlfriend could be Paula Lambert."

"Oh," Gracie said. "Well, that makes sense now."

They both looked at her.

She stared back at them for a moment, then added, "Well, I told her the last time I'd seen Dean was at the Bellemer and that he was with a woman. I said I recognized her but couldn't remember her name. I did like you told me and pretended I was trying to think of it. But Paula got all upset, told me she'd be in touch, and pretty much threw me out of the office. I thought she was just getting emotional about having a murder take place in her hotel, but I guess she was bummed because she thought Dean was with another woman."

"We have to tell Messina," Jenna said, her face lighting up with excitement. "This could help clear me."

Hating to destroy the hope in her friend's face, Vivian shook her head. "We have no proof, and Paula will simply deny it. If they did have a relationship, they managed to keep it very quiet."

"Except for the woman in Natalie's hair salon," Jenna reminded her.

"And whoever told her about it." Vivian thought for a moment. "Maybe we should talk to Florrie again. Ask her if she knows Paula."

"If she's working out of the hotel, she would have to know her," Jenna said. "I think if she'd known about the affair, she would have told us."

"Of course." Vivian sighed. "We seem to take one step forward and two steps back."

Jenna stood up. "Well, I'm going home. I need to think through everything."

"Me too." Gracie jumped up.

"We don't know for sure that Paula was Dean's girlfriend," Vivian said, getting up from her chair. "We could be wrong about this."

"We're not wrong." Jenna walked over to the closet, opened it, and pulled out her raincoat. "Like I told you, I was married to Dean for almost a year before he told me about his dad. And I never knew that about his mother. He and Paula must have been real close for him to tell her all that." She headed for the door. "See you tomorrow."

Seconds later the shop door pinged, and Gracie said quietly, "Poor Jenna. I feel so bad for her."

"She'll be okay. She's a strong lady." Vivian smiled at her, hoping to take away that look of misery on the young woman's face. "Do you have a meeting tonight?"

"No, I'm done with the meetings."

Watching Gracie haul on her jacket, Vivian fought between the urge to ask her what the meetings were for and the knowledge that she'd be prying. "I hope everything's okay with you," she said at last.

Gracie's smile flashed across her face. "Everything's fine." She hesitated a moment, then said, "I promise, you'll know all about it soon."

Vivian had to be content with that, though it wasn't until she was halfway through her glass of wine that evening that she could stop worrying about her assistants and tracking down a killer and just enjoy watching TV.

She was engrossed in a mystery movie when her cell phone buzzed. The temptation to ignore it was strong, but then she thought it might be Jenna or Gracie calling, so she picked it up.

At the sight of Hal's name, she froze. She wanted to talk to him, and she didn't. In the end, common sense won. He'd probably worry if she didn't answer and come pounding on her door. She'd rather talk to him on the phone than face-to-face.

Carefully, she put the phone to her ear. "Hi, Hal."

"Hi yourself. How are things going?"

For some reason, lately the sound of his gravelly voice made her skin tingle. She did her best to ignore the sensation and carefully controlled her tone. "Things are going fine. How about you?"

"I'm okay." He paused, then added, "Actually, I was worried about you. You sounded a bit off last night." Again, the pause. The next words came in a rush. "Look, if I've done or said something to upset you, I'd really like to know."

Guilt flooded Vivian like a cold shower. Softening her voice, she said quickly, "Of course you haven't upset me. I'm sorry, Hal. It's just this thing with Jenna and Dean's murder. It's getting complicated, and I guess I'm getting a little stressed out."

His voice rose in concern. "You're not in danger or anything, are you?"

Remembering the broken window and the words scrawled on it, Vivian briefly closed her eyes. "No, no. It's not that. It's just . . . we're uncovering a few surprises, that's all."

"I can come over, if you want to talk about it."

For several seconds she struggled with indecision, but in the end the desire to see him was too strong to resist. "I'd love that. I've just opened a bottle of wine."

"I'll be there before you can get to the door."

Smiling, she put the phone down on the table. It was time, she told herself, to stop worrying about their relationship and just enjoy it. From now on, she intended to do just that.

Chapter Fourteen

Vivian was still smiling when she went down to unlock the door.

The sight of Hal, standing in the rain with drops of water sliding down his glasses, warmed her all over. She reached out and grasped his arm. "Come on in. You're getting soaked."

"I'm going to drip all over your floor." He stepped inside and shook his head, sending a spray of water flying from his hair. "It's pouring out there."

"I know." She frowned at him. "Why didn't you bring an umbrella?"

"This is Oregon. No one carries an umbrella."

Her frown turned into a grin. "That's what Jenna's always saying. But you could have driven."

"I need the exercise."

Personally, she thought he looked just fine, but she wisely refrained from telling him so. "Leave your jacket down here to dry," she said. "The wine is waiting."

"That's the best invitation I've had all week." He reached inside his jacket and pulled out a package. "But first, I want to give you this."

She stared at the package as if it would bite her. "What is it?"

He laughed. "It's not going to explode. It's just a small gift."

"For me?" She took it from him. "It's not my birthday or anything."

"You don't have to have a birthday to get a gift. Open it."

She unwrapped the package carefully, half afraid of what she might find. Inside the blue-and-white-striped paper was a long box. She stared at the picture on it, then realized she was looking at an electric wine opener. "Oh my goodness! This is great! Thanks so much! I was thinking of buying myself one after seeing yours, but somehow it seemed extravagant. I just love this!" She held the box out for him to see. "Look! It even has a foil cutter. I usually cut mine with a knife."

Hal rolled his eyes. "How archaic."

She gave him a light punch on the arm. "Thank you, Hal. I shall think of you every time I open a bottle now."

Hal pretended to frown. "I'm not sure that's how I want to be remembered, but thanks."

She laughed. "Let's go get that wine."

Intensely aware of him as he followed her up the stairs, she didn't realize she was holding her breath until she let it out at her door. She was trying to remember the last time she'd tidied up the place as she led him into the living room.

Hal headed straight for the couch and sank down on it. "It's been a long day."

"Me too." She glanced at the clock. "Have you eaten?"

"About two hours ago."

"I have cheese and crackers, or some lemon curd tarts if you're in the mood for something sweet."

He gave her a long look. "I'm always in the mood for something sweet."

She could feel her cheeks warming and quickly turned her back on him. "Good. I'll get them."

Hurrying into the kitchen, she cursed herself again for her immature response to him. It was a perfectly innocent remark, and she was reading all kinds of hidden meanings into it. After carefully placing the lemon tarts on a plate, she grabbed a wineglass from the cabinet and carried both back into the living room.

"Those look absolutely delicious," Hal said as he reached for a tart. After taking one bite, he nodded his head. "It tastes even better than it looks. You're a first-class pastry chef."

She flushed at the compliment. "Well, thank you, sir. That's the nicest thing anyone has ever said to me."

The twinkle in his eyes unsettled her even more. "I'll get the wine," she said, and fled back to the kitchen. It took her a moment to compose herself before she carried the bottle back into the living room, where she poured wine for Hal, then refilled her own glass.

"Now," Hal said, as he settled back on the couch. "Come and sit down and tell me what's been going on with you guys."

Thankful that things were getting back to a more comfortable level, she sat down next to him on the couch and reached for her glass. "How well do you know Reggie Lambert?"

Hal stared at her. "Reggie? Like I said, I've met him a few times at the golf club. Can't say I know him all that well. Why?"

"What about his wife, Paula?"

"I've seen her once or twice." He frowned. "What's going on?"

"Would you say they had a good marriage?"

"I don't know. They seem okay together, but I wouldn't say they were all over each other."

Vivian nodded. "We think Paula was having an affair."

Hal's eyebrows shot up. "What? With who?"

"We think it might have been Dean Ramsey."

"That's crazy. I can't imagine a woman like Paula Lambert falling for a deadbeat guy like Dean."

"Well, we can't be sure, of course. This is all guesswork up to now." She took another sip of her wine. "We did find out that Dean bought the negligee he was wearing."

Choking on a gulp of wine, Hal took a moment to get his breath. "Are you telling me Dean's a cross-dresser?"

"No, we don't think so." Vivian put down her glass. "We think he bought it for his girlfriend."

"Ah. I remember now. I think I heard on the local news that the cops believe he grabbed it to cover himself when the killer came at him."

"Right."

Hal frowned at her. "And you think Paula killed Dean?"

Vivian shrugged. "She's obviously a very jealous woman. When Gracie told her she'd seen Dean with another woman, she practically threw her out of the interview."

"Wait a minute. Gracie wants to work at the hotel?"

Vivian smiled. "No, of course not. I just sent Gracie there to ask questions. Paula wouldn't talk to Jenna and me."

Hal rubbed his forehead with his fingers. "You know you're playing a dangerous game. I'm worried about you guys. I wish you'd just let the cops take care of it."

"And where is that getting us?"

He sighed. "I have to admit, they're taking their time. But they have to be careful. If they want to bring a killer to justice, they have to cover all bases before bringing charges. Some of these defense lawyers are pretty clever at finding loopholes."

"I know. I was married to a prosecuting attorney, remember?"

"I do." Hal looked serious. "I know you're all anxious to clear Jenna's name, but you need to be on your guard."

"I know." Vivian smiled at him. "Thanks for caring. Don't worry. I'm sure we'll be fine."

Hal stared down at his hands. "I wasn't going to bring this up, but the more I think about it, the more I believe it's the right decision."

Vivian grabbed her glass and swallowed a full mouthful. Her stomach muscles clenched as she waited for his next words. What was he about to say? Was he going to get personal? Was he, heaven forbid, going to propose, or something ridiculous like that? How was she going to answer him? What was she going to do?

"A friend of mine told me his son is moving to France," Hal said, lifting his head. His expression changed when he saw Vivian's face. "Is something wrong?"

Realizing her mouth was hanging open, Vivian quickly shut it. "No," she said weakly, her mind now grappling with what she'd just heard. "You're thinking of moving to France?"

Hal drew back in surprise. "What? No! I said the son of a friend of mine is moving there."

"Oh. I thought . . ." She broke off, feeling foolish. "I don't get why you're telling me that."

"Oh." Hal's face registered understanding. "The point is, the son has a dog that he can't take with him. His parents have two cats and don't think the dog will fit in, so they're looking for a home for him. I'm wondering if you'd like to adopt him. He's a cute dog, very well trained, and will be some form of protection. At the very least, he'll keep you company."

It took Vivian another few seconds to absorb what he'd said. She was still mulling it over in her mind when Hal spoke again.

"Look, it's just a suggestion. You don't have to make up your mind right now. Only they're thinking of taking the dog to a shelter, so—"

"No!"

Hal shut his mouth, his expression wary. "No, you don't want the dog?"

"No, I don't want him to go to a shelter." Vivian let out a sigh. "What kind of dog is he?"

"He's a borgle."

"A what?"

"A borgle. It's a cross between a beagle and a border collie."

"Oh." She tried to picture that and failed.

"Look," Hal said, "why don't I give Ted a call and ask him if we can go over to Barry's place and meet Felix."

"Who?"

"Barry. He's the son. Felix is the dog."

"Oh." She thought about it some more. "I'd have to leave him alone in the apartment while the tearoom is open."

"That's only six hours. Barry works all day, so Felix is used to being on his own." He picked up his wine. "I could stop by now and then and take him for a walk, if you like."

She met his gaze and smiled. "Well, I was thinking of getting a dog. Yes, I'd like to meet Felix. If we get along, then I'll be happy to bring him home."

"Good." Hal dug into his pocket for his phone, swiped the screen, and thumbed in a number. Seconds later he gave Vivian a quick nod as he quickly explained to the person who answered why he was calling.

A minute or two later he said good-bye and tucked the phone back into his pocket. "Ted's going to talk to Barry and get back to me. I'll let you know when we can go over there."

"Okay." She was beginning to feel a little nervous about it. "I hope I'm doing the right thing. We had dogs when the kids were growing up, but after the girls left home and our last dog died, I never got another one. It was too hard saying good-bye to them."

Hal nodded. "I know what you mean. But years of companionship are worth a few months of heartbreak, right?"

She smiled. "Right. I'm looking forward to meeting Felix."

"Good." He settled back on the couch. "You don't mention your kids very often. One of them is in Seattle, right?"

"Yes." Vivian cradled her glass in her hands. "Rachel's in Seattle. Her husband, Kris, is an architect and doing very well."

"They have kids?"

"Two. Jason, who's thirteen, and Madison. She's eleven. Carrie, my other daughter, lives in LA. She's an actress."

Hal raised his eyebrows. "You never told me that. Well known?"

Vivian shook her head. "Mostly commercials and a couple of movies no one has ever heard of, but she seems happy enough."

"Is she married?"

"Was. To Ken Kiyama. Fortunately, they never had kids. I think Carrie felt they would have interfered in her career."

Hal frowned. "Ken Kiyama. Why does that sound familiar?"

"He's a Californian state representative."

"Ah, yes. So, your daughter is divorced?"

"Happily divorced, as she puts it."

Hal grinned. "Good for her."

"You'd like her. She's enterprising, industrious, and has boundless energy, like her father." Vivian sipped her wine. "Not at all like me."

Hal looked at her over the rim of his glass. "Don't sell yourself short. I know what it takes to build a business. You're more like your husband than you think."

"Not really. I'm far more emotional that he was. He was always in control, whereas I tend to let my heart rule my head. Martin would never do that."

"That's not a bad thing."

"No?" She sighed. "It's landed me into trouble more than once."

"Well, personally, I prefer people who aren't afraid to display their feelings."

He was putting down his glass as he spoke, and she studied him for a moment. One of the things she liked most about

250

him was that he didn't hide his emotions. So different from Martin. In fact, now that she thought about it, she knew more about the opinions and ideals of the man seated next to her than she'd known about her late husband in all the years she'd been married to him.

Once more, the revelation shocked her, and she hastily drained her glass.

"So," Hal said, "getting back to Dean's murder, what are you planning to do about it?"

"I don't know." Vivian stared at her empty glass. "What if Paula really was Dean's girlfriend and was with him that night? She could either have killed Dean or know who did."

"Or she may have left the room before the killer arrived."

"I thought of that too." Vivian sighed. "I can understand why she wouldn't want to tell anyone she was there. I think the only way to get her to talk is to accuse her outright and see what she says."

"And that could get you killed."

"I guess it depends where we are when I ask her."

Hal shook his head. "I don't like it. If she's the killer and you confront her, she doesn't necessarily have to act right away. She could wait until you're vulnerable and then get rid of you. You really need to talk to Detective Messina about this."

A vision of scrawled words on a broken window popped into Vivian's mind. "Maybe I should just hold off on everything until I bring Felix home."

"I think that's a very good idea. Meanwhile, think about talking to the police. Please." Hal glanced at the clock. "I'd better get going. I know you get up at the crack of dawn. I don't want you losing your beauty sleep because of me."

She laughed. "I think it's a little late in my life to worry about that."

He gave her one of his long looks that never failed to unsettle her. "Well, you must be doing something right. You always look good to me."

She laughed again to cover her confusion. "And you always know how to make a lady feel good."

He grinned at that. "It's one of my better qualities." He stood up, stretched, and headed for the door.

She had to agree with him, she thought, as she got up from the couch. She'd watched him interact with his customers, and the women always left the store with a smile on their faces. Charming. That was a good word for Hal Douglass.

She was still smiling at the thought as she unlocked the shop door and opened it. "It looks like it's stopped raining."

Dragging on his jacket, Hal grunted. "Good. All that moisture really messes up my hair."

That made her laugh. "I didn't know you were so obsessed with how your hair looks."

"Obsessed?" He walked to the door and stepped outside. "The only thing I'm obsessed about is a good night's sleep. Hope you have one."

"You too." She smiled at him. "Thank you for the wine opener. I really do love it."

"Then I'm happy. Thank you for the wine, the snacks, and the company."

"I enjoyed it."

"Me too." He gazed at her, looking as if he wanted to say something else, then raised his hand in a mock salute and vanished into the night.

She locked the door again and leaned against it for a moment. For the first time in quite a while, she felt alone again.

That loneliness had been almost unbearable after Martin's death, but once she had thrown herself into the turmoil of leasing the shop, renovating it into a tearoom, and building her customer base, she hadn't had much time to feel lonely.

Now, for some reason, she was once more keenly aware of the emptiness and the silence around her.

It would be good to have a dog for company, she told herself as she walked back into her living room. She tried to imagine a dog greeting her, but it was hard to envision him, since she didn't know what he looked like.

She picked up the empty glasses and what was left of the cheese and crackers, and then, munching on a cracker, she stacked the glasses in the dishwasher. *Felix.* She liked the sound of it. She tried it out aloud. "Here, Felix. Good dog, Felix." The words echoed around the kitchen, and she shook her head. She was going nuts. It was all the stress of the murder. She needed a good night's sleep. Hal's words came back to her, and she smiled.

She fell asleep that night with his voice in her ears and the memory of his reassuring gaze soothing her fears.

*   *   *

Jenna seemed subdued when she arrived the next day, and Vivian fought an unfamiliar feeling of helplessness. She'd been so hopeful that with all of them working together, their investigation would produce results. Now it looked as if they were at an impasse, with no clear way to go forward.

253

She wasn't about to give up, however. There had to be a way to determine if Paula Lambert was having an affair with Dean. Someone, somewhere, knew the truth. Like the woman at the hair salon. Maybe she could somehow get the owner to give her the name of that woman.

She was still trying to figure out a way to do that when the last customer of the afternoon left the tearoom.

Jenna hadn't had much to say all day, and Vivian's maternal instincts warned her not to probe too much into her friend's thoughts.

Gracie, as usual, was in a hurry to leave, but while Jenna was loading tablecloths and napkins into the washing machine, Gracie took the time to ask if Jenna was okay. "She seems awfully down," she said, as Vivian walked with her to the shop door.

"I know." Vivian sighed. "This whole thing is depressing. We started out with such high hopes, and now I'm not sure what to do next."

"You'll think of something. You're so good at figuring out things." She hesitated, then added in a rush of words, "I listen to you like I used to listen to my mom. You're like a second mom to me."

Before Vivian could answer, Gracie rushed out the door and disappeared into the street.

Warmed by her words, Vivian smiled as she wandered back to the kitchen. It seemed that she now had two surrogate daughters.

"I'm off," Jenna announced, as Vivian walked into the kitchen. "I'll see you in the morning."

"Jenna, I'm sorry. I know all this mess is frustrating, but we will get to the bottom of things. I promise."

"Yeah, I know how hard you're trying." Jenna dragged on her jacket as if she were going into battle. "Don't think I'm not grateful, because I am. But even if Messina doesn't have the proof to charge me, he may never find out who killed Dean. For the rest of my life, people will think I killed my ex."

Vivian shook her head. "No. I won't let that happen. If I can't find a way to solve this by tomorrow, I'll go to Messina and tell him everything we know."

Jenna stared at her. "You know he won't be happy to find out we've been investigating his case."

"It could also get you out of trouble. It could help him solve the case."

"And it might not. What if he accuses us of withholding evidence, or something?"

"As long as we're not aiding and abetting a criminal, we're not committing a crime. He'll probably thank me for coming forward. Then again, he's been investigating the case, and he's a lot more experienced at this than we are. He might very well know everything we know. It's just . . ." Vivian shook her head.

"Just what?"

"I hate to give up on this when we've come so far. I have a feeling that the answers are right around the corner, if only I could figure out how to get there."

Jenna sighed. "Well, unless Messina barges in here waving handcuffs, I'm willing to wait until we can get around that corner."

255

"That's very courageous of you." Vivian gave her a hug. "But I will talk to him soon. I promise." The jingle of her cell phone caught her attention, and she dug in her purse. "It's Hal," she said, after glancing at the screen.

"I'll see you in the morning," Jenna said as she headed for the door.

Nodding at her, Vivian spoke into the phone.

"What are you doing this evening?" Hal asked when he heard her voice.

"Not much. I need to clean up the kitchen and get things ready for tomorrow, and I should vacuum my rugs upstairs and do some laundry, but other than that . . ."

"How about you forget all that stuff and come with me to meet Felix? Barry invited us to go over there tonight."

"Really?" Her thrill of excitement surprised her. "I'd love that. What time?"

"How about now? We could go get a bite to eat at the brewery, then go on from there."

She brought up a mental image of how she looked right then. Frumpy gray pleated skirt, plain white shirt, and no makeup. "Give me half an hour?"

"Thirty minutes on the dot."

He hung up, and she found herself smiling again. She'd been doing that a lot lately, she thought as she hurried up the stairs to her apartment. Every time she heard his voice, she couldn't help smiling.

She had to admit, she was a little on edge about the evening. This would be the first time they would be out in public together. Knowing how virulent small-town gossip could be, there could be some speculation going on if any of her regular customers caught sight of them.

In the next instant she chided herself. They were two friends having a quiet meal together, and if people wanted to make something of that, she would soon set them straight.

With that in mind, she changed into black pants and a soft pink sweater. Nothing fancy, she told herself, as she dabbed on lipstick and a touch of blush to her cheeks. *Keep it casual.*

* * *

She actually enjoyed the meal even more than she'd anticipated. Hal, as always, was good company, making her laugh with his account of Wilson's latest goofs.

"I don't know how you put up with him," she said as she laid down her fork on her empty plate. "He would drive me crazy."

"I have to admit, he gives me a headache or two. He's a good kid, though, and he'll learn. He just needs someone to believe in him."

"Don't we all?" She smiled at the man opposite her. Dressed in a black sweater over a crisp blue shirt, he looked classy yet comfortable. Which pretty much summed up the man himself.

"You ready to go?" He was smiling back at her, confusing her.

"Er . . . yes." She made a hurried grab for her purse. "I'm anxious to meet Felix."

"Me too. I've heard some interesting things about him."

"Oh? Good things, I hope."

"All good, I promise you." He signaled to the server. "I think you will enjoy his company."

"I'm sure I will." She hesitated, then blurted, "We'll split the bill." Ducking her head, she scrabbled in her purse for her wallet.

"We'll do no such thing." Hal took his credit card out of his wallet as the server laid the bill on the table. "When a gentleman invites a lady out to dinner, he pays the bill. With pleasure."

Vivian smiled. "Then the lady accepts with pleasure. And many thanks."

"You're very welcome." He waited until the server had left before adding, "I'd like to do this again."

"I'd like that. But next time I'm paying."

"Is that so?" He stroked his chin. "Hmm . . . in that case, I suggest we go to the Bellemer in Newport."

He must have noticed her expression, as his smile vanished. "Wait. It was a joke. Of course, I wouldn't expect you to—"

"No! It's not that." She lowered her voice. "It's just that the Bellemer is somehow significant in Dean's murder."

"Oh? In what way?"

"Natalie told me that Reggie Lambert made reservations there the night before Dean died but never turned up for dinner and never called to cancel."

Hal frowned. "I don't see . . ."

"Reggie told me he got back to town on Saturday morning. It seemed odd to me that he would forget about expensive reservations, especially when it cost him seventy-five dollars."

"Maybe, but not entirely implausible. He could have been delayed and in the hassle of rescheduling his flight, forgotten, or simply not had time to cancel."

Vivian let out a sigh. "You're right. I'm trying to read something into it that isn't there. I guess I'm too anxious to clear Jenna's name. I've pretty much decided to go talk to Detective Messina tomorrow, though I'm not sure I know anything he doesn't already know."

"Well, I'm happy to hear that." Hal smiled and nodded at the server as she returned with his credit card. "Let's hope you can help him put an end to all this turmoil. My customers are talking about nothing else these days. Misty Bay was a nice quiet, peaceful town before this happened."

"I know." Vivian sighed. "I'm afraid Jenna is feeling the brunt of it. Which is why I need to talk to Messina and at least try to help."

Hal leaned forward and laid his hand over hers. "None of this is your fault. You are to be commended for taking risks to help her. I'm sure she appreciates it."

"She does. And thank you." She slid her hand out from under his and took hold of her purse. Hoping that he didn't notice her cheeks were warming, she added, "We'd better make a move if we're going to meet Felix."

"You're right." He glanced at his watch, then pushed back his chair.

Leading the way to the door, she drew a deep breath. It meant nothing, she told herself. It was just a friendly gesture, meant to comfort and reassure her. Nevertheless, she was quite sure the memory of his warm hand on hers would stay with her all night.

They arrived at Barry's house a short time later. Vivian's heart was thumping with excitement, and she prayed that she and Felix would be a good match.

The young man who opened the door greeted them with a grin, one hand holding the collar of a knee-high black-and-brown dog. "Felix has been waiting to meet you," he said, after introducing himself.

At the mention of his name, Felix uttered a soft whine. His tail started thrashing back and forth, while his mouth opened in the resemblance of a smile. He looked up at Vivian with anxious brown eyes, and her heart melted.

She squatted down, offering the back of her hand to his nose, and was rewarded with a wet lick. "Hello, Felix," she said softly.

Felix wagged his tail again.

Barry invited them in and, while Vivian bent down to pet the dog, talked about his plans to move to France. "I wish I could take him with me," he said, looking wistfully at his companion. "But it's just not practical. I'll miss him, though."

"It must be so hard to part with him," Vivian said, fondling Felix's ear. "I promise I'll give him a happy home. We'll take care of each other."

Felix deposited a lick on her nose in approval.

"Then you'll take him?" Barry looked relieved. "Thank you. He likes you. I think he'll be happy with you."

"Anyone would be happy living with Vivian," Hal said, making her blush again. "Don't worry, Barry. Felix will live like a king."

Vivian laughed. "Hear that, Felix? You're coming home to your castle. I have a feeling you and I will have lots of adventures together."

Hal smiled. "I don't doubt that at all. Adventure seems to wait around every corner for you."

"My life isn't dull, that's for sure." She straightened with a sigh. "Is there anything I should know about taking care of him?"

Barry shook his head. "He's a healthy dog. I'll give you what I have left of his dog food, but it's up to you what you feed him. He'll bug you for table scraps. He loves to go on walks, chases birds, sleeps a lot. He's house trained and will go to the door when he needs to go out. He doesn't mind the rain and loves the beach."

Vivian reached down once more to stroke Felix's neck. "He sounds like my kind of dog."

"I'll get his food and leash." Barry took off for the kitchen, and Felix got up to follow him.

"I hope he won't pine for Barry," Vivian said, feeling an ache in her heart for the dog. "Felix won't understand why he's not coming home again."

"He'll soon settle down with you. I heard that it takes three to five days for an adopted dog to get used to new surroundings."

"How long does it take them to get used to new owners?"

Hal shrugged. "He may never forget Barry, but that doesn't mean he won't be happy with you."

"I hope so." The magnitude of what she was taking on suddenly hit her. "I hope I'm doing the right thing."

"Barry is going to find him a new home, one way or another. He seems really relieved that you're willing to take the dog. He really doesn't want to leave him in a shelter."

She was beginning to feel better already. "Right. I'll take care of Felix, and he will take care of me."

"That's my girl."

It wasn't so much what he said as the way he said it. Aware once more of her heating cheeks, Vivian was relieved when Barry chose that moment to come back with a bag of dog food and another bag holding treats, an assortment of toys, and a leash.

Hal took the packages from him while Vivian fastened the leash onto the dog's collar.

"Okay, Felix," she said, as she led him to the door. "Let's go home."

"Oh, wait. I almost forgot." Barry took off down the hallway and came back moments later carrying a bright-purple dog bed. "He doesn't use it much," he said, as he offered it to Vivian. "Actually, he's used to sleeping with me on my bed."

Vivian sighed. There went her peaceful nighttime sleep. On the other hand, if she heard any more strange noises at night, it would be comforting to have Felix by her side. Besides, she wasn't a fan of the purple dog bed.

Thanking Barry, she took it from him, and promised herself she would replace it as soon as possible, just in case Felix would prefer something a little less gaudy for his naps.

Barry squatted down and rubbed the dog's ear. "You be a good boy, now," he said, his voice just husky enough to bring tears to Vivian's eyes. "I'll come and visit when I can." He looked up at Vivian. "If that's okay with you?"

"Sure. Come anytime you want."

She was having a hard time holding back the tears, and Hal ushered her to the door. "We'll keep in touch," he promised as they stepped outside.

"Thanks." Barry shut the door a little fast, and Vivian's heart ached for him. She knew, only too well, the pain of parting with a beloved dog.

Felix seemed a little agitated when Hal loaded him onto the back seat of his car and paced back and forth on the ride home.

"If he's too much to handle," Hal said, as he walked up to the shop door with Vivian, "I'm sure Barry will understand."

Holding on to the leash with one hand, the purple bed tucked under her arm, Vivian unlocked the door. "I've never given up on a problem without a fight. Felix and I will come to an understanding. Won't we, Felix?"

The dog looked up at her with soulful eyes and uttered a faint whine.

That did it. No matter what, she wasn't about to let this animal go to the shelter. "Felix," she told Hal, "is here to stay."

"Good." He shifted the packages in his arms. "I'll bring these up for you."

"Thanks." She led him upstairs, Felix sniffing at every step. Once inside the apartment, he trotted around the room, sniffing at everything, then wandered into the kitchen.

"Do you think he's hungry?" Vivian watched Hal put the packages down on her coffee table. "I forgot to ask Barry if he'd had dinner."

"I'm sure Barry had eaten by the time we got there."

Vivian gave him a mock scowl. "I was talking about Felix."

Hal laughed. "I've got a feeling Felix is going to be mightily spoiled by you."

She smiled back. "Isn't that what dogs are for?"

Shaking his head, he looked at his watch. "Good night, Vivian. Let me know if you have any trouble with Felix."

The dog chose that moment to wander back into the room. Vivian bent down to scratch his neck. "I won't have any trouble. But thanks."

Hal nodded, and walked to the door.

"And thanks for dinner. I really enjoyed it."

He turned to look at her. "Me too. We'll do it again."

She watched him leave, then moments later remembered she needed to lock the shop door. By the time she got down there, Felix at her heels, Hal had gone.

She looked down at the dog. "Well, boy, it's just you and me now. Shall we go upstairs and have a nightcap?"

Felix rewarded her with a slight flip of his tail.

Much to her relief, the night went better than she'd anticipated. She laid the purple dog bed down on the floor next to her bed, but after one disdainful glance at it, Felix jumped up onto her flower-patterned comforter and rested his chin on his paws.

He stayed there all night, apparently, since she awoke the next morning with him still at the foot of her bed.

She took him down to the small patch of grass in her backyard, then led him back upstairs. He was lying on the bed again when she finished her shower and didn't even look at the bowl of kibble she put down for him in the kitchen.

She hated having to leave him alone in the apartment, but she had to bake pastries and prepare fillings for the sandwiches. Promising herself she would check on him as soon as she had a chance, she went downstairs to work.

Chapter Fifteen

Shortly before eleven thirty, the shop doorbell announced a visitor. When Vivian opened the door, she was surprised to see Gracie standing there, a large package tucked in her arms.

"You're early this morning," Vivian said as she stepped back to let Gracie come in.

"I brought you a gift." Gracie danced into the tearoom and thrust the box into Vivian's arms. "I hope you like it."

Hugging the package, Vivian stared at her. "Why is everyone giving me gifts? Is something going on I don't know about?"

Gracie headed for the kitchen, throwing words over her shoulder. "Not that I know. Open it."

Shaking her head, Vivian carried the package into the kitchen. "The scones are still in the oven," she said, seeing Gracie peering at the shelves.

"That's okay, I can wait." Gracie pulled off her jacket, flung it into the closet, and plopped down at the table. "Go ahead. Open the gift."

Vivian placed the box on the table and opened it. Surprised to see brightly colored fabric inside, she lifted it out of the box. "Oh my goodness." She shook it out, exclaiming with amazement as she stared at the massive wall hanging.

In huge white letters on a red background were the words CELEBRATING TWO YEARS OF TEA AND CRUMPETS AT THE WILLOW PATTERN TEAROOM! Three faces were appliquéd on the fabric, which Vivian realized depicted her, Gracie, and Jenna. A teapot, teacup, saucer, and cake stand were all stitched on there, almost overpowered by the British flag.

It took Vivian several seconds to regain her breath. "This is . . . magnificent."

"I'm glad you like it." Gracie's face was flushed with excitement. "That's what I've been doing at the meetings. It was a sewing class. I wanted to do something special for the anniversary, and I thought this would catch people's attention."

It would certainly do that, Vivian thought, as she took another look. "This must have taken hours to make."

"I worked on it at home a lot." Gracie leaned back, looking pleased with herself. "I know we can't keep it on the wall forever, but it will be a keepsake for you after we take it down."

"I will treasure it forever, that's for sure." Vivian started to fold the hanging. "We'll hang it on the back wall. I can take the plates down until the celebration is over." She smiled at Gracie. "It's really lovely. And incredibly thoughtful. You must have worked really hard on this to get it done on time."

"I did." Gracie slumped on her chair. "But it was worth every minute of it."

"Bless you." Vivian laid the hanging back in the box and moved around the table to give the young woman a hug. "Thank you so much. This will give the tearoom a really festive look for the anniversary."

"You're welcome. I just wish we could get Jenna's name cleared before next week. We could have a double celebration."

"That would be wonderful." Vivian sighed. "I don't seem to be making much headway."

"I think you've done a lot. We know now who was with Dean that night."

"We think we know." Vivian hurried over to the ovens, opened one of the doors, and peered inside. "We really don't know anything for sure."

"Yeah." Gracie sounded gloomy. "That sucks. I should have, like, done a better job at the interview."

"You did the best you could." Vivian pulled out a tray of scones. "And you may have broken the case with that remark about Dean's past from Paula. We just have to figure out a way to prove what we suspect." She laid the tray on the shelf. "I'll let these cool off a bit; then you can have one. By the way, I have some news. I've adopted a companion."

"Who is it? Hal?"

Vivian swung around to look at her. "What? No! I'm talking about a dog. His name is Felix, and he's upstairs in my apartment."

Gracie's face lit up. "Oh, cool! Did you get him from the shelter?"

"No, I got him from a friend of Hal's. He's moving to France and couldn't take Felix with him,"

"Felix?" Gracie was practically jumping up and down. "What an awesome name for a dog. Is he cute? I bet he's adorable. Can I see him?"

Vivian had to smile at her assistant's excitement. "Later. Right now, there's a new shipment of cartons in the storeroom waiting to be opened. The anniversary is on Saturday, and I need everything on the shelves."

"Oh, right." Gracie darted off to the storeroom, leaving Vivian alone to begin making the fillings for the sandwiches.

She had just finished slicing the tomatoes when Gracie bounced back into the kitchen.

"Where's Jenna?" Gracie looked around the kitchen as if expecting Jenna to be hiding from her.

Startled, Vivian looked at her watch. She'd been so engrossed in the sandwiches—and, much as she hated to admit it, indulging in recalling every word of her conversation with Hal last night—that she'd completely lost track of the time. She was shocked to see that it was almost twelve thirty. "Oh, goodness. I'd better unlock the door."

Gracie frowned at her. "Are you okay? You never forget to open on time."

"That's because I usually open the door to you both and then leave it open." Vivian was throwing out the words as she hurried across the tearoom to the door. "You were early this morning, and now Jenna is late."

She reached the door, unlocked it, and pulled it open. To her relief, there were no impatient customers waiting to get in. Her first booking for afternoon tea was at two thirty, she reminded herself as she walked slowly back to the kitchen. If any customers looking to browse the shelves had been locked out, they would hopefully return later.

In the kitchen, Gracie stood at the sink, filling a kettle with water. "I'm making tea," she said as she put the kettle on the stove. "Scones taste better with tea."

Vivian nodded, and dug into her purse for her phone. "I'll call Jenna. It's not like her to be late. Oh, wait. There's a message." She tapped the icon and scanned the text. "That's odd."

Gracie twisted her head to look at her. "What is?"

"This message." Vivian read it again. "It's from Jenna. She just says she'll be late. She doesn't say how long or why."

"She must have been in a hurry."

A cold feeling of dread was beginning to settle in Vivian's stomach. Quickly she thumbed Jenna's number and held the phone to her ear. A series of buzzes ended with Jenna's voice telling her to call back later.

Frowning, Vivian shoved the phone back in her purse. "She's not answering," she said. "Something's wrong." She looked at her watch again. "I think I should go and check on her. Make sure she's not sick or something. I—" She broke off with a gasp. "I almost forgot. I need to take Felix out to the yard."

Now Gracie looked worried. "Go take Felix out. I'll keep an eye on the shop until you get back; then I'll go check on Jenna."

"Right. Thanks." Her stomach clenching with anxiety, Vivian hurried upstairs to her apartment. Felix lay in his bed and barely lifted his head when she walked in. He was probably missing Barry, she told herself as she led him down to the yard. She watched him sniff all over the grass before lifting his leg against a laurel shrub. He trotted toward her when she called his name but still seemed listless when she took him back to the apartment.

"I'm sorry, Felix," she said, as he snuggled back on his bed and looked up at her with soulful eyes. "I know you're sad right now, but you'll get used to living with me, and I promise I'll give you as much time as I can, okay?"

He answered with one lazy thump of his tail.

On her way out, she switched on the TV, hoping the sound would make the dog feel less lonely.

The second she got downstairs, Gracie grabbed her jacket and struggled into it. "I'll call you when I get there," she said as she sped out the door.

Left alone, Vivian filled a teakettle with water. Maybe she was overreacting, she told herself. Maybe everything that had been happening lately, with the threats and suspicions and discussions about the murder, was making her overly anxious.

Or maybe her gut feeling was right, telling her Jenna was in trouble.

All this time she'd been warned about the danger of poking her nose in a murder case. She'd figured the threat of danger was leveled at her. She'd forgotten about the note on Jenna's windshield.

She tried not to think about her friend lying somewhere, all alone, hurting, or worse. No, she wouldn't let such thoughts get into her head. Jenna could simply have gone on an errand and lost track of the time.

Then why isn't she answering her phone?

Maybe she'd lost it? Angry with herself, Vivian shook her head to clear her mind. She was clutching at straws. She had to face the fact that Jenna could well be in serious danger.

Paula had been upset at the interview with Gracie. Was she angry because she thought Dean was cheating on her, or was she worried because she had killed Dean and Gracie's questions were getting a little too close for comfort?

Reggie had seen Gracie in the lobby of the hotel. If he'd mentioned to Paula that Gracie worked at the tearoom, Paula would probably have realized that the interview was just an excuse. It wouldn't take her long to figure out that the Willow Pattern women suspected her of murder and were on her trail.

Had Paula kidnapped Jenna? Why Jenna? Vivian closed her eyes. Why not her, or Gracie? What could Paula have to gain?

Feeling sick to her stomach, Vivian tried to reassure herself. Jenna was a sturdy, strong woman. She wouldn't go anywhere without a fight. She'd find a way to escape.

The next fifteen minutes dragged on as Vivian made tea, drank two cups, and called Jenna's phone three times. Just as she was about to call Gracie, her phone buzzed with an incoming call.

Seeing Gracie's name on the screen, Vivian slapped the phone to her ear. "Gracie? Is Jenna okay?"

"I don't know."

Hearing the worry in Gracie's voice, Vivian briefly closed her eyes again.

"Her front door is locked," Gracie said, "and she's not at home. Her car is gone."

The iceberg in Vivian's stomach intensified. "Maybe she's had an accident."

"I didn't see anything on the way up here."

Vivian tried not to envision Jenna's car flying off the cliffs as she took the curve. "Come on back to the shop," she told Gracie, "and check the railings on the way down. Just in case."

Gracie muttered, "Okay," and the line went dead.

Pacing around the tearoom, Vivian tried to think what to do. Her first instinct was to call Detective Messina. But what if she sent off a manhunt that would surely attract the attention of the news reporters, only to find out there was a simple reason for Jenna's disappearance?

All that publicity would put Jenna in the limelight again as a murder suspect.

Vivian sat down again and pulled out her phone. She needed to call Hal. He'd know what to do. She had her thumb over his number when it occurred to her that he would tell her to call the cops.

Sighing, she put the phone back in her pocket. The shop doorbell rang just then, and she shot off the chair, hope rising that Jenna had arrived safely after all. Those hopes sank as Gracie walked across the tearoom toward her.

"I didn't see any damaged railings," she said as she looked around her. "She's still not here?"

"No." Vivian looked at her watch. "I can't just sit around and do nothing. I'm going over to the hotel. If Paula did do something to Jenna, I'll get it out of her."

Gracie made a whimpering sound in the back of her throat. "You don't think Jenna's . . ." Her voice trailed off, as if she found it impossible to put into words what she was thinking.

"No," Vivian said loudly. "I won't even consider the possibility that something bad has happened to Jenna. If Paula is behind this, I think she's playing games, trying to frighten us, that's all."

Gracie nodded but looked unconvinced. "What are you going to do?"

"I don't know yet." Vivian pulled a dark-blue jacket from the closet and pulled it on. "Can you hold the fort until I get back? Our first tea isn't booked until two thirty. I hope to be back by then. If not, everything is ready to go. You just have to make tea and fill the cake stands."

Gracie looked scared to death, but she managed a weak smile. "I'll be fine. Just go ahead and find Jenna."

"I'll call you as soon as I know something." Vivian grabbed her purse and flew across the tearoom to the door. She hated to leave Gracie alone with all the worry about Jenna and the stress of taking care of customers.

But right now, finding out what had happened to Jenna was crucial. She might well be wrong, but somehow she felt certain that Paula Ramsey was behind her friend's disappearance. All she had to do now was get the truth out of her.

* * *

The day had not started out well for Detective Messina. He'd had trouble starting the car this morning, reminding him that he hadn't taken it in for a checkup in almost a year. The chief had been waiting for him when he arrived at the station, demanding to know when he was going to wrap up the murder case. Like he hadn't been busting his butt trying to do just that.

By the time he'd finished telling the chief everything he'd been doing for the past three days and returned to his desk, the coffee was cold and all the doughnuts were gone.

Now he was sitting at his desk, staring at the notes on his computer and wondering where in the hell he was going to find the evidence he needed. The problem with small towns, he reflected as he scrolled down the pages, was that the people were so damned tight-lipped. City folk were a lot more forthcoming when it came to witnesses.

He'd tracked down four people who'd been in the vicinity of the Blue Surf when the murder occurred, and all four had sworn they'd seen nothing and knew nothing. He couldn't be sure if they were telling the truth, if they were protecting someone, or if they simply didn't want to get involved.

Same with the hotel staff. Every one of them told him they didn't know Dean Ramsey all that well and had no idea who might have spent the night with him in the bridal suite. Now the chief was urging him to arrest Jenna Ramsey, since he hadn't come up with any other suspects. He'd told the guy a dozen times that he didn't have enough evidence. Each time he'd been told to find some.

His only hope now was the lipstick. Remembering his interviews of the hotel staff, he'd thought he recognized the color on one of the women's lips. He'd taken her DNA, along with that of the rest of the women to avoid tipping her off that he suspected her, and was still waiting for the results. It was a long shot, pretty much born of desperation, but his gut kept telling him Jenna was innocent. There was no way he was going to arrest her unless he had indisputable evidence that she was the perp.

Meanwhile, he had a vague lead that he intended to follow. He'd heard rumors of a prostitute ring operating out of the hotel. It probably had nothing to do with Ramsey's murder, but it was worth looking into, just in case.

He was halfway out of his chair when Brady rushed over to him, brandishing a paper at him. "I got the DNA report back. We got a match!"

Messina sat down hard. "On the lipstick?"

"Yes, sir." Grinning, Brady handed over the report. "This is going to make things real awkward for somebody."

Quickly, Messina scanned the text. Things were looking up. The report clearly stated that the DNA on the lipstick belonged to Paula Lambert.

He tried not to get too excited. After all, she was the assistant manager at the hotel. She could have dropped it while inspecting the bathroom or something. She could have dropped it weeks ago. He smiled. She could also have dropped it in her hurry to get out of that room the morning she pushed a man to his death.

He looked up at Brady. "I need to take care of a couple of things first, but we'll go over to the Blue Surf and talk to Paula Lambert."

"Yes, sir." Looking pleased with himself, Brady swung around and marched off to his desk.

Messina studied the report some more. Maybe, just maybe, this would clear Jenna of the crime. Aware that he was far happier than he should be about that, he shoved the report aside. Time to get down to business and wrap up this case once and for all.

* * *

Reaching the door of the Blue Surf Hotel, Vivian burst into the lobby and headed straight for the desk. She recognized the clerk immediately as the young woman who had summoned Reggie a few days ago.

The clerk also recognized her, since she gave her a stiff smile and asked, "Do you have an appointment with Mr. Lambert?"

"I'm not here to talk to Reggie." Vivian leaned across the desk. "I want to speak with Paula Lambert."

One of the clerk's eyes twitched. "I . . . er . . . do you have an appointment?"

"I do not." Vivian's worry over Jenna's disappearance made her voice harsh. "I must speak with Paula. Now. It's an urgent matter and concerns this hotel."

Deep wrinkles appeared in the clerk's forehead. "Your name?"

"I'm Vivian Wainwright, Jenna Ramsey's counselor."

"One moment, please." She lifted the phone and spoke into it. "Ms. Wainwright is here to see you. She says she has an urgent message for you." The clerk listened for a moment before saying, "She says she's Jenna Ramsey's counselor." She looked at Vivian. "She says to give me the message."

"Tell her," Vivian said, filling her voice with venom, "that she can either talk to me or to the police."

Apparently Paula must have heard her. The clerk muttered, "Yes, Ms. Lambert," and put down the phone. "You can go up to the office. First floor, first door on your right. There's a sign on the door."

"Thank you." Vivian could feel the clerk's gaze on her back as she crossed the lobby to the elevators. No doubt the gossip would be circulating in minutes around the hotel.

Reaching the first floor, she stepped out onto thick yellow carpeting, decorated with swirls of gold along the edges. The bright lights embedded in the ceiling lit up the hallway like sunlight gleaming through glass.

She saw the sign on the office door right away and gave it a sharp rap with her knuckles. Without waiting for an invitation, she pushed open the door and barged right in.

Paula sat at a mammoth desk that took up a good third of the room. A giant painting of an eagle soaring over mountains hung on the wall to her left. The window behind her looked out at the ocean, and Vivian caught a glimpse of a freighter on the horizon, chugging its way north.

"What do you want?" Paula looked defiant and a little agitated.

"Jenna Ramsey is missing," Vivian said, leaning her hands on the desk. "I think you can help me find her."

Paula's cheeks grew pale. "Me? How would I know where she is?"

"Because you killed her ex-husband."

Vivian held her breath as Paula stared at her with wide eyes. She was taking a chance, attacking a murderer with no real means to defend herself. What if the woman pulled a gun on her? She'd be defenseless against her. Maybe she should have called Messina after all.

Her only hope was the tough-guy approach. Paula didn't look too threatening right now. If Dean's death was an accident, she might not have the stomach to kill another person in cold blood.

"I don't know what you're talking about," Paula said, her fingers crawling toward the phone on her desk.

Realizing her intention, Vivian slapped a hand over Paula's fingers. "You were having an affair with him, weren't you? What happened? Did he try to dump you and you got mad? Was it an accident? Did he hit you and you hit back? Was there a struggle? If so, that's self-defense and—"

"I didn't kill Dean!"

Paula's eyes had filled with tears as Vivian's accusations engulfed her. Now those tears streamed down her cheeks, and she grappled for the box of tissues on her desk.

Vivian waited while the other woman's sobs filled the room. Part of her wanted to rush around the desk and hold her until the awful, wrenching sobbing ceased, but common sense held her back. She couldn't be sure this wasn't all an act to cover her guilt.

After a few tense moments, Paula's anguished weeping subsided and she seemed to be struggling for control.

Vivian softened her voice. "Why don't you tell me what happened." She sat down on the chair opposite the woman, her gaze wandering back to the painting of the eagle. Something about it unsettled her, though she had no idea why.

After a few more hiccups and shudders, Paula said quietly, "I loved him. I would never have hurt him."

Vivian leaned forward. "But you know who did."

"Yes." Paula blew her nose and dropped the tissue into something hidden from Vivian's view. "I know I should have told the police, but I couldn't. The whole thing was my fault. I did something stupid, and it cost the man I loved his life."

"Tell me."

Paula shuddered again. "It was my birthday. Reggie was out of town, and Dean wanted me to celebrate with him. When he asked me to stay the night, at first I said no." Her heavy sigh seemed to linger in the room. "If I had kept to that, Dean would be alive now. But I was in love, it was my birthday, we'd had a few drinks . . . I couldn't keep saying no."

"Did you know that Dean was running an escort service, using this hotel?"

Vivian wasn't quite sure why she'd asked that. Maybe she felt that if she painted a bad picture of Dean, the grieving woman wouldn't be so heartbroken. She was unprepared for Paula's answer.

"Of course I knew. We were partners."

Vivian stared at her. "You were Dean's partner?"

Paula uttered a shuddering sigh. "Yes. The whole thing was my idea. I took care of the management details, while Dean hired the escorts and arranged the appointments."

"What about your husband? Does he know you're doing this?"

"Reggie? He wouldn't see an elephant stampede if it was right in front of his nose. All he cares about is his precious golf games, his poker nights with the boys, and getting his hair styled every week. The only time he pays any attention to me is when I give him the monthly financial report. I'm the one who runs this hotel, while he sits back and lets everyone think he's an exceptional manager. That's why I created the escort service. We were down on our profits, and I needed to give them a boost."

"And Reggie never questions where that extra money is coming from?"

Paula's laugh sounded bitter. "I don't think he ever reads the reports."

"I see." Vivian was beginning to sympathize with the woman. "So, when Reggie went out of town, you went out to celebrate your birthday with Dean." She could understand why now.

"Yes." Paula's voice wobbled as she added, "We went into Lincoln City for dinner." Her eyes misted over again. "It was all very romantic. Dean was making me feel like a woman again, especially when he gave me my birthday gift."

"The pink negligee."

"What?" For a moment, Vivian thought she would deny it; then her shoulders slumped. "Yes." She wiped away a tear. "It ended with Dean begging me to leave Reggie. He said he was thinking of moving to California and wanted me to go with him."

Vivian nodded. "And you agreed."

"I said I would think about it. I needed time to sort things out in my mind."

"I know how that feels." Vivian sighed.

"Well, that's when Dean asked me to stay the night with him. He wanted to stay there in Lincoln City, but I told him I couldn't. I reminded him I had to be at the hotel early the next morning. On the drive back home, he kept trying to persuade me to spend the night with him. By then I was pretty much making up my mind to go to California with him. I couldn't bear the thought of him leaving without me."

"So, you decided to stay at the Blue Surf."

Paula hugged herself, as if trying to stay warm. "When Dean suggested the bridal suite, it seemed sort of significant. Like the start of our new life together. It wasn't until about five the next morning, when I'd sobered up, that I realized it wasn't going to be that simple. I couldn't just take off into the unknown. There were things I'd have to do first. Like get a divorce from Reggie, for one."

"That would help."

"I know, right? So I crept out of bed, got dressed in the dark, and left Dean still sleeping. I figured we'd have a serious talk later and work things out. I left the negligee on the bed. I didn't want to risk taking it home. Reggie would know I would never buy something like that for myself."

"So, you went home?"

"Yes. I went home to change. The dress I wore to dinner wasn't exactly office attire." Paula stared down at her hands. "As soon as I drove into the driveway, I knew I was in trouble. Reggie's car was sitting there. He wasn't supposed to arrive in Portland until eleven thirty that morning."

"So he did come back on Friday," Vivian said, congratulating herself on a good guess.

"Yes. He'd booked dinner in Newport for my birthday. He'd told me he wouldn't be back until Saturday morning, planning on showing up Friday evening to surprise me."

"Instead of that, he was the one who got the surprise," Vivian murmured.

Paula shuddered. "He was so cold. Just sat there when I walked in. Never said a word. Just sat there looking at me."

Vivian tried to imagine what it must have felt like, and shivered.

"I told him I had dinner with a couple of my friends to celebrate my birthday. I said I'd had too much to drink and stayed the night rather than risk driving home."

"But he didn't believe you." Vivian shifted on her chair. She was beginning to see where this was going. Now she desperately needed to know where Jenna was, and time could be running out.

She looked back at the dark-gray feathers of the eagle in the painting and suddenly realized what it was that bothered her. Reggie's tattoo. The eagle on the back of his hand wasn't tinted. The dark blue was a bruise. She should have realized that.

She switched her attention back to Paula, whose voice had risen with tension.

"Reggie said he'd called my friends," Paula said, "and they hadn't heard from me. He asked why I was lying. I'd finally had enough. I yelled at him. Told him I'd been with Dean and that I was leaving him." She began to cry again. "Reggie flew into a rage. I've never seen him so angry. He tore out of the house, and I knew he was going to the hotel to have it out with Dean. I tried calling Dean on his cell, but he must have had it turned off. So I drove over there."

Her voice rose to a wail. "Reggie was there, fighting with Dean on the balcony. I rushed over there, and when Dean saw me, he let down his guard for a moment. That's when Reggie punched him in the jaw." She was sobbing now, her arms clenched across her chest as she rocked back and forth.

Vivian felt sick to her stomach, but she had to hear the rest, just in case Paula clammed up when Messina questioned her.

She could barely make out the next words, and Paula struggled to get them out. "Dean hit his head on the marble table out there. When Reggie . . . told me Dean was . . . dead . . . I couldn't believe it." Her sobs drowned out the next words.

Vivian took out her phone. "Where's Reggie now?"

Paula managed to control herself long enough to answer. "I don't know. He was here this morning, but he left a while ago." She caught sight of the phone in Vivian's hand. "What are you doing?"

"I'm calling Detective Messina." Vivian dialed 911 as she spoke. "You need to tell him what you told me."

"I can't! Reggie will swear I killed Dean!"

Ignoring her, Vivian spoke into the phone. "This is Vivian Wainwright. Please tell Detective Messina to meet me right away in the lobby of the Blue Surf Hotel. Tell him it could very well be a matter of life and death."

She tucked the phone back into her purse and glared at the sobbing woman. "Now you're going to tell me where Reggie is and what he's done with Jenna."

"Jenna?" Paula cut off a sob to stare at her. "Jenna's with Reggie?"

"I think Reggie realized we were getting close to the truth. I think he's kidnapped Jenna. I just hope and pray he hasn't hurt her."

Paula's wail hurt Vivian's ears. "No! I can't bear the thought of him hurting someone else."

"Think!" Vivian surged up from her chair and leaned over the desk. "Where would Reggie take her?"

"I don't know! I can't—"

She broke off with a gasp.

Vivian leaned closer. "What is it?"

"I think . . . I don't know . . ." Paula shook her head, then continued in a rush, "Whenever Reggie gets mad at someone, he threatens to send him over Lookout Edge. Maybe . . ."

Vivian straightened, feeling as if her entire body were encased in ice. Lookout Edge was a viewpoint about a mile or so from the hotel. It was the highest point of the cliffs in that area, towering above the ocean and the jagged rocks below. Anyone falling from that height wouldn't have a chance of surviving.

"If anything happens to Jenna," she said through gritted teeth, "I promise you, I will bury you both." With that, she flew out of the office.

Chapter Sixteen

Waiting for the elevator, Vivian jiggled back and forth on her toes. She still had trouble imagining that overblown twit overpowering Dean Ramsey. If Paula hadn't burst into the room when she did, there could have been a different ending to that story.

The important thing now was to find Jenna. As quickly as possible. The elevator door finally slid open, and she darted inside. As the door closed again, she pulled out the phone and quickly dialed 911. A voice answered as the door slid open again, and she spoke quietly as she stepped into the lobby. "Please tell Detective Messina . . ."

She broke off, staring in amazement at the door as Messina strode through it, followed by the same officer who had been with him at the tearoom. The man he'd called Brady.

Catching sight of her, Messina headed straight toward her, his usual grim expression making him look formidable. "What's this all about?" he demanded when he reached her. "This better be a real emergency."

"I think it might be." Still wondering how he'd managed to get there so fast, she gave him a brief update on her conversation with Paula. "I have it all on here," she said, waving her phone at him. "I recorded everything she said."

A gleam of approval appeared in Messina's dark eyes. "I'll need to check that later. Right now, I'm going to take a look up at the viewpoint. I'll contact you if we learn anything."

"I'm coming with you." Vivian gave him a look that dared him to contradict her.

"That's not a good idea," he said, as she'd expected. "The situation could be dangerous."

"Which is exactly why I'm coming with you. I'll follow you in my car." She marched to the door, ending the conversation.

To her relief, neither man made an attempt to stop her. Out in the parking lot, she spotted the police car parked near the entrance. By the time she'd climbed behind the wheel of her own car, found her keys, stashed her purse, fastened her seat belt, and started the engine, Messina was already pulling out onto the street.

She lost sight of him around a curve as they roared down the coast road but wisely refrained from stepping on the gas. She wouldn't be a help to anyone if she drove herself off the cliff.

The thought brought another vision to her mind, of Jenna's body hurtling down toward the rocks a hundred feet below her. Vivian gulped and, clutching the wheel, began to pray.

She rounded the last curve to see three cars parked at the viewpoint. She recognized Jenna's car immediately. The police car was parked behind it, and next to it was a sleek, red Mercedes. It wasn't the cars that held her attention, however.

Messina stood by his car with Brady right behind him. They were staring at Reggie, who stood at the low wall at the edge of the cliffs. Jenna was slumped in his arms, her eyes closed, her face as white as the foam capping the waves of the ocean behind her.

"I'm warning you," Reggie shouted, as Vivian clambered out of her car. "Go away. Leave me alone, or I'll dump her over the wall."

Vivian clamped a hand over her mouth to stop from crying out. She couldn't tell if Jenna was still alive. All she wanted to do was rush over there and grab her friend out of that monster's arms.

Messina, however, caught her eye and raised his hand, signaling her to stand still.

Certain she was about to throw up, Vivian leaned against the hood of her car.

"Give up, Lambert," Messina called out. "You can't get away with this, so why waste your time? Let the woman go, and we'll talk."

"I'm done talking!" Reggie sounded hysterical, his voice rising almost to a scream. "My life is over. I've lost it all— my wife, my job, everything. All because this woman couldn't keep her man happy. It's her fault. He went looking for another playmate, and he chose my wife. *My wife!*"

The last words were a howl of despair. A sea gull, flying low overhead, screeched back at him, and he looked up.

Vivian never could remember exactly what happened after that. Messina moved with the speed of Superman. He seemed to fly through the air as he made a dive for Reggie's legs. Brady was a few steps behind him and was there to catch Jenna as she dropped to the ground.

Messina had Reggie pinned under his knee while Brady cuffed him, and then the detective scooped Jenna up in his arms and carried her to his car.

Tears almost blinded Vivian as she ran up to him. "Is she . . . ?" She couldn't say the word.

"Unconscious." Messina looked down at the woman in his arms, his expression close to tender. "No visible injuries. I'm guessing she's drugged. I'm taking her to the hospital, if you want to follow me out there."

Vivian desperately wanted to do just that, but the thought of Gracie, alone and anxious at the tearoom, loomed large over her own desires. "I have to get back to the Willow Pattern." She stroked Jenna's limp arm. "I'll call the hospital later."

Messina nodded and looked at his officer, who had led Reggie to the police car. "Take him to the station." He nudged his head at Reggie. "I'm taking his car to the hospital."

"Hey," Reggie whined, "I don't let anyone drive my car."

Messina ignored him. "Get his keys," he said, "and get the damn door open."

Brady hastily stuffed his hand in Reggie's coat pocket and came up with a bunch of keys. Seconds later the car beeped as the locks sprang up.

Brady pulled the passenger door open, and Messina gently lowered Jenna onto the seat, propping her up with the seat belt. He closed the door and looked at Vivian. "Good work, Ms. Wainwright. You probably saved her life."

"I couldn't have without you." Vivian managed a smile. "Please, call me Vivian."

For a moment he looked uncomfortable; then he nodded. "Vivian." With that, he strode around to the driver's side and climbed into the car.

Meanwhile, Brady had stuffed a complaining Reggie into the back seat of the police car. "He won't be going anywhere for a while," Brady said as he slammed the door shut.

"Good." Vivian shivered. "He was going to kill her."

"Yeah, looks like it. But he's going down for the murder of Dean Ramsey, that's for sure. Thanks to you recording that conversation you had with his wife."

"Oh, I forgot to give my phone to Detective Messina." Vivian pulled it out of her purse. "Do you want to give it to him?"

"Nah. Keep it for now." Brady opened the car door. "I'm guessing Messina will want to collect it himself."

He disappeared inside the car, leaving Vivian frowning. She wasn't quite sure what that meant, but right now she had to get back to the tearoom and rescue Gracie. She just hoped she'd have time to fill her assistant in on everything before they got too busy to talk.

She arrived back at the Willow Pattern just in time to see the first afternoon tea customers walk in the door. A flurry of making tea and sandwiches followed, with Gracie carrying loaded cake stands out to the tables and hurriedly clearing away everything before the next hungry clients arrived.

Jenna was on Vivian's mind all afternoon, and she sighed with relief when she could finally close the door behind the last satisfied customer. While they cleaned up the tables, she filled Gracie in on her conversation with Paula and the subsequent events at the viewpoint. Until then, she'd had no time to tell her assistant much except for the fact that Jenna was possibly drugged and in the hospital.

"I'm going to check on Felix," she said as she pulled off her apron, "and take him out to the yard. Then I'm going to the hospital. I need to know she's okay."

"Me too." Gracie snatched her jacket out of the closet. "I'll follow you out there."

Later, as she drove along the coast road to Newport, Vivian finally had time to go over everything again in her mind. It must have been Reggie who'd followed them home from the parking lot of the hotel the night Jenna found the note on her car. And Reggie who'd broken her window and left the note there.

What she didn't understand was how Jenna had ended up drugged and unconscious, on the brink of falling to her death from the viewpoint. That was something she was dying to find out.

Gracie was right behind her as she pulled into the parking lot of the hospital. Once inside, a receptionist directed them to the ward, where they found Jenna, pale and a little drawn, hooked up to a monitor.

She managed a smile when she saw them, but the nurse in the room warned them not to stay long. "She's still feeling the effects of the drug," she told them, "and she needs to rest."

"But she's going to be okay?" Gracie asked, her voice hoarse with concern.

"We're keeping her here overnight for observation." The nurse walked over to the door. "She should be fine to go home tomorrow."

She left them alone, and Gracie rushed over to the bed. "We were so worried about you," she said, sounding close to tears.

"I'm fine."

Jenna sounded weak, and Vivian quickly reached for her hand. "Hang in there, hon. We'll take care of you."

Jenna's eyes filled with tears. "Misty. I . . . she needs . . ."

"Don't you worry about Misty." Vivian gave her friend's hand a squeeze and let it go. "I'll run over there and make sure she's fed."

"Thank you." Jenna closed her eyes, then opened them again. "Reggie?"

"Messina has him locked up by now."

"He killed Dean."

"I know. Paula told me everything."

"He blames me for Paula's affair."

Vivian leaned over the bed. "Listen to me. None of this is your fault, okay? You're not responsible for what happened. You were divorced. Dean was free to do what he chose to do."

Tears trickled down Jenna's cheeks as she nodded.

Vivian's heart broke for her. Jenna was a strong, proud woman. To see her so vulnerable like this was hard to bear.

"Vivian said Messina carried you over to his car," Gracie said. "Do you remember that?"

Jenna's eyes opened wide. "He did? The nurse said he brought me here."

"I thought that was so romantic. I wish I could have seen it."

Vivian tugged at Gracie's arm. "We should be going. You need your rest. I'll be back in the morning to take you home. Your car is still up at the viewpoint. I'll get Hal to go up there with me, and he can drive it back to your house. We'll check on Misty while we're there."

"My keys." Jenna waved a weak hand at the locker next to her bed.

"I'll get them."

"Do you remember anything about what happened?" Gracie asked, as Vivian searched the locker for Jenna's keys.

"I found a note as I was leaving to come to work," Jenna said. "It was on the windshield of my car. It said, if I wanted to know who killed Dean, to be at the brewery by twelve thirty, to come alone, and not to tell anyone or I'd never know who killed him."

"So that's why you just left that cryptic text to me," Vivian said.

"Sorry. I couldn't tell you where I was going." Jenna's voice faded, and she seemed to make an effort to keep talking. "I got to the brewery early, ordered a beer, and waited. It got to almost one, and I was just about to leave when Reggie came in."

She paused again, and her eyes closed. Vivian thought for a moment that she'd dropped off to sleep, but then she opened her eyes again. "He bought me another beer and kept talking about Paula and how she was having an affair with Dean. I thought he was going to tell me that Paula killed Dean, but I was getting sleepy and not following everything he said. I think he must have put something in my beer when I went to the restroom. I didn't feel good, and he said he'd help me to my car. That's when he told me what he'd done. I don't remember anything after that until I woke up in here."

"He almost killed you," Gracie said. "Messina saved your life."

"How . . . did he . . ." Jenna's voice trailed off, and she closed her eyes again.

"Got them," Vivian said, as her fingers closed around Jenna's keys. "Let's go, Gracie. Let Jenna sleep. We can catch her up on everything tomorrow."

Gracie followed her out to the parking lot. "Do you think she'll be okay?" she asked as they walked over to their cars.

"I think she'll be just fine." Vivian gave her a hug. "Don't you worry about her. I'll come back here tomorrow and take her home. She probably won't feel like working tomorrow, so we'll be on our own again."

Seated in her car, she watched Gracie drive off before pulling her phone out of her purse.

Hal answered right away. "Sure, I'll help," he said, when she told him what she needed. "I'm closed up, so you can come get me right away."

Minutes later they were driving up to the viewpoint while she told him everything that had happened.

"You friend had a lucky escape," he said as they pulled in behind Jenna's car. "A few minutes later and she could have been lying on the rocks down there."

"I know." Vivian shuddered. "Reggie must have slipped the date drug into Jenna's beer while they were talking. I always figured Jenna could take care of herself. I'll never take anything for granted again."

"Well, I, for one, am very happy this mess is all over. At least now I won't have to lose sleep worrying about you."

She thought he was joking, but when she looked at him, she could see he was totally serious. "I'm sorry," she said softly. "I hate that I worried you, but I'm awfully glad to know someone cares about my well-being."

"I do care, and I thank the good Lord everything turned out okay in the end. Though I'm not sure how long it will take the town to recover. The local news was just coming on TV as I left."

"Did we make the headlines?"

"Front and center."

"Wonderful."

Hal laughed. "All this notoriety will probably bring customers pouring into the tearoom."

"I hope so. Our anniversary celebration is on Saturday." She pulled the keys from the ignition and tucked them in her purse. "I hope you'll find time to stop by?"

"I wouldn't miss it for anything. How's Felix doing?"

"A little depressed, I think." She sighed. "He's missing his master."

"He won't for long. He'll soon find out how lucky he is to have such an amazing woman to take care of him."

He never failed to unsettle her, she thought as she murmured her thanks. And she wouldn't change that for all the tea in China.

Acknowledgments

There are many people involved in producing a book, and I want to thank my Crooked Lane editors, publicists, and especially the artist who created such a beautiful cover. Thank you all for your hard work on my behalf.

Thank you also to my agent, Paige Wheeler. In spite of a difficult year, you've continued to advise, encourage, and fight for me. I hope you know how very much I appreciate it.

Most of all, I want to thank my readers. Your constant support, your generous compliments, and your friendship mean the world to me. Bless you all. I hope my work gives you a glimmer of light in a sometimes dark world.